HONO
BOUN

Helen Dickson

MILLS & BOON LIMITED
ETON HOUSE   18-24 PARADISE ROAD
RICHMOND   SURREY   TW9 1SR

First published in Great Britain 1990
by Mills & Boon Limited

© Helen Dickson 1990

Australian copyright 1990
Philippine copyright 1990
This edition 1990

ISBN 0 263 76847 3

Set in Times Roman 10 on 11½ pt.
04-9006-78880 C

Made and printed in Great Britain

PROLOGUE

ELLEN SLADE stood on the cliffs searching the sea as she had been doing for the past few days. Her tired grey eyes scanned the black ocean that spread out before her. The huge, angry waves rolled and swelled and came crashing on to the rocks far below where she stood. Black, thunderous clouds were scurrying across the sky above her—as if at any moment they would burst. The storm which had been threatening all that day was sure to come. The wind had risen and was howling menacingly, whipping her skirts about her as if it were trying to blow her off the cliffs and into the turbulent, frothing waters below.

Despite all this around her, Ellen stood firm and insensible. Clutching her shawl tightly about her thin shoulders, she kept her eyes fixed on the distant horizon, although it was difficult to distinguish where the sea ended and the sky began. Her heart was heavy and sad and she was weary of this troublesome land. So full of misery and hatred. If only her son would come for them, as he had promised. He must, she thought wretchedly. Time was growing short and she could feel fear creeping into her heart, clutching at it like an ice-cold hand. She did not fear for herself, only for those close to her—her husband and children—and she knew that at all costs they must escape from Ireland.

Her eldest son, Francis, was sailing from Holland and would take them to London. There he was to marry Anne Sinclair. Ellen had never met her, but she knew by the way Francis spoke of her that she would like her. Her

5

family owned vast quantities of land in the West Country but also kept a house in London. Francis had come to know and love her when he had served under her father during the Civil War. Ellen sighed, full of impatience to leave Ireland forever. But even in England, the land of their birth, their troubles would be far from over now that King Charles had been so cruelly executed and the country declared a Commonwealth.

William Slade, her husband, was a staunch Royalist and was now desperate to leave Ireland. It was already several months since Oliver Cromwell had landed at Dublin with an army of twenty-thousand men, and had begun his bloody campaign to recover Ireland for the Commonwealth and to put down the people who had risen in arms on behalf of Charles, the eldest son of the King. He had also set out to stop Ireland being used as a beach-head for the invasion of England on behalf of the Royalists. Drogheda, twenty miles north of Dublin, had fallen to him. The garrison, including Catholic priests, English Royalists and even civilians, had been shown no mercy as Cromwell had begun his policy of terror—a dire example to others of what to expect if they did not submit. He and his triumphant army had gradually moved further south, and Wexford had fared even worse than Drogheda where at least two thousand people had been slaughtered. By this time he had already written his name in blood and fire across this miserable and unhappy land.

William Slade and his family were not Catholics but had much to fear, being Protestant settlers who had come over at a time when there had been some law and order in Ireland, when Thomas Wentworth, the Earl of Strafford, had been Lord Deputy. William's family owned land in Devon, and because his older brother was heir to the estate he had decided, like many others, on the request of the King, to seek a new life for himself and his family in Ireland. But now his older brother had died without issue and the estate, or what was left of it after the sequestrations exacted by Parliament during the Civil War, had passed on to William. So far they had been lucky in Ireland, but the downtrodden Irish hated the English settlers and there were constant rebellions in which many of their friends had perished. Why, even now they had the two daughters of their dearest friends staying with them—Louise and Elizabeth Cranwell. They had only been in Ireland for five years, and now both their parents were dead. Their father had been killed at Marston Moor fighting for the King, and their mother had died of a fever just a few weeks ago. They were to go back to England with the Slades to live with a spinster aunt in Worcester.

Ellen sighed, wondering who could blame the Irish for being angry. Their lands had been taken from them and given over to the English settlers. Why, they themselves lived in a large, fine house with beautiful gardens and overlooking the sea. No one knew what had happened to its previous Catholic owner.

Suddenly the rain began to fall. At first slow and sharp, but gradually it began falling heavily, and it wasn't long before it was lashing about her, wetting her skirts and face and hair until it clung to her face. Slowly she covered her head with her shawl and reluctantly tore her eyes from the sea, knowing her son would not come that night. She turned and slowly walked up the path that led to the house—but suddenly became alert. So preoccupied had she been with her thoughts and so great was the noise of the storm that she hadn't heard the sounds that now came to her. She stopped and listened, knowing in her heart what it was. Shouts and screams of complete terror came to her over the noise of the

storm. As the torrential rain swirled about her and the
wind tore at her skirts, she looked towards the village
which clung to the cove. Already flames were leaping up
into the sky as homes were set alight, and in the streets
people were running in all directions, trying to escape
the soldiers whose helmets she could see shining in the
firelight. How quickly this force of evil had come, and
without warning.

She turned towards her own home, and could see her
seventeen-year-old son Christopher and fifteen-year-old
daughter Clara running out from the warm comfort of
the house, running out into the storm, uncaring that they
were soaked to the skin. Seeing her, they ran towards
her. Their father followed, along with Louise and
Elizabeth, who was the same age as Clara—but already
they were too late. Soldiers were riding swiftly from the
village, their bloody swords swinging at their sides.
William Slade caught his wife and clutched her to him,
seeing the fear and panic in her eyes. What could he do
now? He was powerless. He held his sword by his side,
but what use could it possibly be against so many? His
one and only hope was that the soldiers might show them
some compassion when they learned they were English
settlers. They faced the soldiers, who were now almost
upon them. They looked a sorry little group, wet and
bedraggled and all huddled together.

The soldiers came to a halt, their tunics muddied and
wet with rain and spattered with blood. The man at the
head of the column rode forward until he stood directly
in front of William, who held his head high and proud.
His two children and Elizabeth stood behind him, their
eyes large in their ashen faces, transfixed with terror.
Only nineteen-year-old Louise stood by his side un-
flinching, tall and slender like a young willow, her
chestnut hair spilling in abundance down her back. She

stood with her eyes fixed with icy contempt on the evil countenance of the stranger, unaware of the cold and the rain lashing about her body. She felt a sudden rush of rage at their helplessness, which was to melt a moment later when sheer terror struck her. The stranger's eyes flickered over her with interest, but it was only fleeting, before they came to rest once again on William Slade.

The sounds coming from the village were now horrible to hear: terrible screams as people were mercilessly slaughtered. Suddenly William froze when his eyes, which had searched the face of the man who now looked down upon him, recognised the hard, lean features and cruel eyes from long ago, and a cold dread crept through him.

'Robert Grey,' he said, his voice scarcely above a whisper.

'Oh, God, no,' said his wife, clutching her shawl beneath her chin when she too recognised this evil man.

When he spoke his voice was low and cold as steel, and his lips twisted cruelly. 'Well, well. If it isn't William Slade. So this is where you've been hiding all these years. I wondered when we would meet again.'

His soldiers encircled the wretched group and in their eyes was the lust for more blood. They had shed so much since they had come to Ireland that they were drunk and besotted with it. Robert Grey looked at them and laughed mirthlessly.

'Well, men, here we have William Slade—a Royalist and a gentleman,' he said, bowing his head to William in mock respect. 'Perhaps he is ignorant as to what has taken place in England during his absence.'

'No,' said William, trying to suppress the anger that was almost choking him, but he had to appear calm for he realised that the lives of his family depended upon him. 'We are not ignorant of the fact that our King is now dead.'

'Good. And do you know why we are here in this accursed land?'

William knew perfectly well why Cromwell was in Ireland, but chose to remain silent, his arm still about his wife's trembling shoulders.

'Perhaps I should enlighten you,' went on Robert Grey. 'We are here to wipe out the Papists.' He spat the word 'Papist' as if it were something dirty he wished to rid his mouth of.

'Yes, we have heard what is happening in other parts of Ireland,' said Ellen, suddenly gaining courage from her anger and remembering the fearful tales she had heard from travellers and small, ragged bands of refugees who were trying to escape the oncoming force. 'We have heard how you have plundered and burned, and have massacred men, women and little children without mercy.'

At first Robert Grey seemed to shrink from the hatred in this woman's eyes, and he remembered how lovely she had been as a young woman. His sudden weakness maddened him. 'Silence, woman,' he snarled. 'You let your tongue run away with you. Perhaps I forgot to tell you. To me your sort are far more despicable than this Irish scum.' He now laughed softly, and looked at the soldiers who were beginning to dismount and move menacingly towards them. 'Come—let us show William Slade what we do when we catch a nest of Royalists.'

Then everything happened so quickly that there was nothing William could do. He made a futile attempt to defend himself with his sword, but his hand was cruelly severed from his arm by a brute of a man as he raised it to strike at Robert Grey. His scream was high-pitched and terrible, and his wife ran to him, only to find herself caught in a grip of steel. Louise bravely ran to his aid, but a hard blow crashed down on to her head and she fell to the ground unconscious. Ellen called her husband's name in vain as he was pulled to his feet and dragged towards a huge oak tree a few yards from her. A rope appeared and was thrown over one of its strongest branches, and William was roughly hoisted on to a horse and the noose placed around his neck. So great was the pain in his arm, with blood pouring from his wound, that he didn't seem to realise what was happening. Ellen could hear screams behind her and, half turning, saw her son and daughter and Elizabeth stumbling and falling down into the mud as they were dragged away by the soldiers.

'Oh, God, no,' she moaned. 'Please, God, don't let them hurt my children.' And then she turned back to her husband, only to see the horse leap forward and William's body swing in mid-air. It was then that she threw back her head and opened her mouth, letting out a scream of indescribable anguish and terror, before falling to the ground when a sword was thrust into her chest.

The soldier left her lying there with Louise, believing them to be dead and impatient to offer his assistance to his comrades, who had thrown burning torches into the house and were hoisting the struggling children on to their horses. Elizabeth, her once beautiful blonde hair matted and covered in mud, was crying and screaming for her sister, for her to get up from where she lay with blood running down her cheek, for her not to be dead— but after a time her cries and screams were nothing but a mere whimper.

Slowly, Ellen opened her eyes. She couldn't move. She just lay there, dirty and sodden with her own blood, and watched as her children were taken away by the soldiers.

Eventually it all became too much, and darkness engulfed her. She fainted away, but before she lost her senses she caught sight of Robert Grey. He was calmly seated on his horse watching the scene before him, with a smile on his thin lips and madness in his eyes, looking like a demented devil. And still the rain poured down and the storm raged about them.

Now that the soldiers' work was done, Robert Grey ordered the two girls and the youth to be left alive. They would be taken as prisoners and shipped, along with hundreds of other poor creatures, victims of Cromwell's purge, to the West Indies, there to be sold as slaves.

How long Louise lay on the ground before regaining consciousness she had no way of knowing. She was stiff with cold. Slowly she opened her eyes and winced at the pain in her head, quickly remembering the blow given her by one of the soldiers and also the horror that had taken place before it. She coughed, and felt her eyes smart with the effects of smoke. Puzzled, she looked about her. She was bathed in firelight. Alarmed, she sat up quickly, looking around in desperation, half expecting to see the soldiers to still be there. But no—they had gone. Her eyes took in the pitiful, swinging body of William Slade where he still hung from the branch of the great oak, but she quickly averted them and they came to rest on Ellen, lying in the churned-up mud close by. A red stain was spread on the front of her dress, showing that she was wounded. Louise slowly crawled towards her, her head feeling as if it would explode at any moment. She heard a faint moan come from the inert form and sighed, relieved to find Ellen still alive. She must try and get her away from the fire which had completely engulfed the house and besides, she thought fearfully, how was she to know the soldiers wouldn't return?

With all her strength she somehow managed to drag Ellen to some bushes, far enough away from the house for them not to be in danger from falling timbers, and well hidden should the soldiers return. Exhausted, she fell beside Ellen, who had not opened her eyes but continued to moan softly. Gently Louise lifted and cradled her head in her lap, fearful as to what could have happened to Elizabeth and Christopher and Clara—but she couldn't think of that now. The roar of the fire blotted everything out of her mind, and her head hurt so much. She closed her eyes to shut out the sight of the burning house, huge flames leaping grotesquely up into the night sky, flames whipped up into a frenzy by the howling wind. Sharp red and white lights flashed and danced in front of her closed lids as once again she slid into a merciful oblivion, plunging her into an enormous black chasm.

CHAPTER ONE

FRANCIS SLADE stood on the wet and slippery deck of the *Seafarer*. He clung to the rails of the ship and kept his eyes fixed on the land that was slowly becoming larger as they sailed closer. It had taken the *Seafarer* many days of hardships and bad weather to reach his home on the south coast of Ireland. They should have docked yesterday, had not the terrible storm of the night before prevented them from entering the bay. The day was misty and a light drizzle was falling steadily, but he thanked God that the sea was now calm enough for them to risk putting into port. He had been absent from his family for too long and was impatient to see them again.

They were drawing close to land, and he could just make out the ghostly shapes of the buildings of the small village nestling on the hillside. He strained his eyes in an attempt to see his home, which stood a little way from the village, but to no avail. Activity went on all around him as the crew prepared to dock, and he could hear the creak of the ship's timbers and the wash of the sea as she ploughed her way through. At twenty-eight years old Francis was tall, taller than the average man. All the fighting he had done during the Civil War, coupled with the hard work he had done since, had given him an athletic frame, full of vitality, with strong, muscular shoulders. His hair, which was black and thick, curled down to his shoulders, and his eyes were blue, bold and searching and a merry light shone in them. His lips were hard, but would soften when in the company of a pretty woman and would curve up in one corner when he

14

smiled, which was often. He had great magnetism and
ability as a leader, but although he always maintained
order and discipline among the men under his command
he also liked to enjoy himself as much as any other man.
He had changed his clothes for his return home and the
meeting with his family, and they looked expensive and
were of the finest materials.

Richard, on whose ship he had sought passage and
who was also a close friend, came to stand beside him
at the rails. He said nothing and, like Francis, kept his
eyes fixed on the land. Francis had a frown on his brow
and his eyes were troubled. It was strange that there were
no people crowding on to the quay to welcome the ship.
He had a peculiar feeling as he looked at the buildings,
now becoming clearer as they emerged from the thin,
clinging mist. He could see smoke rising from the
buildings, but there was something odd about that
smoke. He watched, growing suddenly colder and feeling
the first pangs of fear as he realised what it was that was
troubling him. The village had been burned—not completely, for the rain had gutted a lot of the fire and now
the smoke was all that remained of life within it. His
knuckles showed white as his hands gripped the wooden
rail, and his chin set hard.

'There has been trouble, Richard. It appears we have
come too late.'

'Aye,' said Richard, and followed Francis' eyes with
his own as they searched for his home. And then they
saw it. Just a burned-out shell standing on the cliffs, the
faintest sign of smoke rising from the ruin. Francis'
throat tightened and he swallowed hard. 'Oh, God, no,'
was all he said.

Slowly the *Seafarer* moved towards the deserted quay,
and Francis searched the village with his blue eyes,
frantically looking and hoping for some sign of life—

but there was none. Not even any ships on the quay. The crew stood at the rails of the ship and all had eyes fixed and staring, as if in a trance. None was willing to be the first to step ashore on to the quay. What horrors were they to discover when they did?

Francis pulled himself together and tried to put on a brave front when he faced Richard. 'Tell half the crew to stay with the ship,' he said, 'and the others to come with me.' He felt inside his jacket for his pistol, to make sure it was there, but it was his sword he clutched in his hand when he jumped down on to the quay.

The men left on the *Seafarer* stared after Francis and the others as they bravely walked towards the village, glad they were not going into those strangely quiet streets.

It wasn't long before Francis learned the full horror of what had happened. Bodies were strewn everywhere, covered in mud and blood, and down the gutters which ran in the middle of the narrow streets blood mingled with rain-water. There was not a sound to be heard anywhere, and he thought then that whoever was responsible for the mass slaughter of the people of this village must have gone long since. Slowly he walked up the street towards his own home, dreading what he would find.

They had to stride over bodies that had been killed and mutilated in the most horrifying manner. Whoever had done this had shown no mercy for either man, woman or child. No crime had been too atrocious for the bloody butchers. The newcomers strode on up the street, the stench of blood strong in their nostrils. They saw charred and blackened bodies of whole families who had been burned alive in their homes, which would have come alight like tinder-boxes with their dry thatched roofs and rushes on the floor. They saw children who had been spitted on long knives and men who had been decapitated.

They walked on. Francis experienced a new kind of anger and rage. He remained silent, taking in everything around him, for what his eyes now saw was to be imprinted on his mind for all time. Several of the men, who were tough and hardened sailors, and who had been in some of the bloodiest skirmishes ever fought on the high seas, had to turn away from the dreadful spectacle and vomit in disgust. This mass slaughter of women and children was something quite new—even to them.

They climbed on, Francis a few strides ahead of the rest, his face devoid of any expression. He tried to still the trembling in his stomach. They left the carnage and burned-out ruins of the village behind and climbed up the slippery path, muddied and rutted by the many horses' hoofs which had trampled over it the night before. Francis had his eyes firmly fixed on his blackened home, fully expecting his beloved family to have been murdered like the rest. But when he stood in what had once been the garden, the beautiful green lawn and flower-beds now just a churned-up mess, he stopped and slowly let his eyes wander over the ruin. At first, when he couldn't see anything, he thought that they must have perished in the blaze, and he took a step forward. His foot kicked at something, and he looked down. It was his father's hand, with his sword still lying on it. On seeing this he wretchedly covered his eyes, but felt a light touch on his arm and turned to find Richard beside him. Richard didn't speak. He was looking ahead, and Francis followed his gaze with his own. Then he saw his father's body, still hanging where his murderers had left him. There was a congealed pool of blood on the ground where it had dripped from his wrist. Francis walked forward, staring at his father's face, which was blue and bloated. His hair was wet and lank, a dishevelled mass above his blank, staring eyes which protruded from their sockets.

'Cut him down,' Francis said hoarsely.

Two men ran forward and cut the rope which suspended the body, and gently lowered it to the ground.

'Cover him,' commanded Francis, turning his face away. 'I'll look for the others.'

He turned away, feeling a terrible, fierce hatred for the butchers who had dared do all this. He walked towards the ruin of the house. The red brick of the tall chimneys were blackened by the fire. The thin drizzle had soaked his hair, which clung to his wet face, and his eyes now blazed with a murderous fury. His heart thudded in his chest as he stared about him. His eyes became fixed on some bushes a little way ahead of him, and it was then that he heard something. He stopped and listened, straining his ears until the sound came again. It was a faint groan. Whether it was animal or human he had no way of knowing. Quickly he rushed forward and forced his way through the bushes, which cruelly tore at his hands and clothes. And there was his mother, lying on the ground with her head still cradled in Louise's lap.

Louise had her large brown eyes fixed on him, full of terror, believing him to be one of the soldiers who had come back. She did not recognise him, never having seen him before, but watched in terror as he moved closer and she shrank back. It was only when he reached out for Ellen that a strangled cry broke from her frozen lips.

'No!' she cried, clutching Ellen tightly to her. 'No—you'll not harm her.'

It was then that Francis, believing her to be one of the servants who had survived, realised what was going through her mind and paused, seeing before him a young woman who had almost reached the limits of her endurance, her face white and motionless and her fear-filled eyes shining with an unearthly brilliance as she stead-fastly refused to relinquish her hold on his mother.

'Don't be afraid,' he said softly in an attempt to dispel her fear. 'I mean her no harm. I am Francis—her son.'

Very slowly the terror faded from her eyes, and she looked at him in disbelief. Francis—Ellen's son, who she had heard so much about from Christopher and Clara that she felt she already knew him. By what manner of miracle he had come at this time she did not question. It was enough for her that he had.

Francis looked down at his mother, tenderly wiping the damp hair from her eyes. 'Mother,' he whispered, 'it's I—Francis.'

Very slowly her eyes flickered open and she looked about her until they focused on her son. She looked be-wildered and afraid. Her eyes were full of the horror they had witnessed. 'Francis?'

'Yes, Mother,' he whispered, feeling choked and so full of emotion.

'Francis,' she said, and then her eyes rested on his face. Very slowly, huge tears rolled down her sunken, grey cheeks. 'Oh, Francis—you came too late. It was so terrible,' and she closed her eyes tightly, trying to shut out the face of her husband as he had been hanged.

'I know. Are you in great pain?' he asked, removing his cloak and gently placing it over her.

'Pain? The pain from my wound is nothing compared to the pain in my heart,' and again she looked up into her son's face.

He took her cold hands in his big, brown, lean ones and held them, trying to infuse into them some of the warmth from his own. He then asked the terrible question that was gnawing at his heart. 'Where are my brother and sister?'

Again she closed her eyes, and the tears continued to
flow. 'They have gone.'

'Gone? Gone where?'

'They—the soldiers—took them away.'

'Where? Where did they take them?'

'I—I don't know, Francis,' she sobbed, clutching at
his hands tightly. 'But I did hear someone say that they
could be shipped along with others to the Indies—and—
and there to be sold as slaves.'

'Slaves? Good God!' said Francis.

'You—you must find them. You must,' said his mother
fiercely.

'I shall. I shall find them, Mother. I swear I shall find
them. But who did this—and why?' He looked at Louise
for the answer, but before she could reply the crew came
and stood about him, silently looking down at him as
he knelt beside his mother. He looked up at them, and
Richard stepped forward.

'I'm sorry, Francis, but I think we should get back to
the ship. Whoever is responsible for all this may come
back if they have seen the *Seafarer*.'

'Yes, you're right.'

'Would you like us to bury your father's body?'

Before Francis could reply, his mother had raised her
head and looked wildly at the men gathered about her.
'No. My husband's body shall not be left in this accursed land.' She looked at her son. 'Take him, Francis,
and bury him at sea. You know how much he loved the
sea.'

'I know, Mother, and it shall be as you say. Would
the pain be too great if I carried you back to the ship?'

'No. I would face anything rather than die here,' and
all the hatred she felt for this terrible Ireland showed in
her eyes.

And so Francis raised her up in his strong arms and carried her as carefully as he could, knowing she was experiencing much pain, but not one sound passed her lips. His father's body and dismembered hand were wrapped and carried by two of the crew. As quickly as they could they passed through the village, and their eyes did not dwell on the terrible sights they passed. Francis, closely followed by Louise, drew his cloak about his mother's face so that she would not witness the horrors that lay about them. Thankfully, they all climbed on board the ship, and Francis carried his mother down the narrow stairs to his cabin and his bed where he placed her gently. Louise knelt, silent and motionless, by her side, her face as white as death.

Ellen was so still that at first Francis thought she was dead, but slowly she opened her eyes and again looked at her son. Weakly she raised her arm, and stroked his face with her hand. 'You are handsome, my son. How I wish your father could have seen you once more. But it was not to be.'

Francis caught her hand and pressed it fiercely to his lips. A hard lump had risen in his throat. 'Tell me,' he whispered. 'Tell me who did this and why.'

Richard handed him a small glass. 'Here, Francis—give her some brandy. It will warm her a little.'

Francis took the glass from him and gently placed his hand beneath his mother's head, raising it a little from the pillow. She sipped the fiery liquid and gradually a faint redness crept into her thin cheeks. She then lay back and sighed. 'Do you remember Robert Grey, Francis?'

He looked at her and slowly shook his head. 'I don't think so.'

'He was the one who did this. He—he——' But she faltered and closed her eyes, finding it difficult to speak. Francis looked at her in alarm.

'Don't talk now, Mother—you must rest.'

'No—I must tell you,' she gasped. 'I know I don't have much time.'

He remained silent, knowing she spoke the truth. No human being could lose so much blood and live.

'Your father and Robert Grey grew up together. They were good friends as boys and their families were close. They lived not far from us in Devon. Do you remember now?'

Francis thought hard, his mind going back to the past and the few short years of his childhood he had spent in England. Robert Grey? He did now remember the name and then the lean, hawk-like face. 'Yes—I do remember,' he replied.

'You were very young. When your father and I married, they were still friends—but I always disliked him. Something came between them as they grew older. They were torn apart by their beliefs. His family farmed a great deal of land. But his beliefs verged towards Puritanism.' She shuddered slightly as she said this and her voice was low and bitter. 'When you were a child and the great struggle began in England between the King and his Parliament, Robert Grey raised a troop of horses and went to fight against him. Your father never forgave him for that—he said Grey was fighting him also. And so they became deadly enemies. Their friendship turned into a bitter hatred. When we came to Ireland, the name of Robert Grey was never mentioned—neither by your father nor by me. But I knew he thought of him—often.' She fell silent and closed her eyes, exhausted.

Francis gently took her hand and she slowly opened them again, fixing them on her son. They burned with anger, and when she next spoke her voice was fierce. 'He came over to Ireland with Oliver Cromwell, intent on destroying all the Catholics, and it was he who butchered the people in the village. He showed no mercy for your father or myself when he came upon our home. He hanged your father gladly, knowing who he was, and allowed his soldiers to carry off Christopher and Clara.' She raised herself painfully from the pillows and looked closely at her son. Her voice shook with savage anger when she spoke again. 'A creature such as he has forfeited all rights to live.' Again she closed her eyes, the effort of speaking becoming too much, but there was more she had to say before the end came. She took a deep breath, and when she again opened her eyes this time she fastened them on Louise and gripped her hand, but it was to Francis that she spoke. 'Francis—you must promise me that you will take care of Louise. She is the daughter of my dearest friend, Mary Cranwell, who— God willing—I shall see quite soon. Her sister Elizabeth was taken along with Christopher and Clara. She has no one except an aunt in Worcester. Promise me that you will take care of her.'

'Of course,' said Francis, looking down at the girl kneeling by the bedside but without really seeing her. The terrible anguish he was feeling for his mother, knowing she would breathe her last at any moment, filled him so that he had no room for any other thought.

CHAPTER TWO

THAT night, Francis stood alone on the deck of the *Seafarer*, his eyes directed towards the distant coastline of Ireland, which had vanished into the sea mist. The rain had now ceased and the moon was breaking through, making a silver pathway on the calm black sea. But he saw none of this. Gone was the unconcealed anguish he had felt earlier when he had watched as the great black ocean had closed over his father and mother—taking with them part of his life. The heartbreak and pain had been replaced by a deep and terrible hatred. Indeed, it was so great that night as he looked towards the distant land, he vowed vengeance and swore that he would not rest until he had found his brother and sister and wreaked his vengeance on Robert Grey.

When he came on deck later it was to find it almost deserted, apart from the watch and a single figure standing alone at the bow, gazing out to sea—so still that she reminded him of some ship's figurehead silhouetted against the night sky. Slowly he moved towards her, but she did not turn although she knew when he stopped behind her. Francis had hardly been aware of her until now, apart from when the bodies of his parents had slipped into the sea. Then she had raised her hand and brushed a tear from her cheek.

It was a cold night and he saw that she was wearing the same clothes as when he had found her, the mud and blood having dried on them long since. But as ragged

24

and dirty as she was, there was something strikingly lovely and dignified about her tall, slender form.

'Why don't you come below and warm yourself?' he said softly. 'It's a cold night.'

'Is it? I hadn't noticed.' There was a moment of silence between them before she continued. 'Where do you think they have sent Elizabeth and your brother and sister?'

'I don't know exactly. Mother said the West Indies, but I'm afraid that could mean any one of a number of islands ruled by the English.'

'I cannot believe I shall never see her again,' she whispered, feeling a hard lump rise in her throat and hot tears well in her eyes. 'What will happen to them?'

'They will be put to work on the plantations.'

'Will they be sold—like slaves?'

'Yes,' said Francis hoarsely, finding it difficult to think of Christopher and Clara being forced to perform hard labour on the sugar plantations. They would be badly fed and obliged to work in close company with negro slaves. And then there were the masters, some too cruel to imagine. The best they could possibly hope for would be to be put to work in the owners' houses as domestic servants. A fierce hatred for Robert Grey and Oliver Cromwell burned through him for what they'd done to his family, but now he looked at the girl before him, at her bowed head and the dejected droop of her shoulders. Something of her anguish and despair penetrated his mind and he reached out and placed his hands on her shoulders, turning her slowly to face him. Her face was awash with tears, her eyes big and dark in her face, a face whiter than death. He drew her into his arms as a tearing, strangled sob broke from her and she cried wretchedly as she clung to him and all the horror and pent-up grief poured from her. Francis held her tightly, his cheek resting against the softness of her hair.

'Oh, Francis—I keep thinking that this is all a bad dream and that soon I shall wake up but—but deep down I know I shan't—that all this misery is real. But I—I shall not be able to bear it,' she said between her muffled sobs against his chest, 'knowing that somewhere Elizabeth is alive—suffering God only knows how much. I must find her—I must.'

Francis tightened his hold. 'You shall find her, Louise,' he said fiercely. 'One day we will find all three of them—together. I promise you that I shall not let them fester on any one of those islands for longer than I have to.'

Louise raised her head, her tears frozen on her cheeks, and although she was tall she still had to look up at him. She was strangely comforted by his strong arms about her and the warmth in his voice. She had never met Francis before, but had heard so much about him that she felt as if she had known him all of her life and now, as she tilted her head back, her eyes enormous in her pale face, each was aware that something passed between them, something so strong that it took them completely unawares and for one mad, glorious moment Francis wanted to bend his head and place his lips upon her full, soft mouth—and he was correct in thinking she would not have resisted. She searched his face with a kind of wonder, and very slowly and reluctantly pulled herself from his arms and stood back from him.

'I'm sorry I cried like that. What must you think of me?'

What did he think of her? He didn't know. All he knew was that he wanted to hold her and go on holding her, but it was sheer madness. He shook his head tiredly and lowered his gaze, knowing he would be unable to look into those deep brown eyes for much longer without beginning to lose all reason. He ran his fingers through his tangled hair, and she noticed how they trembled slightly.

'After what you've been through it's hardly surprising you cried. But come,' he said, 'let's go below. You must be exhausted, and we will see if we can find you something suitable to wear. We can't have you arriving in London like that.'

'London?'

'Yes,' he said, averting her questioning eyes. 'There is something I must take care of, and perhaps when we are not so tired we'll be able to think how to go about getting Christopher and the girls back.'

When Louise lay in bed later, sleep eluded her at first, and she stared up at the ceiling, all the horrors of the last twenty-four hours crowding into her tired mind. But strangely it was Francis who troubled her, and what they had both felt when he had held her. She turned and buried her flushed face in the pillows, knowing he was pledged in marriage to another—Anne Sinclair—who would be waiting for him in London. But then that hadn't mattered, because she knew that if he had kissed her her body would have responded gladly, that she would have behaved like some kind of wanton, and she was deeply ashamed.

The skies under which the *Seafarer* sailed on the final stage of her journey to London were grey and heavy, like Louise's heart, and all the fears and uncertainties of the future flooded her mind. She spent many solitary hours on deck gazing at the cold waters of the ocean, insensible to the work of the sailors going on all about her or the wind billowing out the big sails high above or the creak of timbers and rope and the smell of pitch. She was shrouded in a warm woollen cloak, covering the coarse skirt and bodice which had replaced the fine

French blue silk dress she had worn on her last night in Ireland and been more than thankful to discard, with its blood and mud stains a constant reminder of that night.

It was as if she had just emerged from some kind of nightmare and for a time she was desolate, hardly able to believe what had taken place on that terrible night, and she knew it would haunt her for the rest of her life. The thought that perhaps she might never again see Elizabeth nearly tore her apart. Only Francis could understand what torment she was going through, feeling the same cruel loss, experiencing the same kind of hopeless misery, but his mere presence gave her comfort and, whatever the future held for either of them, there would be no escaping the strong bond that had been forged between them during these few days on the *Seafarer*. A bond created by their mutual loss and grief, which had drawn them closer together than they otherwise might have been.

Francis found his eyes constantly drawn towards her still figure and he experienced a strange concern, wondering how deeply what she had gone through would affect her. The emotional scars would be almost impossible to erase.

Often Louise would feel his distinct gaze on her shoulders, penetrating the thick material of her cloak and bodice, almost burning her bare skin. On turning, she would meet his stare without any embarrassment; his deep blue eyes would be troubled, but then he would smile, a smile which could melt even the coldest heart. He had never spoken to her of his future bride, and she had a strange feeling deep down that he didn't want to. That he was avoiding speaking of her. But she knew he would—some time—and waited for him to do so with deep apprehension and misgivings.

It was when the *Seafarer* was slowly moving up the Thames, a journey which was long and tedious because of the large number of ships of many descriptions and nationalities—small boats and merchant ships and slow barges laden with coal and grain—all sailing either up or down, that he came to stand close beside her. She was staring absently at the river, and he was deeply moved by her sheer loveliness. She pushed a strand of thick hair back from her face wearily, but then she looked up into his tanned face and met his deep blue eyes. So blue, she imagined them to be the colour of some far-off tropical sea.

'We'll be docking shortly,' he said, 'although it will be quite some time before we will be able to leave the ship.'

'Where are we going?'

'I'm taking you to stay with some friends of mine in Bloomsbury. They're good people— I know you'll like them.'

'What are they called?' she asked, knowing perfectly well who they were, but she dreaded the moment when he would tell her.

'Sinclair. I served under Sir Thomas Sinclair during the Civil War. He's a fine man, Louise, although how he's fared recently under the new Commonwealth I have yet to find out. I—I also hope to introduce you to his daughter Anne,' he said quietly, suddenly finding it difficult to meet her steady, questioning gaze and wondering why he should feel so hesitant at telling her. 'We— we were to be married on my arrival in London.'

'Were?' she asked, hope suddenly filling her heart.

'Yes. You see, she was expecting to return with me to Devon along with my family, to begin a new life but— well,' he said, his eyes clouding, 'I'm not sure what we'll do now. It's going to be difficult telling her what's happened.'

'Yes,' she whispered, staring at the river but without really seeing anything, feeling a great emptiness inside her. He had spoken of his bride-to-be at last, and her name caught Louise's consciousness and filled her with dismay. But why should it? she asked, furious with herself. Why should she mind that he loved another? Hadn't she already known that? Why should she want their relationship to be anything deeper than what it was? He had saved her life, but that gave her no reason to assume she could ever mean anything more to him than a devoted friend. She had fallen victim to her grief and, reaching out, had found Francis. They were like kindred spirits, and she told herself that what she felt for him had been born out of gratitude. That was all. It could never be anything else. She turned and looked at him steadily.

'Do you love her, Francis?'

He didn't answer right away, but he knew that if anyone had asked him that question before he'd set foot in Ireland and met Louise, he would have said 'yes' without hesitation. Now, when he looked into her eyes, he didn't know any more, but a picture of Anne as she had been when he had last seen her, happy at the prospect of their marriage but sad at his leaving, sprung before his eyes and he was filled with self-loathing and guilt. Guilt for not having thought of her as often as he should during the last few days, although he could not deny that his impatience to see her was no longer as strong as it had been.

'Yes—yes, I love her,' he said but, Louise thought, without much conviction. 'Anne and I have known each other for a long time, Louise, and indeed I owe her family a great deal.'

'Then surely there is no reason why you can't still marry, why you can't marry and leave for Devon as you first intended. I'm sure it's what your parents would have wanted.'

'Perhaps,' he said quietly, looking deep into her eyes. 'But I'm not sure that I want to any more.' After excusing himself, he turned from her and walked away, and wondered why fate should have brought them together in such a cruel way. He was drawn to Louise in a way he had never been to any other woman, but there was nothing he could do. It was too late. The fact remained that he and Anne were promised to each other, and she loved and trusted him implicitly. He could not abandon her. He had no right to make her suffer because of what he knew he was capable of feeling for Louise, and with her he must make a deliberate effort to put up all his defences.

It was only when Louise was alone that she also became determined that, on reaching London, she would waste no time in going to her Aunt Katherine in Worcester. She must, she thought wretchedly, otherwise it would be too late and she would fall hopelessly in love with him. She must put an end to something that had hardly begun.

At her first sight of London, Louise was almost struck dumb by its sheer size. Never had she envisaged it as being so big, seething and throbbing with life. The wharves were thronging with people, all going about their various tasks. Tall, skeletal masts were all of a tangle in the sky, and the great gilded hulls of many ships, men-of-war and merchant vessels, were all jumbled together.

When Francis at last managed to leave the ship, they climbed inside one of the many hackney carriages that travelled the streets of the city. It was certainly not the

most comfortable carriage, but Francis assured her she
would not have to endure it for long.

They headed north-west, away from the river, and for
the first time since leaving Ireland Louise became spellbound by what she saw. They travelled through a lab-
yrinth of narrow alleyways and streets overhung by black
and white, timber-framed gabled houses. An open gutter
filled with decaying garbage ran down the middle of the
streets, and she wrinkled her nose at the acrid stench
that rose from it. The noise of the street criers, monot-
onously intoning their cries, bearing their merchandise
in barrows and trays, became almost deafening at times.
Often the carriage had to stop when the streets became
too congested, but they eventually left the crowds behind
and the bustle of London gave way to a more fashionable part where the well-to-do lived, and they travelled down country lanes passing many fine houses.

'How much longer before we're there?' she asked
Francis, who had watched her closely throughout the
journey.

'We're almost there. I only hope we find the family
at home. They didn't know when to expect us. Until
recently they divided their time between their home here
in London and their estate in Gloucester, but not any
more. Parliament has confiscated all their land.'

Almost as soon as he had said this, the carriage turned
in at a tree-lined driveway at the end of which stood an
elegant rose brick house with white-painted sash
windows. Box and yew evergreen shrubs adorned the
gardens, and a few fashionable Italian marble statues
were placed among them, the white stone contrasting
beautifully with the dark green of the leaves. But Louise
only had eyes for the house and her throat had gone
very tight. She had a tremulous fluttering in the pit of
her stomach. She suddenly felt very lost and helpless,

and looked to Francis for support. The door of the house was opened by a servant, who stood aside when an elderly gentleman in a white curled wig emerged. Aware of Louise's confusion, Francis held out his hand and assisted her from the carriage, leading her up the stone steps until they stood in front of the gentleman. The two men embraced each other with genuine warmth, and then Francis stood back and drew Louise forward.

'Louise, I would like to introduce you to Sir Thomas Sinclair. This is Louise Cranwell, Sir Thomas. I have brought her from Ireland.'

'Welcome, my dear—but where are your family?' asked Sir Thomas, looking past them towards the carriage which was preparing to leave. 'Are they not with you?' He fell silent, reading what was in Francis' eyes, and he understood something was gravely wrong. 'Come inside where we can talk.'

Inside the oak-panelled entrance hall, Louise looked about in amazement. The first thing that took her attention was the elegant wooden staircase with ornately carved balustrades rising grandly to a gallery up above. She looked up just in time to see a young woman emerge in a flurry of petticoats and with a joyous cry run down the stairs, her soft slippers hardly making a sound on the hard wood. She ran straight into Francis' arms, and Louise was suddenly aware of a terrible ache wrenching her heart.

'Anne—I would like you to meet Louise Cranwell. She has come with me from Ireland, and I hope you two will become friends.'

'Oh, I'm sure we will.' Anne smiled, a warm, welcoming smile revealing small, even white teeth and, reaching out, she placed a hand on Louise's. There was a naïveté about her, but also something that inspired trust, and Louise was drawn to her, although she would have found it so much easier if she could have disliked her. Slowly the smile faded from Anne's lips, and her eyes became puzzled when she glanced searchingly about the hall.

'But where are your parents—and your brother and sister? Francis?' she asked, and her eyes flew to his in alarm. 'Where are they? What has happened?'

Before Francis could reply, her father had stepped forward.

'Come in here,' he said, ushering them into another room, 'and you can tell us what has happened—although I must tell you that we are not unaware of what has been taking place in Ireland.'

He closed the door and Francis told them, as briefly as he could so as to spare Louise's feelings, what had happened. She sat with her back straight, staring ahead, her dark eyes filled with pain and fixed on Francis' face. It was only when he had finished speaking that she lowered her head.

Thomas Sinclair couldn't speak for a long time—he was too full of angry emotion, which was eventually replaced by a deep sorrow. There was silence in the room, apart from Anne's quiet weeping. Eventually her father went to her and patted her shoulder gently.

'Come, Anne—I think Francis and Louise will be in need of some refreshment after their journey.'

Anne wiped her tear-drenched face with her handkerchief and turned to Louise, her eyes full of an infinite sadness and pity. 'Of course—I'm sorry. Would you like to come with me, Louise, and I'll ask the servants to prepare a bath for you and some fresh clothes?'

Louise rose and smiled softly. 'Thank you—I'd appreciate that. I'm afraid I left everything I own back in Ireland.'

The two men watched them leave the room. Louise followed Anne up the stairs, knowing it was going to be more difficult than she had imagined remaining for long in this house and being forced to watch her and Francis together.

The days that followed in the Sinclair household passed so slowly that Louise felt as if she were suspended in another world. The time spent in the quiet solitude of the house should have been a time for healing, but it wasn't. She became restless and impatient and found that it only intensified her situation, increasing her determination to find Elizabeth—but to do this she needed money to pay for her passage to the West Indies, and she didn't have any. She must go to her Aunt Katherine at Bessington Hall in Worcester. She would help her. She could figure out no other way of getting the money— apart from asking Francis or Sir Thomas. But she had no intention of doing that. She had imposed upon their hospitality for too long as it was, and besides, she thought bitterly, it was better that she disappeared out of their lives for good instead of waiting in vain for some miracle from heaven to bring her and Francis together.

It was one night when Louise and Anne had retired that Francis and Thomas sat facing each other, one on either side of the fire, drinking their home-brewed ale. Francis, his long, booted legs stretched out lazily in front of him, looked across at his one-time commander with warm respect. A deep and lasting friendship had developed between them during the long years of the Civil War, and he thought how lucky he'd been when his father had sent him into Thomas' service. A chest wound acquired two years previously had aged the older man prematurely, and his breathing was laboured, but his intelligent grey eyes still sparkled and were full of life. Francis had always admired his consistent and steadfast loyalty to King Charles and had been proud to serve under him, until he had been given his own command and had come to know the young Prince Charles—the Prince of Wales—to whom he bore a striking resemblance with his uncommon height and black, curling hair. He had been mistaken for Charles many times, and they had never been together without people commenting on the likeness.

The two men had just finished talking over old times, winning and losing hard-fought battles all over again, when their thoughts turned to the uncertain future.

'So, Charles is back in Holland,' said Francis.

'Aye, at Breda—and wondering what to do next, I don't doubt. He's certainly had his share of troubles for one so young.'

'Will he be persuaded to sign the oath of the Covenant with Scotland?'

Thomas nodded, a grave expression in his eyes. 'If he wants to sit upon the throne of England, then it's his only way, although his father would turn in his grave if he knew. He had hoped to do it with the help of foreign forces and Ireland—without the conditions imposed on him by the Scots commission—but that man Cromwell has put a stop to that with his policy. The appalling savagery he is using to suppress the Irish will be remembered for all time. You mark my words, Francis, it will be an ineradicable stain on his character. Oliver Cromwell is a man of great courage and military genius—there is no denying that. But what he did in that land was unbelievable and unforgivable. The man must have been crazy.' He looked at Francis, who had paled significantly. 'Forgive me, Francis—I had forgotten for the moment that you witnessed it at first hand. Come—tell me what you intend doing now. Will you go to Devon and claim your inheritance?'

Francis' tone was full of irony when he spoke. 'Inheritance? What inheritance? After our defeat at Naseby in forty-five, and the enormous fines Parliament exacted on Royalist properties, my uncle—like yourself—was forced to sell off most of the land to pay them, and now there is a danger that the house and the rest of the land will be confiscated. Besides, I do believe there is a price upon my head, because it is known that I was the leader of several Royalist uprisings and also because of my close association with Charles Stuart. So—I think it wise to keep a low profile for the time being. There are Parliamentary spies and informers everywhere. Already many well-known men and their families loyal to the memory of King Charles have been thrown into prison and more than a few executed.'

'Then what will you do?'

'I mustn't remain here. I am aware that my presence in your household puts all of you at risk. I have a mind to go to the West Indies and find my family, and also Louise's sister Elizabeth. I have grave doubts that they will survive the sort of life forced on them, and must do all in my power to get them back—and besides, I am not willing to conform with laws and a way of life under the rule of Cromwell which is completely alien to me.'

'And what of Charles Stuart?' asked Thomas, looking Francis straight in the eye. 'What if he goes to Scotland—as I am sure he will—and puts his hand to the Covenant, committing England to Presbyterianism, tolerating no other religion? Don't you think he will have need of all those who have remained loyal to him? And—what of Anne?' he asked, looking at Francis quizzically. 'How much longer does she have to wait before you make her your wife?'

Francis shook his head. 'I cannot make Anne my wife until I have something to offer her—much as I want to. And of Charles—well—I shouldn't have to tell you that I have no intention of deserting him. My whole life is dedicated to avenging the memory of our murdered King, and I shall not rest until his son sits upon the throne of England, as is his right.' He sighed deeply, a serious frown creasing his brow. 'But—you are right, Thomas. You always were. Charles will be in need of all the support he can get, and perhaps with the support of Scotland he might just rally enough Royalist loyalties to win England.'

'Then go to him in Holland, Francis, and find out what he intends,' said Thomas, an excited gleam entering his eyes. He slapped his knee hard, spilling some ale on to the hearth where it sizzled with the heat. 'By God, if I were a younger man, that is what I would do. My years of fighting and adventure are over, but I never had any doubt in my mind about the justice of the King's cause. The most I have to hope for now is that Parliament will leave me be, to live out my life in peace—but somehow I don't think it will. My days are numbered. Although— I worry for Anne, with her mother gone. Perhaps I should send her to her brother and his wife in Holland until things settle down. It's just not safe for her here.'

'I know, and I have given it a great deal of thought. I agree with what you suggest. She will be safe with George and his wife, but I think you should both leave— and——' he hesitated, lowering his gaze '—I would be grateful if you would take Louise with you. It was intended that she would go to her aunt in Worcester, but after making discreet enquiries I have discovered that she is no longer alive. I don't think she has any more close relatives she can go to.'

Thomas shook his head sadly. 'Poor lass—so now she has no one. As if she hasn't been through enough. Does she know?'

'No, I haven't told her.'

'Then of course she must come with us. She will be company for Anne,' said Thomas, observing how Francis' manner and look changed when he spoke of the young woman he had brought with him from Ireland. He suddenly found himself feeling very sorry for his daughter.

It was two days later that Francis asked to see Louise in the drawing-room. Anne was out visiting a friend and Sir Thomas was resting, as he usually did most afternoons. Louise entered the room quietly to find him standing by the fireplace, and her heart gave a joyful leap at the sight of him. The bronzed features and deep blue eyes would remain buried in her heart for all time.

He watched her move gracefully across the polished wood floor until she stood before him. He had seen little of her since their arrival, and this was the first time they had been alone together. There had been a great deal to occupy his time in London, not to mention the arrangements for them all to leave unobserved for Holland. It had proved difficult, because already he knew he would be arrested when found, and he was certain that the house was being watched, which made coming and going tedious. But now he looked at Louise, and something stirred in the region of his heart when he looked into her clear brown eyes. Her beautiful, deep chestnut hair was drawn off her face, revealing the long, slender column of her throat. As a sign of the times she wore a plain dark grey dress which emphasised her slender waist. It was relieved only by a fine white linen collar. He could not deny that what he felt for her was more

primitive than anything he had experienced for any other
woman before. She was looking at him, her eyes never
leaving his face, and he saw the sorrow and sadness still
there.

'How are you, Louise?'

'Well, thank you. And you?'

He shrugged slightly, moving a little away from her,
finding it difficult to stand so close without touching
her. 'I, too, but there is something I wish to discuss with
you.'

'Yes—I've been meaning to have a word with you
also.'

'Oh?'

'Yes. I—I wish to go to my Aunt Katherine in
Worcester.'

'That's what I wanted to see you about, Louise. I'm
afraid I have sad news concerning your aunt.'

'What is it?' she asked, feeling a chill creep through
her.

'I made certain enquiries concerning her, and I am
deeply sorry to have to tell you that she is dead.'

'Dead?'

'Yes. She died four months ago.'

'Four months? But—but she can't be,' she whispered,
all the blood having drained from her face. One hand
rose and froze at her throat when she realised the grim
reality of his words. 'Oh, dear God—what am I to do?
I have no one. What—what did she die of?'

'It seems there was a fire one night. How it started
remains a mystery, but your aunt died in the blaze. The
house was burned to the ground.' He looked at her
stricken face, wishing he could have softened the blow,
but there was no easy way to tell her. 'Her affairs were
placed in the hands of her friend and trustee, a Mr James
Beamish,' he went on, 'although I must tell you that she

died leaving very little. The land had already been sequestered by Parliament, and what little wealth she had went to funding the Royalist cause.'

Louise stared at him, trying to comprehend what he was saying. At first she couldn't believe that her Aunt Katherine and Bessington Hall—that well-remembered and loved house of her mother's family, where she and Elizabeth had spent so many enjoyable summers when they were little—was no more. That quiet, beautiful house with its mellowed brick and stone walls and beautiful gables. Francis was telling her that it had gone—gone forever. She lowered her gaze sadly.

'Then there doesn't seem much point in my going to Worcester after all,' she whispered.

'You'll have to—eventually. It may be that you're her only surviving relative.'

'No!' she cried, looking at him fiercely. 'Don't forget there is still Elizabeth. I will not believe she's dead.'

'Yes—of course. I'm sorry. But Louise, listen to me. I've made arrangements for Anne and her father to go to Holland. Go with them. George—Anne's brother— lives there with his wife. They will be more than pleased to have you stay with them, and I know Anne would be glad for you to accompany her.'

Louise felt the room reeling about her ears. What he had said seemed absurd, and she looked at him in confusion. 'Holland? But why should I want to go to Holland? That's impossible.'

'You must,' he said earnestly. 'Don't you realise how dangerous it is for us to remain here a moment longer— for all of us—and if you go to Worcester alone there may be nothing for you? Louise—there is something I have not told you because I did not want to add to your worries, but there is a warrant out for my arrest. It's only a matter of time before we are all arrested for the parts we played during the Civil War. You must understand that we have to leave here at all costs—before it's too late. Please come with us.'

'But—to Holland,' she whispered, her eyes misting with tears.

'Yes, there you will be safe. I shall go and join the King at Breda.'

'But—but what about Christopher and our sisters? Surely you cannot have forgotten so soon what they are going through? That we must get them back?'

At her words his eyes filled with pain. 'Don't you think I haven't thought of them—all the time? But I cannot go chasing halfway across the world until I know for certain where they are. I shall go and look for them, Louise—I promise you—but not now.'

'But why?' she cried, uncaring that she angered him. 'Because of your loyalty to Charles Stuart? Perhaps if you had not been in Holland, dancing attendance upon him, then you would have heard about what was happening in Ireland and it would not have taken you so long to get there. Perhaps they would all be here now if you had. Can you not show them some loyalty also? You have served the King relentlessly for the past ten years, and now his son is in exile. Francis, the Royalist cause is in ruins—can't you see that? There is nothing you can do to change it, but you can remember the promise you made your mother and find your brother and sister.'

'I know,' he flared, and he suddenly reached out and seized her roughly by the shoulders. He looked at her hard, violent rage and anger burning in his eyes, his whole body taut, and she trembled at the sudden force she had unleashed inside him by her cruel accusation, one she hadn't known existed. His tone was mercilessly cutting. 'Don't you think I blame myself all the time for not getting there sooner? I go through hell every time I think of it, but there is nothing I can do. You are right to blame me and your accusations are just, but I do not need to be reminded of it. It is I who will have to live with it for the rest of my life. But I also remember the promise I made my mother concerning you, Louise,' he said, his lips twisting cruelly. 'That I would take care of you. That is why I am asking you to go to Holland.'

Louise stared at him incredulously, and the tears that had misted her eyes earlier now flooded her cheeks. His words had hurt her deeply. 'And for no other reason? Well—you can forget the promise you made to your mother, Francis, because I am not your concern. I am not a child and am quite capable of taking care of myself, and if you think I shall go to Holland merely as a salve to your conscience—then you are mistaken.'

'You little fool,' he said, his expression softening, deeply moved by her distress. 'You know that is not the reason,' and the next instant she was folded in his arms. Something like madness exploded in his brain, and he was kissing her wet cheeks and then he found her mouth, soft and sweet, and tasted the salt of her tears. They kissed each other hungrily, aware of nothing any more but each other and the moment. Louise trembled against him, and he awoke hundreds of demons inside her head as she was swept along on a delicious tide of ecstasy. She forgot everything, her sorrow and pain and even their disloyalty to Anne, and she wanted to abandon herself to him completely. But somehow she managed to summon the strength to struggle free from his embrace.

She pulled herself from his arms and swayed slightly, dazed by what they had done. 'No!' she cried. 'This is not right.'

Francis stood quite still, his face full of unconcealed passion. He saw the desperate hunger mirrored in her eyes. 'So,' he said quietly, 'it's like that with you too.'

'Yes, and I am ashamed of what I feel. I cannot do this to Anne—she has been so good to me. I am unworthy of her friendship. Have you any idea what it will do to her if she finds out?'

'Yes. It would destroy her.'

'And together I believe we would destroy each other,' she said softly.

He nodded, understanding, and their eyes locked together. 'Please, Louise—I beg you to go to Holland. You must go. Will you promise me that you will think about it? What alternative is there?'

'None,' she said, sighing deeply, and she suddenly felt very weary. 'But have you not thought how hard it will be for us—to see each other often—feeling as we do?'

'Yes, I have thought about it,' he said fiercely, 'and I cannot deny that I want you. I shall probably go out of my mind with wanting you. I want you so much that a moment ago I would have forgotten one of the sweetest girls a man could ever hope to marry. But I will not— I cannot betray her love.'

A sharp pain pierced Louise's heart at these words, and she bowed her head in defeat. 'I am not asking you to do that.' She turned and moved sadly towards the door, but there she paused and looked back at him. She squared her shoulders and lifted her head proudly, and that gesture nearly broke Francis' heart. 'I shall think about going to Holland if there is no alternative—I promise,' and she went out, leaving him staring at the closed door.

*   *   *

Louise did think about it. She thought about it a great deal, but in the end she decided against it. She believed what he had told her about her aunt's death and thought it was useless going to Worcester now. She paced her bedchamber in an effort to sort out her situation, but came to no conclusion. When she thought of Francis and their kiss, she flushed crimson and was filled with shame, angry with herself for behaving as she had. And the accusation she had flung at him, almost blaming him for the death of his parents and the awful fate that had befallen his brother and sister, was unforgivable. How could she have said those terrible things? How could she, when she now knew that she loved him more than life itself? A great emptiness engulfed her when she thought of him and she felt a deep, physical pain—rather like an insatiable hunger which she would never be able to satisfy. It was at that moment of realisation that she made her decision to leave. It was clear to her now that she alone must change the course of her life—however lonely or frightened she was to be in the future. She could not live near Francis and not be able to love him, so she must learn to live without him. She would not see him again.

CHAPTER THREE

LOUISE waited until after dark, when the candles had been lit and the big house was quiet, before wrapping herself in a dark cloak, and picking up a small bundle of clothes from the large four-poster bed. She was about to cross towards the door when at that moment someone tapped on it quietly. Her breath caught in her throat and she froze. It was Anne who entered.

'Louise, I just came to say goodnight and to see if there was anything you wanted before—oh!' she said, her eyes widening as she took in Louise's appearance. 'Where are you going?'

'I—I——' Louise turned away from her wide, questioning stare. Oh, why did she have to come in now? 'I'm leaving, Anne. I can't go with you to Holland.'

'Oh, but you must. It's far too dangerous for you to stay here alone.'

'I can't go with you,' stressed Louise. 'I must try to find my sister. Please—try and understand.'

'I do understand, but she is on the other side of the world. How can you find her?'

'I don't know. I only know that I must try.'

'But—but what about Francis? Shouldn't you tell him?'

Louise's eyes flew to Anne's in alarm. 'No—no, he mustn't know—not until after I've gone. He'll only try to stop me.'

'He'll be so angry.'

'I can't help that. I've written a letter to you all,' she said, indicating the neatly folded letter propped against

46

the mirror on the dresser, 'thanking you for everything you've done for me. I shall always be grateful. But I must go.'

'But where? Where will you go? And you have no money. Will you go to Worcester?'

'No. There's nothing for me there.'

'Then what will you do?'

'I'll find work.'

'What kind of work?'

'I don't know, but if the worst comes to the worst then I shall offer myself for employment on one of the plantations in the West Indies. At least it will be a way of getting there, and my passage will be paid.'

Anne looked at her in horror. 'To become an indentured servant, you mean? But that will mean your having to work for at least three years to pay it back before you'll be free to go and look for Elizabeth. Why, you might not even survive that long.'

'I know, but that's a chance I'll just have to take.'

'Oh, Louise—listen to me,' said Anne, reaching out and gripping her arms, looking hard into her eyes in an attempt to force some sense into her. 'You cannot go there—especially alone. It's far too dangerous, and have you any idea of the sort of work you'll be forced to do on any one of those plantations, and the sort of people you'll have to work and live with? Why, I've heard that even the prisons of Newgate and Bridewell send convicts to the islands to provide labour. Only vagrants and destitute people go there.'

Louise's lips twisted with irony at her words. 'And isn't that what I am? Destitute?'

'Oh, no—no, you're not, Louise. You have us. Please come with us to Holland. I believe Francis has arranged for us to go tomorrow night. I shudder to think what

he'll say when he finds you gone, or his anger when he
discovers I knew about it and failed to stop you.'

At the mention of his name Louise's heart almost
stood still, and the shame she had felt earlier was replaced by remorse. Remorse for the hurt this sweet and
gentle creature would feel if she ever found out that she
herself was in love with Francis. Perhaps then Anne
would not be so eager for her to go to Holland with
them. She became even more convinced that she was
doing the right thing by leaving.

'You don't have to tell him you knew.'

'I cannot lie to him.'

'I'm not asking you to do that,' and she sighed at the
unhappiness on Anne's face. 'You love him very much,
don't you, Anne?'

She nodded. 'Yes—yes, I do. I love him so much that
without him I would die.'

Louise lowered her head so that Anne wouldn't see
the hurt her words had caused her, and hastily she began
pulling on her gloves.

'I can see that your mind is made up and nothing I
say will change it,' said Anne.

'No.'

'Very well, then wait here—I have something to give
you,' and she went out quickly but returned a moment
later. She pressed a purse full of coins into Louise's hand.
'Take this. It's not much, but at least you won't starve,
and it should pay for a decent room at an inn for a few
days.'

'But—but I—I can't,' protested Louise.

'Please—take it. I couldn't bear to think of you wandering the streets with nowhere to go. Anything could
happen to you.'

A lump of gratitude rose in Louise's throat, and
reaching out she embraced Anne warmly. How she

wished circumstances could have been different. She would have treasured Anne's friendship.

'Thank you, Anne. Please don't worry about me. I'll be all right,' and she stood back and looked into Anne's eyes, swimming with tears. 'Thank you for all your kindness, and I do hope you and Francis will be happy.' It was with a heavy heart that she turned and, picking up her bundle of clothes, went quickly out.

She pulled the cloak about her, covering her head with the large hood, and hurried along the landing, careful not to be seen, towards the narrow back staircase used by the servants. She went down them and unlocked the door to the outside. Silently she pulled it open and slipped through, and like a shadow disappeared into the night.

The following morning found Louise in London amid the pealing of what seemed like a hundred church bells, all with their own distinct ring. She had entered the city at dawn along with people from nearby hamlets and villages, all with heavily laden carts and wagons of fresh fruit and vegetables and dairy produce to sell to the street traders. She was thankful that the air was warm, and looking up through the overhanging gables she could see the sky, a translucent blue with only a few fluffy white clouds drifting along on the gentlest of early summer breezes. The cobbled streets swarmed with people. She passed booths selling freshly baked bread and hot meat pies and the air was filled with their delicious smells, which reminded her of how hungry she was. She was also extremely tired and her feet hurt. She had walked nearly all night, and unless she rested and got something to eat soon she would be unable to walk much further.

She paused when she emerged into what seemed to be a large, open space, and gazed in awe at the unmis-

takable building of St Paul's Cathedral, topped by a
tower and a slender spire. The buildings around it were
dwarfed in comparison. She walked on down the wide
thoroughfare of Westcheap, lined by two long, irregular
rows of half-timbered houses, three and four storeys
high, each storey overhanging the one below it. It was
a popular, busy market street, noisy and full of carts
and coaches. She weaved her way through the throng of
people, past beggars, and ragged, barefoot street urchins
darting through the crowd. Apprentices stood outside
their masters' shops bawling their wares. There were
booths and stalls selling all kinds of merchandise from
eggs, cakes and rabbits to lace, ribbons and pots and
pans. If only she had not been so tired and hungry she
would have loved to linger and browse, but she must
find somewhere to rest.

There seemed to be numerous taverns, but none that
she had the courage to venture into. She walked on and
the street began to narrow. She came to a small tavern,
quieter than some she had passed, and looking up at the
sign swinging above the door saw that it was the Nag's
Head. She paused, and looked down at a young woman
vigorously scrubbing away at the doorstep. She looked
up when Louise approached and smiled broadly.

'Hello, love,' she said, getting to her feet. 'Want to
come in?'

'Yes, please. I'd like something to eat.'

'Then you've come to the right place. Come on in and
sit yourself down. It's quiet just now, but you wait until
later—when the traders want their dinner.'

She led Louise inside the dimly lit tavern to a long
table. Louise seated herself on the hard bench, placing
her bundle beside her, and looked around. There were
only two more customers besides herself, both elderly
men contentedly smoking their clay pipes as they talked

over the politics of the day. Louise relaxed and leaned back against the wall.

'My—you look done in,' said the girl.

She nodded tiredly. 'Yes, I am. I've been walking most of the night. Do you have a room I could have?'

'Aye—but I'll fetch you something to eat first,' and she moved towards another room, wiping her hands on her white apron. An appetising aroma wafted through the half-open door.

After Louise had eaten eggs and lashings of ham, and buttered oat-cakes dipped in honey, she sat back and sipped a delicious cup of steaming coffee, a new beverage she was acquiring a liking for. The girl came and sat across from her, folding her arms on the table and fixing Louise with a friendly stare.

'Feel better now?'

'Yes, thank you. It was just what I needed.'

Louise liked the girl and felt completely at ease with her, drawn to her by her open friendliness, and she thought that, with her soft grey-green eyes and luxuriant auburn hair escaping beneath a white, starched cap in rebellious curls, she was extremely attractive.

'Do you live here?' asked Louise.

She nodded, her curls bouncing. 'Yes. My father's the innkeeper. My name's Jane, by the way—what's yours?'

'Louise,' she replied, liking this girl's open frankness and admiring her obvious self-confidence and vitality.

'That's a pretty name. You said you'd been walking all night—come far?'

'Not really. Just west of the city. I'm here to try and book a passage to the West Indies.'

Jane's eyes opened wide in amazement. 'Lordy me—that's a bit ambitious, isn't it?'

'Yes, I suppose it is, but I have to go and look for my sister.' Louise found that she liked talking to Jane, and she talked as she had never talked to anyone in her life. Before she was shown the way up the rickety stairs to a spotlessly clean bedchamber, she had told her all about her life in Ireland and what had taken place since. Everything, that was, except her feelings for Francis. That was something she couldn't discuss with anyone. When she lapsed into silence, Jane reached out and squeezed her hand comfortingly.

'That's an awful story,' she said, 'but it's a crazy thing you're thinking of doing—going to the Indies by yourself—why, anything could happen to a girl on her own. She could be raped or even murdered. Binding yourself to those plantation owners will be like a prison sentence. You'll be condemned to be miserable for as long as you live. Do you know that?'

Louise blanched at her words and nodded. 'Yes, but I can think of no other way of getting there and I must find her.'

At that moment the tavern began filling with people, and Jane rose. 'Come on—let me show you up to your chamber. We can talk later when you've rested.'

Louise smiled at her gratefully, and it was not until she laid her head on the soft pillows that she allowed her thoughts to turn to Francis. He would know that she had gone by now. Did he miss her? Was he angry with her or merely relieved that she had taken it upon herself to go, exonerating him from any further responsibility where she was concerned? She sighed and closed her eyes, determined that, however difficult it would be, she would put him and the past behind her. The time for tears was over, and she shuddered when she thought of the dark, uncertain future looming before her, but she was determined to face it. With a firm resolve, she told herself fiercely that she would find Elizabeth. If she had to swim every inch of the way to the West Indies she would find her.

Louise spent several days at the tavern trying to decide what to do next, but whatever she decided she knew she must reach a decision quickly because the few precious coins Anne had given her wouldn't last forever. Jane had little time for conversation, being kept so busy, and she had told her, quite candidly, that until recently her mother had helped run the tavern, but that she had been convicted of felony for a petty theft and was now serving time in Newgate. At the shocked expression on Louise's face she had merely laughed, and said they would have to get someone else to help out in the tavern, as if it were an everyday occurrence for one's mother to be sent to gaol.

Not surprisingly, Louise found herself helping out at busy times, and oddly enough she began to enjoy it. The tavern was a lively place, and played host to many different kinds of people. Merchants, writers, lawyers, to name but a few, and Jane was extremely popular with her lovely form sauntering between the tables, swinging her hips provocatively and balancing plates of food and mugs brimming with ale.

Every Sunday since the beginning of the Commonwealth the taverns were closed—in fact, all music-making and most of the old festivals were banned. Everything that had been an occasion for people to enjoy themselves was frowned upon. It was on the first Sunday since Louise had come to the tavern that Jane asked her to take a walk with her, saying there was something she wanted to show her.

They left Westcheap behind and walked in the direction of the river. The streets became infested with poor tenement buildings and the upper storeys leaned so closely together that they almost shut out the light of day. It got worse as they went along, and Louise held a delicately perfumed handkerchief to her nose in an attempt to shut out the appalling stench of the gutters. The streets became alleyways and dirtier and darker, places of unhealthy dwellings where filth and squalor led to diseases like the plague and all kinds of deadly fevers. Places where cut-throats and thieves lay in wait for the unwary and at night were safe for no man who dared venture out alone in the narrow, dimly lit alleyways.

Louise knew that she was close to the river when she heard the hooting of barges, and it was then that Jane halted in front of a tall gateway and turned to Louise, gripping her hand tightly.

'Why have you brought me here?' asked Louise curiously.

'Because I want you to take a good look beyond these gates and tell me afterwards that this is the way you want to get to the West Indies. Go on—look.'

Puzzled, Louise looked. She saw groups of people, showing poverty in their filthy rags, mainly young men and hollow-eyed, lice-ridden children, all showing abject misery and despair in their faces. Louise turned to Jane. 'Who are these people?'

'You see that building over there?' She pointed towards a house where people were going in and out.

Louise nodded.

'That's the office where people bind themselves to servitude on the plantations in the West Indies—and you see those men?' she said, pointing to some better-dressed fellows.

'Yes—who are they?'

'They're the kidnappers. They walk the streets in order to seduce people into employment on the plantations.

Unknowingly, all these young boys, mainly runaway apprentices, are selling themselves into slavery. They have no idea what they are letting themselves in for, being drawn by false promises to a land flowing in milk and honey. Poor fools—they believe that once they have worked off their passage after four years or so they will be allotted so many acres of land and will eventually grow rich, but most of them are signing their own death warrant. The only people who grow rich are those finely dressed fellows, and for every unfortunate person they trap into misery they are paid so much a head from the ships' masters.'

Louise was staring at the piteous scene before her as one paralysed. She felt chilled to the bone. What Jane had told her had gone straight to her heart, and she realised what a blind fool she had been to even contemplate going to the West Indies when faced with these stark facts of reality. Why, she didn't even know which island Elizabeth was on, and for all she knew they were probably hundreds of miles apart.

Jane gripped her arm fiercely. 'For the love of heaven, Louise—look at them. Look at them good and hard, because most of them won't live to see the end of their servitude. Do you want to be killed by hard work before you can help your sister? Because you probably will if you go into that office and sign on to become an indentured servant.'

Louise was engulfed with a hopeless despair and felt as if her whole world were crumbling to pieces before her eyes. She looked at Jane with a sad resignation, tears blurring her eyes.

'Yes—you're right. It would be sheer madness. I can see that now. But what else can I do?'

'You could stay on at the tavern. It's not much, I know—but it's better than nothing, although I am aware that, with your background, working in a tavern is as far removed for you as my becoming the Duchess of York is for me but—well—we would love to have you, and we do need somebody to wait on tables until my mother gets out of Newgate. You could give it a try for a while—after all, you've nothing to lose. Father can be a bit of a tyrant at times, I know, but deep down he's a soft old thing really and besides,' she said, a twinkle in her eye and a mischievous smile playing on her lips, 'he likes you. Even said you'd be good for the tavern, as you have a certain way with the customers.'

Louise flushed scarlet. 'Jane—what on earth do you mean?'

Jane laughed at the confusion she had caused her friend. 'He's seen the way they look at you—and, just in case no one's ever told you, you're a very attractive lady—in a refined sort of way, of course.'

Louise sighed and laughed lightly. 'How can I refuse after that?' and she gave her a grateful hug. 'Thank you, Jane. I can't tell you how much your friendship has meant to me these last few days. I think it must have been fate that brought me to your tavern.'

'So do I, love, and now—what do you say? Will you stay?'

'Yes, for now, anyway.'

'Good, and don't worry—you'll have all the customers eating out of your hands in no time.' She linked her arm through Louise's. 'Come on—it's a glorious day. Let's stroll down by the river. I love watching the ships.'

The days gradually melted into weeks, and very soon Louise fitted into the routine of tavern life as if she had been born to it. Jane was clearly an expert in dealing with men. Louise watched her, and it wasn't long before she too learnt how to deal with any lewd or ardent advances from drunken customers. She discovered a new kind of life and savoured every moment of joy, and was thankful to be kept so busy that she didn't have time to dwell on her unhappy thoughts. It was only at night, in the darkness of the bedchamber she shared with Jane, that they came creeping out of the dark recesses of her mind to torment her. Even during the light-hearted moments of the day she felt all the while as if she were living under an invisible cloud. But she did begin to laugh again and she and Jane talked for hours when the tavern was closed, and on Sundays there were always their strolls and new, exciting areas of London to discover.

It was a quiet day at the tavern when the invisible cloud hanging over her finally burst. She had just emerged from the kitchen when she noticed a man enter and move to the centre of the room. He wore a long dark cloak and his face was shadowed by the wide brim of his hat. He stood head and shoulders above any other man in the tavern, and she had noticed how he had had to bend his head to pass through the doorway. Louise stared at him and, although he had his head bowed, she would have recognised him anywhere. At first she thought she must be suffering from some kind of delusion, brought on by her constant desire to see him, but when he raised his head and looked directly at her, their eyes locking, she knew it was no delusion. Those darkly handsome features, the lean face and deep blue eyes and firm lips, lips which could soften—oh, how they had softened when he had kissed her—were deeply implanted in her heart.

She stood there and stared at him for what seemed an eternity, her heart palpitating madly and the blood pounding in her ears. At first the expression on his face had been one of surprise and then relief, but now it was cold and there was no mistaking the anger in his eyes as

they briefly took in her appearance, travelling down over
her soiled blue apron and back to her face. He made a
move towards her, but at that moment something
snapped inside her brain and she had a frantic desire to
get away from him. On impulse she turned and ran from
the tavern, out into the crowded street.

She looked desperately one way and then the other,
wondering which way to run so that she could escape.
She ran into the crowd, not turning, but knowing instinctively that he followed. In desperation she ran down
a narrow alleyway, one thought only in her mind and
that was to get away. She slipped several times on the
shiny, uneven cobblestones but managed to keep her
balance and she ran on, through a maze of now quiet
passages, her heart pounding so hard it almost burst.
All the while she kept asking herself over and over again
how he could have found her, and why—oh, why—had
he come when she was just beginning to live without
him?

She could hear him behind her now and she was sure
she heard him call her name, but she did not turn. He
was gaining on her and finally his hands clamped down
on her shoulders, bringing her to a halt. He turned her
to face him and pinned her against a wall, his fingers
biting cruelly into her soft flesh.

'You little fool,' he spat. 'Did you really think you
could escape me?'

She said nothing as she gasped for breath and closed
her eyes to shut out the blazing anger on his face. Her
hair had come undone from its pins and tumbled about
her shoulders. Somewhere along the way the white cap
that covered it had been shaken off.

'Why did you run from me, Louise? Tell me—why?'

She shook her head slowly. 'I don't know why—truly I don't. I only know that when I saw you—back at the tavern—I just wanted to get away.'

'But why? Didn't you want me to find you?'

'No. I never intended seeing you again—ever.'

'But I nearly went out of my mind when I found you gone. I thought I had lost you forever. Have you any idea what I went through when Anne told me? Not knowing where you were? I have searched every ship bound for the Indies and every tavern in London.'

'But you shouldn't have,' she cried. 'It's far too dangerous for you. You should have gone with Anne to Holland. Oh, why couldn't you just forget me—forget you ever knew me?' she said wretchedly.

'Don't you think I haven't tried?' he said fiercely. 'But I can't—damn you. You haunt me every minute of every day, and no matter how hard I've tried I cannot get you out of my mind.'

His expression softened as he gazed down at her, her face flushed from exertion under the heavy mantle of her hair, her beautiful dark brown eyes wide and her mouth soft and slightly parted as her breathing became quieter. He thought then that she was breathtakingly lovely, perhaps the most beautiful woman he had ever seen, and he wanted to take her in his arms and crush her to him and kiss away all the misery in her heart. He became aware of the soft flesh of her shoulders beneath the material of her dress and he let his hands fall to his sides, as if it had burned him.

'Does Anne know you're trying to find me?' asked Louise.

'No. She believes me to be with the King. But tell me— what are you doing working in that tavern? It's not the kind of place for you.'

'There was nothing else I could do. Jane and her
father—he owns the tavern—have both been very good
to me. In fact, if it had not been for them I would
probably be halfway to the West Indies by now.'

'It is still not too late for you to go to Anne in
Holland.'

'No,' she said firmly, shaking her head. 'No—I can't
do that.'

'But you can't stay in that tavern.'

'Why not?' and she sighed. 'I don't expect you to
understand this, Francis, but I have been happier there
than I have been for a long time, and perhaps when I've
saved enough money I'll be able to pay for my passage
to the Indies to search for Elizabeth.' She smiled wistfully up into his pain-filled eyes. 'Go to Holland,
Francis,' she said gently. 'Go to Holland and marry
Anne. You must forget about me.'

He shook his head slowly. 'No—you know I can never
do that, and besides, I am going to Scotland. The King
has gone there to sign the oath of the Covenant.'

Louise looked at him in disbelief. The oath of the
Covenant? What did she know or care about that? When
she spoke there was no hiding the bitterness in her voice.

'Patriotic to the end, aren't you, Francis? As usual
thinking only of Charles Stuart and the Royalist cause,
when your brother and sister are probably going through
hell at this very moment.' She had the satisfaction of
seeing his eyes fill with anguish, but she went on
relentlessly. 'I only hope he is worth the gallant sacrifice
you are making, but somehow I don't think so.'

'You are wrong—but don't judge me too harshly,
Louise, for whatever your feelings are concerning him
you cannot deny that he has a moral duty to recover his
kingdom—the one he inherited from his father. The
Commonwealth has confiscated almost all Royalist lands,

and unless the King regains his throne then they are gone forever. I cannot desert him. He needs support now more than ever, but there are few Anglican Royalists who will rally to his side this time.'

'Why? Have they become disillusioned?' she mocked cruelly.

'No, it's because after much soul-searching he has finally agreed to take the oath of the Covenant—however much he hates doing so. To them it is a dishonourable deed, and they are outraged that he has compromised with the Scots in this way when his father stood firmly against it. That they will have to suffer the Presbyterian religion—no other being lawful. It was not for this that they sacrificed their estates or spilled so much blood on the battlefields.'

'Then why is he taking the oath?'

'If he doesn't accept the Covenanters' terms, then he will have to abandon all hope of his restoration. It's as simple as that. He would be forced to live his life in exile—and I with him, because I will not conform to the laws of the land under the Protectorate—although,' he said grimly, 'even if I wanted to I do not believe they would let me. There is still a high price upon my head, and if I am caught I shall be imprisoned and no doubt hanged.'

His words brought cold fear to her heart, fear that he might be caught, and she didn't think she would be able to bear it. She could only stand and stare at him. She had listened to his voice, clutching at words, trying to understand what he said. Since going to Ireland she had been so far removed from the politics in England, being too young to understand the struggle that was taking place between the King and his Parliament, that truth to say she had thought little of it. Although she had to admit that she greatly admired Francis for his steadfast

loyalty to his King and country, why couldn't they see
that their cause was lost?

'But surely life under the Commonwealth is better than
all the fighting and killing?'

He smiled down at her ruefully. 'How can you say
that when your own father gave his life fighting for the
King? Life under this new Commonwealth means that
everything as we know it has gone forever. There is no
music, no dancing, all our old traditions will be
forgotten—and look at you, Louise. Why, you should
be dressed in the finest of silks and brocades with lace
at your throat and ribbons in your hair, not these dour,
miserable clothes. It's as if the whole of England is in
mourning.'

'Oh, Francis, I wish I could understand you—but I
can't.'

'I'm not asking you to understand.'

'Does Anne?'

'Yes,' he said, looking at her steadily. 'She always has.'

Louise felt her heart constrict at his words. She tried
to visualise his life as it had been before he even knew
of her existence, when he had met and eventually fallen
in love with Anne all those years ago, when they had
been drawn together by common interests. Of course she
would understand him. It was foolish of Louise to have
asked. She sighed and lowered her gaze. 'Then it's a good
thing you're marrying her and not me, isn't it?'

Francis didn't answer her question, not knowing how
to. 'There is another reason why I am going to Scotland,
Louise. One which—I believe—you will be interested in
knowing about.'

'Oh? How can anything that is happening in Scotland
possibly be of interest to me?'

'Cromwell—in case you don't already know—has
returned from Ireland. He's moving north to Scotland

and has taken sole command of an invading force. With him is Robert Grey.'

Louise's eyes, dilated with horror, flew to his, and in spite of herself all the blood drained from her face, leaving it deathly white. Her mouth formed the name Francis had spoken, but no sound came. Her feelings were in a turmoil as once again she visualised the evil countenance of the fiend who had almost destroyed her life.

Francis, standing over her, watched her anxiously.

'So,' she whispered when at last she was able to speak. 'For that reason you are right to go to Scotland. I shall go with you.'

He looked at her as if she had lost her mind. 'No, Louise—I won't let you. It would be insane to let you go north when we might be on the brink of another war. I shall not let you be caught up in it. I shall find Robert Grey—never fear—and I swear I shall make him wish he'd never been born.'

Louise looked at him as if she could not have heard right. Had he really said she couldn't go? 'I don't care,' she said stubbornly. 'I don't care whether it's safe or not. I shall go to Scotland with or without you and there is nothing you can do or say to stop me.' Angrily she tossed her hair back from her face and turned and began walking back in the direction of the tavern, blinded to the groups of passers-by who were staring at them curiously.

Francis sighed and followed, halting her by taking hold of her arm and turning her once again to face him. 'Don't be a fool, Louise. How would you get there? A woman alone is prey to all kinds of rogues.'

'By coach,' she snapped, a determined tilt to her chin. 'I do have a little money saved.'

'By coach could take forever.'

'Then how are you going?'

'By sea.'

'Then I shall go by sea,' and once again she turned from him, dragging her arm from his grasp and walking on.

Francis followed, cursing her stubbornness softly, knowing that she would do exactly as she had said and go alone. 'Louise, wait.' She ignored him and walked on, but again he caught up with her and seized her by the shoulders, spinning her round to face him. At any other time she would have shrunk from the anger mirrored in his eyes, but not now. She glared up at him, equally angry. 'Listen to me, will you? You're not going. What the devil do you think you will do if you do reach Scotland unmolested and find Robert Grey? What will you do? Confront him? Kill him? What? For God's sake, Louise, be sensible.'

'All right,' she flared, 'then take me with you if you're so concerned for my safety. I must go to Scotland—can't you see that? Robert Grey is the only man I know who knows where Elizabeth was sent. Oh—please, Francis,' she pleaded. 'I—I think I should go mad having to wait here for news. Please let me go with you.'

Some of his anger faded and he frowned slightly, his eyes narrowed. He looked thoughtfully down into her beautiful face, which eagerly awaited his reply. He pondered over her words, knowing it would be folly to take her with him—but then, how could he bear to part with her so soon now that he had found her? And what had he intended doing with her anyway? He refused to leave her working in that tavern, where she came into contact with all forms of unsavoury characters, and he understood her reasons for not wanting to go to Anne in Holland—and deep down he couldn't blame her. He sighed and nodded slowly.

'Very well, Louise, I will take you with me—but,' he said, when he saw gladness fill her eyes, 'it will not be easy. There are Commonwealth spies everywhere on the lookout for Royalists, and there will be no comforts on board the ship we will sail on from Dover. Are you prepared to endure the hardships and—perhaps—even death if we are captured?'

She nodded.

'Very well, but I need not impress on you the need for secrecy. There will be several Royalists who have been in hiding all going to Scotland to join the King, and a woman among them will not help matters.'

'What do you suggest?'

'Perhaps if you were disguised as a youth you would not attract so much attention,' and he let his eyes rove boldly over her slender but curvaceous body, visualising her long, slim legs encased in close-fitting breeches and hose. The thought was indeed pleasing and brought a smile to his lips, one corner of his mouth lifting, revealing a flash of white teeth. There was an unusual softness in his narrowed eyes. 'However,' he said gently, 'we must ensure the clothes are on the large side, otherwise people may take some convincing.'

An embarrassed flush flooded Louise's cheeks, but before she could reply he laughed softly and, taking her arm, began walking towards the Nag's Head.

'Come—let's walk back. I shall have to leave you for a while, but will come back after dark with some suitable clothes. When we reach Dover and the ship I'll pass you off as the son of a friend of mine, and that I'm taking you to Scotland to join him.' He looked down at her, frowning. 'Do you think you'll be able to play the part?'

'Of course—or,' she said, sounding not altogether certain, 'at least I'll try.'

'Good.'

Reluctantly he left her at the tavern door, promising to be back after dark and insisting she tell no one of their plans.

Back inside, Jane was waiting for her, having kept a worried eye on the door, and when Louise entered she uttered a sigh of relief and was full of questions about the man who had come. Briefly, Louise told her about Francis and that she was leaving, and begged her not to ask any more questions but assured her that she would be all right. Jane respected her wish, but being of a curious nature found it extremely difficult.

When Francis returned, thankfully the tavern was quiet. He handed Louise a bundle of clothes. 'Here— get these on and hurry. We must be away as soon as possible.'

Louise hurried up the stairs to her chamber, and when she came back down it was difficult to recognise her. The clothes were plain and simple, if a little on the large side to avoid attracting unnecessary attention. Her thick hair was coiled and pinned beneath a short black wig, and a wide, floppy-brimmed hat sat on her head. Jane's mouth opened wide in amazement, and Francis took in her appearance and nodded approvingly, ushering her towards the door. But there she paused and turned to a tearful Jane. They hugged each other and stood back, and Louise had to swallow a hard lump that had risen in her throat.

'Goodbye, Jane—I'm going to miss you so much. I've already said goodbye to your father. Thank you for all you've done. I dread to think where I would be now if I hadn't come to your tavern that day.'

'Go on with you,' said Jane, sniffing back her tears and giving Louise's hand a tight squeeze. 'I'm going to miss you too.' She glanced at Francis, waiting impatiently a little way off. 'I don't know who he is, love, but I like the look of him. Now off you go, and don't forget me if you're ever in London.'

'I won't,' said Louise, and slipped away with Francis.

CHAPTER FOUR

LOUISE had had little time to prepare her feelings for the oncoming long and dangerous journey first to Dover and then to Scotland, all in the proximity to Francis whom she had once vowed to put out of her mind forever. But all the feelings she had felt for him before leaving the Sinclair household, the ones she had buried deep in her heart, came flooding back, having increased a thousandfold the moment she had set eyes once more on his darkly handsome features. She loved him—this she knew with a certainty—and there was absolutely nothing she could do about it, and she knew that when he finally left her for Anne it would be like losing her very heart and soul. How she was going to endure their long hours together and remain detached she didn't know, but she must try, and only the thought that perhaps she would discover precisely where Elizabeth was would sustain her throughout the weeks, perhaps months, ahead. But she could not deny that the thought of being with him filled her with happiness.

They attracted little attention to themselves on their journey, carrying little in the way of baggage, and their clothes were such that they in no way marked them out from any of the other passengers on the coach. By the time they reached the inn, the Coach and Horses, where they were to spend the night, the rain was coming down in torrents. They and their fellow passengers almost tumbled from the coach out into the muddy yard and hurried towards the welcoming warmth of the inn, its impressive-looking sign swinging above the door, squeaking loudly in the wind. Inside they found themselves in a low-ceilinged but large, welcoming room with a number of tables and benches. A good fire blazed cheerily in the hearth at the far end, its light gleaming on the copper pans. There were few people at the tables and, after taking a cursory look around and having a quiet word with the innkeeper, Francis led Louise towards a table in the corner by the fireplace, where he hoped they would be inconspicuous.

Louise thankfully sat on the hard bench across from him, feeling the warmth of the fire on her back. She was so weary all she wanted to do was creep into bed and go to sleep, but she had to wait until they had eaten. Francis had spoken little all day, seeming uneasy all the while and discreetly looking at every face of every stranger, trying to discern if they could be Parliamentary spies.

A rosy-cheeked girl in white starched cap and apron brought them two steaming bowls of mutton stew and Francis began eating hungrily, breaking his bread into it. Louise was too tired to eat and merely toyed with it, stirring the greasy, unappetising meal with her spoon, unable to take a mouthful. Slowly her eyelids began to droop as drowsiness spread over her. Francis paused with his spoon halfway to his mouth and looked across at her, smiling softly, remembering the way she had struggled to keep awake throughout the journey but was finally losing the battle. He looked at her flushed face framed by the black wig, which gave her an unusual elfin look. He placed his spoon in his bowl and leaning forward touched her hand. She came awake with a start.

'Oh—oh, I'm sorry—I——'

Francis laughed softly. 'You were falling asleep. Come on—let's go and find which room we're in.' He half rose from his seat and saw Louise's eyes widen in alarm at his words.

'Room? What do you mean?'

'Precisely what I say,' and he looked at her with one eyebrow cocked in faint amusement. 'You don't mind sharing a room with me, do you?' he asked quietly, carefully keeping his voice low so as not to attract attention to themselves.

Burning colour flooded her cheeks. 'No—yes—oh, I don't know what I mean. I just hadn't thought——'

'Come on,' he said, looking down at her and laughing lightly at her confusion. 'It is the only spare room so we really have no choice, and if I insist they find one it will only draw attention to us—and that is the last thing we want, so come along—and I promise to sleep on the floor.'

She followed him towards the stairs which led to the upper storey, completely unaware of the room having filled with people and the serving maids dashing from table to table, it being their busiest time when the coaches pulled up to stop for the night. Her heart was beating strongly beneath her disguise and she was becoming increasingly nervous. Sharing a bedchamber with Francis was something she had certainly not bargained on.

It wasn't very big and had only one comfortably large bed in it. She stood in the doorway and watched Francis kneel on the floor and pull a smaller truckle-bed from beneath it. Indeed, it was so small she couldn't imagine Francis' large frame fitting on to it with any degree of comfort.

'But you can't sleep on that,' she gasped incredulously. 'It isn't big enough.'

'I don't mind—I've slept on worse, believe me. This is absolute luxury to some of the things I've been forced to sleep on during my campaigns.'

Louise watched as he removed his doublet, tossing it carelessly into a chair. He was wearing a loose white shirt with long billowing sleeves gathered at the cuffs. It was open in a V to his waist, and she fastened her eyes on the forest of thick black hair on his chest. A soft flush spread over her cheeks and the room had suddenly become a warm and very intimate place. He was about to remove his boots but became aware of her stillness, and he looked at her, still standing with her back to the door. Tired and weary as he was, the sight of her almost took his breath away, and something in her face made him pause for a moment and then move slowly towards her. He took a deep breath and looked down at her, his eyes darkening, and there was something in their depths that made her tremble. He reached out and removed her wig, dropping it on to the bed, and then very slowly began removing the pins which fastened her hair, releasing it from its tight coil. It spilled down her back like a snake in heavy waves, the candlelight emphasising the deep chestnut colour, giving it a rich, luxuriant texture. All the while he never took his eyes from hers and a sudden rush of warmth pervaded her whole body, bringing it alive beneath the exquisitely gentle touch of his fingers. There was a look in his eyes which betrayed his feelings for her, a look which made her even more aware of her own, and they were so strong she could not hide them from him.

Very slowly his hands left her hair and cupped her face, holding it as one would something infinitely fragile. He bent his head to hers and covered her mouth, cherishing it with his own. He kissed her long and deep, and so great was Louise's joy that she truly believed she would die of it, and she passionately responded to his kiss. Her hands stole upwards over his chest, finally fastening themselves about his neck. His kisses grew more

and more demanding and his arms were about her,
holding her tighter, crushing her to him. The tenderness
of moments before had left him and his kisses became
hard and almost violent. She didn't draw back but clung
tighter.

After what seemed an eternity they drew apart,
stunned by the depth of feeling they had aroused in each
other. The silence of the room was broken only by the
persistent rain beating against the small leaded window-
panes and their breathing, as they looked at each other
as they had never looked before.

'I never meant this to happen,' said Francis, gazing
passionately at her lovely face, all the love she felt for
him in her heart shining from her eyes.

'No—neither did I,' she replied in a shaken whisper.

'I want you, Louise—you know that now—and I
believe it's the same with you.'

She nodded. 'Yes—but we cannot. We would only hate
and despise ourselves afterwards. You are still betrothed
to Anne and we cannot either of us forget that. I wish
I could say that nothing else matters but us, but I can't.
There is such a thing as honour and decency. It would
be sinful, Francis—in a way like committing adultery. I
could not do that to her—she does not deserve it.'

At the mention of Anne's name a look of frustration
mingled with guilt came over his face, and sighing he
turned from her and moved slowly to the window,
banging the sill fiercely with his fist. He turned and faced
her. All the softness had gone from his blue eyes, which
were now hard, glaring at her from between narrowed
lids, and when he spoke it was with precision.

'You are right, Louise, and you were quite correct to
remind me that there is still such a thing as honour and
decency, but what I feel for Anne has nothing to do with
you and me. I know that I want you so much it's sheer

torture. I always believed I was strong where women were concerned, but with you it's different. I am obsessed and bewitched by you in such a way that if I'm not careful it will poison what I feel for Anne, and I cannot—must not—let that happen, and besides,' he said quietly, 'I would also lose all respect for myself if I did. So—I shall not touch you again, because I swear that if I do and we become lovers then I shall be truly lost. Nothing must deter me from getting to Scotland—for both our sakes. I must keep my wits about me at all times, and if I weaken in any way then it may cost us dearly.'

Louise said nothing. She merely stared at him by the window, at the broad set of his shoulders and the anguish on his lean, handsome face. She nodded wearily, eventually speaking in a soft whisper. 'Yes—you are right. We must not let what we feel for each other come between what we have set out to do. There is too much at stake.'

His expression softened and he moved towards her, seeing the misery in her eyes. 'At least we both understand what we have to do. But we cannot deny that whatever happens a spark has ignited between us, lighting a flame that is not going to be easy to extinguish—and, who knows, we may not to able to.'

They fell silent, brought back to reality by the noise of people on the landing coming to their respective rooms.

'Come—let us try and get some sleep. We have an early start tomorrow. I'll slip downstairs while you undress and get into bed.'

She watched him go out, and waited until she could no longer hear his boots on the landing before mechanically removing her clothes and slipping between the cool sheets. She thought sleep would elude her, but by the time Francis returned she was sleeping like a child. Her face was flushed against the whiteness of the pillows, and her hair spread about her in a silken mass. Her soft lips were slightly parted and the covers rose and fell with her rhythmic breathing. With great difficulty he tore his eyes from her and turned to the uncomfortable truckle-bed, cursing softly beneath his breath, fighting the desire to creep into the large bed beside her.

After passing through Rochester and the city of Canterbury, often called the cradle of English Christianity, the roofs of the dwellings clustered around the ancient cathedral with its lofty towers reaching up into the sky, they finally reached the little coastal town of Dover with its irregular mile-long street.

Louise was both relieved and exhausted, and her body ached and felt bruised all over by the constant bumping and swaying of the coach on the badly rutted roads. On the hills high above the town stood an impressive-looking castle with cold, thick walls, standing guard over the busy harbour and the rickety, ramshackle dwellings.

The steaming horses passed through a stone archway and came to a halt outside a large but dingy-looking tavern. Thankfully, Francis and Louise climbed out followed by the other passengers, most of whom had travelled with them from London. The sky was loud with gulls and the air full of the smells of the sea. The day was heavy and oppressive and a hazy mist hung over the town. Francis had told Louise that the time spent in Dover waiting for the vessel which was to take them to Scotland would be the most dangerous. They would have to be very careful who they conversed with and what they said. She knew that Parliamentary agents, all on the lookout for escaping Royalists going to the aid of Charles Stuart, would be everywhere. Indeed, Dover itself seemed to be swarming with troops. The inn yard was full of them but, undeterred, Francis pushed his way boldly through, followed closely by Louise.

The inside of the inn was one of the worst she had been in and was far removed from the Nag's Head. It was a large, dimly lit room reeking equally of smoke, from what seemed like innumerable clay pipes, and ale, which was slopped all over the table tops. The place was full of all kinds of characters. Sailors and fishermen drinking, some falling about and drunker than others while some were with over-painted women, their coarse, ribald laughter ringing out above the din.

'Follow me,' said Francis and began climbing the stairs. Louise breathed a sigh of relief, thankful she didn't have to remain in that awful room. She made to follow him but became separated by the crowd, and was pressed with her back to the oak panelling, and the stench of unwashed bodies and stale ale turned her stomach. A man attempted to push past but stopped in front of her, and she shuddered when she looked up into his big, ugly face with its square forehead. He was thick-set with a broad, shapeless face and wide, thick lips. His black hair was dirty and unkempt, but it was the eyes which looked down into hers that made her go cold. They reminded her of an animal's and seemed to be a separate part of the man. They were grey and piercing and glittered like ice, and seemed to penetrate her very soul. She was momentarily startled when he reached out and placed one hand firmly over her breast. She flushed crimson and his lips parted in a grisly smile. She shuddered in disgust. Here was one man who had not been deceived by her disguise. The incident lasted for no longer than a moment, but no matter how hard she was to try to dismiss the man from her mind she was unable to do so.

She went on up the stairs, still able to feel the firm pressure of his hand on her breast. She turned and looked back. He was still staring after her.

Francis knocked softly on a door at the far end of a long landing, and a deep voice called out for him to enter. They went in quickly. A man was seated at a table engaged in eating a meal, but when he saw Francis he rose, moving quickly towards them. He was not as tall as Francis and perhaps a few years older, and stockily built with a cleanshaven, pleasant face. She could see how difficult it must be for him to conceal his aristocratic distinction although he obviously tried hard with his drab, ill-fitting clothes.

'Come in, Francis,' he said, looking warily past him on to the landing before closing the door. 'Thank God you've come. I hoped you'd be on that coach, although I was beginning to think we'd have to leave without you.' He looked directly at Louise. 'Who's this?'

'John Cranwell,' said Francis, drawing Louise forward. 'He's accompanying me to Scotland where he hopes to join his father. John—this is Sir Percival Lennox.'

Louise nodded while Sir Percival considered her thoughtfully, and she prayed he wouldn't see through her disguise which was becoming increasingly uncomfortable. Thankfully he seemed to accept the name Francis had given him.

'Glad to have you with us, John.' He turned his attention back to Francis. 'Come—be seated, and I'll tell you how the land lies over a glass of wine—although,' he said, pouring some of the deep red liquid from a decanter into two glasses and handing one to each of them, 'it's difficult getting a decent wine these days since the embargo on France, and most of these damn Parliamentarians are so pious they consider it a sin to drink anything stronger than milk or coffee.'

Louise took her glass of wine over to the window and seated herself, watching the activity in the yard below. Francis appeared to forget all about her, fixing his attention on Sir Percival.

'Tell me, Percy—have you managed to secure a vessel?'

'Yes. If all goes to plan then by this time tomorrow we should be on our way to Scotland, although I must tell you that it's not going to be easy. As you will have seen for yourself, the whole of Dover is teeming with redcoats. They're all over the place.'

Francis looked at his friend gravely. 'Yes, I saw. Perhaps we should have arranged to leave from a less conspicuous port.'

'I agree with you, Francis, but it's too late now. We've managed to charter a vessel from Folkestone—at great expense, I can tell you—but it is commodious and owned by a loyal merchant who is prepared to take us to Edinburgh at great risk to himself.'

'Where are the others who are to go with us?'

'Scattered about Dover. It would have been too dangerous for us all to be seen together, but by now they will know what they have to do.'

Francis nodded. 'You seem to have it well planned, Percy. What time are we expected to leave?'

'As soon as the vessel is sighted, word will come to us here. We will leave immediately. I hope the boat will be waiting on the shore to take us out to the ship. No time must be lost, although once at sea it's going to be extremely difficult dodging the Commonwealth fleet which—as you know—has almost doubled in the last two years. They constantly pursue ships thought to be Royalist carrying Royalist supporters to Scotland—

whether they be English or French. I must also warn
you,' he said, his face white and grim, 'that I believe
I'm being watched and if so then I am certain your
coming here will have been noted. There is a man downstairs who has taken to following me. An odious creature,
and I find it exceedingly difficult giving him the slip.'

'Is he big with an ugly face and black hair?' asked
Louise, looking down into the yard at the man she had
encountered on the stairs. He was leaning casually on a
wall looking directly up at their window, a smirk on his
thick lips.

Both men turned simultaneously and looked at her.

'Yes,' said Percy, going to the window and following
her gaze. 'That's him.'

'I met him on the stairs,' said Louise, shuddering at
the memory of the man's hand on her breast. 'I must
admit he looked at me oddly—almost as if he recognised
me—but he couldn't have. He's so dirty—he doesn't look
in the least like a spy.'

'Don't let his appearance fool you, John. We're going
to have to be careful. At least the innkeeper is a good
man, a Royalist sympathiser, and when the time comes
to leave we will do so by a back way. But until then I
suggest we try and get some rest. It's going to be a long
night for all of us.'

With the dark came the dense, clinging fog. Thick
enough to lose oneself in completely. At any other time
Francis and Percy would have cursed it, but not tonight.
As things turned out it was to prove a blessing in disguise. Providence was indeed on their side. They only
hoped the fog would stay with them and not go out with
the tide.

After they had eaten they began their long night's vigil,
waiting for word to come to them that they should make

haste to the shore as soon as the vessel was sighted. Louise was tired and lay back in a chair, one in which Francis had ordered her to try and rest, but it was useless. How could she possibly sleep with all the noise coming from the tavern beneath them and when she felt such excitement tingling through her veins, as if she were on the threshold of some new discovery?

The night passed incredibly slowly and the flickering candles cast a dim light in the room. Gradually the tavern became quiet and Francis and his friend Sir Percy sat patiently at the table, talking softly. It was in the early hours that their patience was rewarded and the knock came on the door. At once all three were alert. Percy went to the door and opened it a crack. He exchanged a few quiet words with someone and closed it again, turning to Francis.

'It is time,' was all he said.

Hurriedly they donned dark, heavy cloaks and went out on to the landing and down the stairs. They left the tavern silently by a back way and went out into the street where they moved swiftly and where the fog wrapped itself about them like a shroud. None of them saw the man with the cold grey eyes regarding them from the shadows or the evil twist to the thick lips. As they hurried on down the empty street he was never far behind.

They were breathless by the time they reached the shore and Louise felt the soft sand beneath her feet. A ghostly figure emerged from the clinging mist. It was the man who was waiting to take them to the boat, but he was only expecting two of them. A few quiet but angry words were exchanged but eventually he seemed to relent, not wanting to waste time, and ordered them to go to the boat at the water's edge one at a time. First Sir Percival went and then Francis, who believed he was being closely followed by Louise. But he was wrong and she suddenly

found herself alone, apart from the fog and the wild
beating of her heart. She waited for the man who had
taken the others to the boat to return, but in an instant
and before a sound could pass her lips a hand was
clamped roughly over her mouth and she felt herself
being dragged along the sand. She was terrified and
struggled frantically, but the vile-smelling hand over her
mouth and the arm clamped around her shoulders did
not relinquish their hold.

She lost her hat and cloak in her desperate struggle
to free herself, and after what seemed like an eternity
managed to bite the hand over her mouth, drawing
blood, which brought a curse from her assailant and
caused him to throw her forcefully to the ground. She
hit her head on something hard and stars exploded before
her eyes. A searing pain shot through her and for a
moment she seemed to lose consciousness. When she
came to and opened her eyes it was to see the mist
swirling all about her and a large, grotesque shape
looming over her. She could just make out his big, ugly
face beneath the black, greasy hair and she was stricken
with abject terror when she recognised her assailant. It
was the same man she had seen back at the inn. The one
she had encountered on the stairs and who had spent
the greater part of the day watching their window. At
first she was petrified with fear, feeling helpless before
this monster, and she shrank away trying to get to her
feet, but she couldn't. Her head was swimming and she
felt sick and faint. She heard him laugh, a hideous noise
which sent a chill through her body, and menacingly he
advanced towards her.

'So, my little Royalist,' he said, his voice thick with
lust. 'You thought to escape, did you? Thinking you
would not be quite so noticeable if you hid your pretty
body. But we both know what secrets are hidden beneath

those shapeless breeches, don't we? And I for one shall enjoy seeing for myself. And don't worry about your friends—they won't have time to get far, because afterwards I shall raise the alarm.'

Before he fell on top of her she managed to open her mouth and utter a choking scream, and with what seemed like her last ounce of strength she resumed her futile struggle and they rolled over and over on the cold, wet sand. His heavy weight almost crushed her and the reek of sweat and rancid ale filled her with revulsion and almost made her faint away. His hands were all over her body, tearing at her clothing as he pinned her to the sand. She grew weaker by the second and was unable to defend herself against his brute strength. She ceased struggling and firmly believed her last moment on earth had come, but suddenly, through half-open lids, she saw a dark shape emerge silently through the mist.

Her attacker was caught off guard. She was vaguely aware of a struggle taking place beside her, followed by an animal-like grunt from her attacker as a knife was thrust between his ribs and then, as if by some miracle, Francis was kneeling beside her, staring down at her figure stretched out before him, her clothes torn where her attacker had tried to rip them from her body. Surprisingly her black wig was still in place, but her beautiful face was streaked with blood. He cursed himself for not having made sure she was following him to the boat. How could he have left her alone as he had—if only for a moment? He should have known better, and he prayed she wasn't badly hurt. He would never forgive himself if she was, but thank God he had heard her cry out and managed to get to her before she was raped.

He was talking softly to her, but she couldn't make out what it was he was saying because the swirling mist had somehow got inside her head, and with a little sigh she closed her eyes and gave herself up to it, feeling her body lifted in two strong arms. With her head against his chest he carried her along the shore and down to the water's edge, where she could hear the gentle sloughing of the waves as they broke on the sand.

Francis waded through the water to the boat with Louise in his arms. It was full of fugitives, all waiting anxiously for Francis, and the tension between them could have been cut with a knife. No words were spoken as he passed her to Percy before climbing in himself. Two men took up oars and began rowing swiftly out to sea and the waiting ship.

'What happened?' asked Percy softly, looking anxiously at Louise's stark white face and the blood still wet on her cheek.

'We were followed by the man you suspected as being a Parliamentary agent. He attacked John, but luckily I got there in time. The man is dead, so you needn't worry about his raising the alarm.'

'Thank God for that. How badly hurt is John?'

'I can't tell. He's taken a nasty blow to his head.'

Percy's eyes took in the torn clothing, and at the same time as Francis' his eyes rested on the soft swell of Louise's firm young breast, which had become partly uncovered when her jacket had been brutally ripped open. He took off his cloak and wrapped it closely about her before anyone else should see it. He raised his eyes and looked meaningfully at Francis.

'It seems he put up quite a struggle, Francis, and he is wondrous fair for a youth.'

Francis looked deep into his friend's eyes and nodded slowly. So—Percy knew this was no youth, and he would not deny it. But he knew he could trust him to remain silent. There had already been enough trouble caused by bringing an extra person on the journey without the captain's knowledge, but if he were to discover that the extra person was a woman then no doubt he would order her off the ship.

As they drew further away from the shore, nothing could be heard but the laboured breathing of the rowers and the gentle splash of the oars. Louise was propped between Francis and Percy, unaware of what was happening or where she was. The faces around them were still and silent and might have been carved out of stone. All shared a common goal and possessed a grim determination to reach Scotland quickly and unhindered, and so be of service to their King.

With the help of Percy, Francis managed to persuade the captain to let himself and Louise have a small cabin to themselves. He explained that the young man had been set upon and badly beaten by a Parliamentary agent before coming on board, and would need looking after. At first the captain had objected strongly, but at the sight of Louise's deathly white face and the blood on her cheek as she lay unconscious in Francis' arms, and also the promise of extra money, he relented.

The journey to Scotland was fraught with danger and many times they were pursued by Commonwealth ships, but skilfully managed to outrun them. They had to make considerable detours to keep out of their way. At first they made slow progress, being plagued by bad weather, and only a few hours out of Dover, when the fog cleared, they ran into a terrible storm and the ship was like a cork being tossed about on the heaving, turbulent sea, its decks awash with spray. The pitching of the vessel brought several of the fugitives prostrate with seasickness, but the frightful illness mercifully left Francis and Louise alone. Louise remained in the cabin, looking out of the small porthole at the huge world of grey water.

The shoreline had disappeared long since and the towering waves fell in deep hollows into which the vessel would sink, only to be thrown back up again. But she struggled bravely on, stretched to her limits.

Louise kept to the cabin for the entire journey. The wound she had sustained during her attack and the deep purple bruises on her body didn't affect her nearly as much as the mental torture she was being forced to suffer at being set upon and almost raped by that vile creature. But she was fiercely determined to put it behind her— she must. Thank God, Francis had found her in time, but she felt a deep regret that he had been forced to kill a man because of her.

She saw no one but Francis, and occasionally Sir Percy. Francis had told her that his friend knew of her subterfuge, and at her alarm had told her not to worry— Percy would keep her secret for the time it would take them to get to Scotland. Ever since the attack on Louise, Francis had blamed himself bitterly for bringing her with him, remembering how his reasons for doing so had been purely selfish ones. How could he have been so stupid as to put her life at risk in this way? He should have forced her to go to Anne in Holland no matter how much she objected. For that brief time after he had brought her on board ship, he had waited through those terrible hours for her to regain consciousness. Everything had ceased to exist, nothing else had mattered to him then, nothing but Louise and her recovery. He was no longer blind to the fact that he loved her desperately—more than life itself—but because of Anne he told himself there could be no future for them together, and when she began to recover he was determined, no matter how difficult it would be, to treat her as a friend and nothing more. And this he did. On reaching Scotland he would see to it that she got some decent clothes to wear and take her to stay with some good friends of his, with whom he would leave her while he went to the King.

During the days that followed, Louise would have been a fool not to notice the sudden change in him. He had become remote from her, cool and indifferent, and spent little time with her. He was always considerate, but somehow he had put an invisible wall between them and she knew he was beginning to regret bringing her with him. But no matter how deeply this hurt her she said nothing, realising why he was doing it and not wanting to make it more difficult for him than it already was. When she was alone and the tears came she would dash them away angrily, telling herself to be sensible and be satisfied that she was with him for now—no matter how short the time was to be. It was a great relief to her and everyone else when the journey was almost over and they sighted the coast of Scotland—where they would part company from Sir Percy and the others.

CHAPTER FIVE

FROM Scotland's capital city, Edinburgh, where they lodged for a few days, and after fitting Louise out with some new clothes, they travelled north to Perthshire, first by coach and then across the River Tay by ferry. Once across, Francis purchased two horses and they went on to Kilcrae Castle, which had been the family seat of the Lairds of Kilcrae for generations. It perched precariously on a huge promontory overlooking the beautiful River Tay. There was nothing furtive about this small castle. It stood open and proud and was reached up a rocky but thickly wooded slope from a low-lying green glen. They clattered over a wooden drawbridge which hadn't been raised in a hundred years, past a small gatehouse and into the cobbled courtyard where they drew rein and dismounted from the sweating, panting horses.

Kilcrae Castle in no way resembled a castle in the normal sense of the word, having no central keep. It was more like a fortified mansion, a grey stone house with a broad terrace dropping down to a beautiful garden with carefully clipped hedges overlooking the river, all enclosed by a thick retaining wall.

Sandy Kilcrae threw the big oak door open wide and came out to greet the travel-stained visitors. He was a man of middle years with a massive barrel chest and a florid complexion. He had red hair surrounding a bald, shiny pate. Like many more of Francis' friends they had met during the Civil War but now, too old for campaigning, he left it to his three sons who were with David

Leslie in the south. Leslie commanded the Scottish army in support of Charles Stuart.

Sandy's wife Mary came and stood beside him, dressed in a dark grey woollen dress. She was a big woman with silver-grey hair drawn from her full, round face. Her eyes were a faded blue and settled on the unexpected visitors warmly.

'Why, Francis,' she said, her face breaking into a welcoming smile when she recognised him immediately. 'This is a surprise.' He had often come home with her husband and sons in the past, spending many happy days hunting and fishing with them, and she was more than glad to welcome him now. She looked at the young woman by his side and never having seen her before assumed her to be Anne Sinclair, his betrothed, who might now be his wife. He had always spoken of her with a deep love and affection, and if this was she then Mary could understand why.

Louise still wore her male clothes but had discarded the wig, there being no longer any need for disguise, and she found it easier riding in the breeches without the encumbrance of skirts. She watched the two men embrace each other with obvious affection and exchange hearty, good-humoured slaps on the back.

'So,' said Sandy, his voice deep and booming. 'I might have known you'd follow Charles Stuart. I said to Mary, you try keeping him away—he'll not be far behind.' His eyes came to rest on Louise. 'Ah—and who is this wee lassie, Francis? Can it be Mistress Sinclair?' he asked with a mischievous twinkle in his eyes.

'Er—no,' said Francis, suddenly discomfited and noticing the soft, embarrassed flush spread on Louise's cheeks. 'No. Anne is in Holland with her family. It was no longer safe for them to remain in England. This is Louise Cranwell. She has accompanied me to Scotland to look for someone but—it is a very long story, which I will tell you later.'

Mary's sharp eyes had also noticed Louise's embarrassment and threw her husband a cross look for his careless blunder. 'Of course,' she said, taking Louise's hand and drawing her inside the large hall.

The stone walls were hung with shields and claymores, the large double-edged broadsword wielded in battle with such expertise by the Scottish Highlanders, and all kinds of cruel weaponry. Rich, colourful tapestries hung, depicting long-past battles. Louise shuddered slightly, feeling that Kilcrae Castle was very much a male-dominated household.

'I'm very happy to meet you, my dear, and welcome you to Kilcrae Castle. My husband and myself are the only ones at home at present—apart from the few servants, of course. Our sons are all away with David Leslie in the south somewhere. Come—you must be in need of refreshment after your journey, and afterwards I'll show you your room. You must feel quite at home at Kilcrae and come and go as you please.'

'Thank you,' said Louise, relieved to hear a friendly voice after the past few days of having to endure Francis' cool indifference. 'You are very kind. I hope we're not imposing on you and your husband.'

'Och—imposing indeed—why, the very idea,' said Mary, laughing and throwing her hands up in the air. 'It's a rare pleasure for us to have visitors, I can tell you. But,' she said, sighing and letting her gaze rest warmly on Francis, 'it gladdens my eye to see Francis again. He's almost like one of my own.'

Francis laughingly placed his arm about her ample waist, giving her an affectionate squeeze and planting a kiss on her cheek. 'Ah, Mary,' he said softly. 'Thank God you haven't changed.'

It was growing late and darkness was already creeping over the hills. The many candles had been lit, and by the time supper was over conversation was almost exhausted—but not as much as Louise, who could hardly keep her eyes open. She was utterly worn out following her journey and, after saying goodnight to their host and giving Francis a weak smile, she followed Mary wearily up the big old staircase to her bedchamber.

Louise had been at Kilcrae for two days when Francis came to her room and informed her that he was leaving later that day. She was dressed in a simple gown of golden silk, which was such a beautiful contrast to the unflattering male attire she had worn on her journey to Scotland that for a moment her loveliness almost took his breath away. He had purposely made a point of seeing little of her since their arrival at Kilcrae because of the desire which filled him whenever he was with her. He had spent his time riding and hunting with Sandy and catching up on events concerning the King and Covenanters, and also learning as much as he could about the military situation between David Leslie and Oliver Cromwell's invading force who—because of sickness and lack of provisions—were faring badly in the south of Scotland.

When he entered, Louise was sitting on the bed, but at his words she rose and stared up at him hard, at first with alarm and then with growing anger when she realised what it was he had come to tell her.

'But where are you going? Surely you're not leaving me here?'

'Yes—for now. I'm going to Perth to see the King and afterwards I shall travel south to offer my services to Leslie, and also I hope to make enquiries concerning the whereabouts of Robert Grey.'

'I see. And what am I supposed to do? Can I not go with you?'

'No. I want you to remain here where I know you'll be safe. I've talked it over with Mary and she's more than pleased to have you stay at Kilcrae.'

Louise had become so angry it almost choked her. It could not be true. How dared he think of leaving her here on the top of this desolate rock with just a middle-aged man and woman for company for what could turn out to be months? His eyes, which looked down into hers, were cold and without emotion and could have been those of a complete stranger. His tone was formal, and she knew he had fought to keep her at a distance ever since they had been on board ship, but when he looked at her like this it was almost as if he hated her.

'And what am I expected to do?' she asked cuttingly. 'Have you forgotten that Robert Grey is as much my concern as yours?'

'No, I haven't forgotten, but be sensible, Louise. How can you come with me?'

'I could disguise myself again. No one will notice me.'

'No,' he said sternly. 'I forbid it. For once, do as I say. I cannot have you trailing about Scotland with me now. It's far too dangerous and it is more than likely there will be more fighting.'

'Why don't you stop lying to me, Francis?' she said, throwing back her head, her thick mane of hair shimmering down her back. She fixed him with a furious stare, her eyes blazing. 'We both know why you don't want me with you. Isn't it because you see me as a threat to your happiness with Anne, and no matter how much you try you cannot deny it? But if I had known you were going to leave me on the top of this God-forsaken rock then I would have stayed in London.'

'Yes,' he blazed, his face contorted both with fury and desire. 'There are times when I wish you had. There are also times I wish I'd never laid eyes on you because I've had no peace since. I think that if I'm not with you that I shall be able to put you from my mind, but I can't. I find myself thinking of you all the time—I can't help myself. The longer we are together the worse it gets. You're like a poison seeping through my veins. Like a witch haunting me night and day.'

'And do you think marrying Anne will stop my haunting you? Well—I can tell you it won't,' she said cruelly, wanting to hurt him as much as he had hurt her by his almost total rejection. 'When you are with her you will be wishing you were with me. Your desire for me will grow stronger by my absence, and not even with the passing of time will my memory fade. I tell you, Francis, that whatever happens you will never forget me—ever.'

'Be quiet!' he shouted, his eyes filled with pain because he suspected she spoke the truth.

'No, I won't be quiet,' she cried, her beautiful brown eyes blazing rebelliously. 'Why should I? Before you go I want you to know this, Francis,' she said, moving closer so that she stood directly in front of him. 'I want you to know that I love you. I have never loved anyone else and never will. I love you so much that I would risk anything to stay with you—always—and if that is not to be, then I would gladly die beside you.'

'Stop it. Stop it, do you hear? I've told you before that my future plans cannot include you. You say you love me——'

'Yes—yes, I do,' she interrupted passionately, giving a triumphant, mocking little laugh as she tossed her head insolently. 'And I could tell when you kissed me that you loved and wanted me. Don't you remember?'

His face paled suddenly and deep lines appeared at
the corners of his mouth. His blue eyes glittered angrily
through narrowed lids. 'I would be grateful if you would
not remind me of that,' he said between clenched teeth.
'I am ashamed of my weakness on those occasions and
have reproached myself many times. But whatever my
feelings are towards you, that does not mean I love Anne
less, and it is her that I shall marry. I shall not allow
my desire for you to prevent my going to her when this
is over.'

They fell silent, their chests heaving angrily as they
glared at each other across the short distance that
separated them, like two combatants on a battlefield.
They were so close that they could have reached out and
touched each other, but Francis took a step back,
although secretly he longed to reach out and draw her
into his arms—he knew that if he did then he would be
lost forever. Abruptly he turned and left the room,
leaving her staring at the heavy wooden door.

When he'd gone, her anger evaporated and she sank
on to the bed. Her eyes were misty with tears and a
painful lump appeared in her throat. A lump of misery
which she tried hard to swallow down. She closed her
eyes and let the tears stream down her face, and even in
her wretchedness she knew that nothing she could say
or do would persuade him to take her with him. She had
no option but to stay at Kilcrae and wait for him to come
back—however long it might be. At the awful thought
that he would be gone a long time, and remembering
the angry words which had passed between them, she
became even more miserable. But then she remembered
her true reason for coming all this way, which for a while
had eluded her. He was going to look for Robert Grey,
and it was as important to him as it was to her that he
find him. She wiped the tears from her eyes, her instinct

to carry on reviving inside her, and she knew she couldn't let him go with any animosity between them. She must see him before he left.

Later that same day Louise stood by her open window. The day was warm, and a heady scent of roses from the garden drifted up to her. She saw a man walk on the terrace and go down the stone steps to the garden below. He had his back to her, but she could see that he was tall and broad-shouldered with black, curling hair falling to his shoulders, and her heart beat joyously. There was only one man in the whole world she knew to be as tall as that, and she had thought he'd already left Kilcrae for Perth. She spun round and ran out of her room and down the stairs, her slippered feet so light it was as if they had wings and they barely touched the steps. She saw two men in the hallway talking quietly to Mary, but scarcely gave them a second glance. She ran outside and on to the terrace and down the stone steps into the garden, towards the place where she thought she had seen Francis overlooking the river. She paused, breathless, looking around, wondering where he was. And then she saw him.

'Francis!' she called and, holding the golden silk skirt of her dress off the ground, ran towards him. 'Oh, Francis—thank God. I thought you'd left without saying goodbye.'

When she was close, the person she had believed to be Francis turned, and she was confronted by a total stranger. She stopped directly in front of him and gasped, her eyes opening wide when she realised her mistake. From behind he could have been Francis, but when he turned round this man was so different. For a fleeting moment she caught a look about his face as he turned. It was sombre and the black eyes which looked down

into hers out of a dark, swarthy face were full of sadness
and melancholy. But suddenly the wide, full, sensual
mouth broke into a smile and he bowed his head slightly,
his eyes never leaving hers.

She was indeed a delightful vision, with her rich
chestnut hair contrasting beautifully with her golden
gown of pure silk. He had seen the disappointment mirrored in her lovely liquid-brown eyes when she realised
her mistake, and he felt a pang of dismay that his name
wasn't Francis.

'Oh—oh, I'm sorry—I thought——'

'That I was Francis,' he said, his voice rich and deep.
'Then I am sorry to disappoint you. I too am waiting
for Francis, and it is not the first time that we have been
mistaken for each other.'

Louise felt the colour mounting in her cheeks beneath
this stranger's close scrutiny, and wondered who he was.
He was immaculately dressed in a dark blue velvet suit
but, apart from his unusual height and black hair, there
the similarity to Francis ended. He was also younger in
years, but older in the fact that he appeared to have all
the troubles of the world upon his broad shoulders, and
she wondered what could have happened to make him
look so unhappy. Before hearing his voice, she had
thought he must be foreign because of his dark good
looks. Perhaps Italian or Spanish, but he spoke with no
accent. He emanated a great physical power and the
muscles of his hard shoulders rippled beneath his clothes.
His movements for one so tall were graceful, in a lazy
kind of way, and there was an air of mystique about
him. She didn't object when gently he took her hand in
his own, keeping his eyes firmly fixed on hers.

'Come,' he said. 'Perhaps you will walk with me in
this delightful garden and together we will await Francis.'

She allowed him to lead her along the paths lined with borders of fragrant flowers, and the sodden earth, after all the rain which had fallen during the past weeks, steamed beneath the warmth of the sun. The day was unusually warm and humid, and bees hummed lazily as they flitted from flower to flower.

'Do you know Francis well?' asked the stranger.

'No—not really,' she answered truthfully, 'although I knew his family for a long time in Ireland before I met him.'

So, thought the stranger. From her words he was led to understand that there was no romantic attachment between herself and Francis, and if that were so then she could prove to be a delightful diversion for a time.

She looked up at him sideways. 'Don't you have a name?' she asked curiously.

'Of course. My name is Charles.'

'Charles? But is that all? Don't you have another name?'

'Oh, yes,' and he smiled down at her, a slow, secretive smile. 'And no doubt you shall learn that later. What is your name?'

'Louise—Louise Cranwell.'

'Ah—a pretty name. Now come—tell me what a delightful creature like yourself is doing in Scotland with Francis. Could it possibly have anything to do with King Charles?' he asked, and he cocked a sleek black eyebrow as he surveyed her quizzically.

'Good Lord, no,' she said honestly. 'At least, not me. Why, I don't even know what the King looks like, and anyway, how anyone can possibly call him the King when he hasn't even been crowned baffles me.'

He listened to her with an amused smile playing on his lips. 'And Francis? Why did he come to Scotland?'

'For two reasons. One is personal, but the other—the main reason—is because of the King. He will not rest until Charles Stuart sits upon the throne of England.'

At her words the expression on her companion's face became grave, and he looked down at her seriously. 'Yes,' he said. 'That is just like Francis. He hasn't changed. So—tell me—if it isn't because of Charles Stuart, then what brings you to Scotland?'

'I never wanted to come,' she said, sighing deeply. 'It always seemed so far away, and I always imagined its people as being wild and untamed.'

He nodded slowly, his black eyes brooding and thoughtful, and once again Louise thought she could detect a hint of sadness in him.

'I can't say that I blame you,' he said. 'I myself shall never understand the nature of this country or the Scots.'

'There is someone I must find,' she continued.

'A friend?'

'No—far from it. More like Satan, I think,' she replied, pausing and gazing wistfully down at the shining waters of the River Tay where it meandered its way through the valley below. There was a faraway look in her eyes and Charles paused beside her, looking down at her lovely face.

'Would you like to tell me about him?'

She looked up at him. His eyes were kindly, and something about him inspired confidence. The next moment she was telling him all about her years in Ireland and that awful night.

He listened to her soft voice calmly, his eyes intent on her face. Her gaze was all the while fixed on the river. When she told him of the night Robert Grey had come to the village and the terrible outrage which had fol-lowed, a deep pain wrenched his heart and something of her hatred for the man conveyed itself to him. His face bore a sombre expression, but his eyes had become hard and glittered with anger when he thought of Ireland and what its people had been forced to suffer beneath the crushing hand of Oliver Cromwell.

When she had finished speaking a long silence stretched between them, and when at last she lifted her eyes and looked at him she was shocked by the expression of deep sadness, and she truly believed that what she had told him had sickened him.

'I'm sorry,' she said. 'Perhaps I shouldn't have told you.'

'I'm glad you did. Word has spread to us about the atrocities which took place in Ireland under Oliver Cromwell, but it's the first time I've met someone who has experienced it at first hand. You must have suffered greatly—and Francis also. Well,' he said, shaking his head sadly, 'I really had no idea. 'So—you are here to seek revenge?'

She shook her head slowly. 'I don't know any more. All I know is that I must find Elizabeth, and to do that I must first find Robert Grey to discover where she was sent. But Francis,' she said, her face grim and her eyes darkening. 'I believe he will kill him when he finds him.'

'Yes—I can understand that. But even if this man is here in Scotland, then short of riding straight into the Parliamentary camp I cannot see how you can reach him.'

'I'm sure Francis will find a way,' she said softly.

They had entered a rose arbour, the air full of the flowers' heady scent. Roses clambered and trailed in abundance over the trellising. Luxuriant scarlet ones, dripping their petals on to the path, intermingled with yellow and some as white as the purity of driven snow. Charles bent down and plucked a half-open deep velvety-pink one and, after carefully removing the prickly thorns,

placed it in the low-cut bodice of her dress where it rested
between her creamy breasts. The action was casual and
light-hearted, and Louise wasn't at all embarrassed by
it. She felt completely at ease with her companion. He
suddenly laughed lightly, for a while his sadness gone.
He slipped an arm casually about her slim waist.

'Come,' he said, 'let us resume our walk and I promise
I shall try and cheer you.'

This he did, and when Francis returned it was Louise's
laughter that directed him to them. He paused on the
terrace, looking towards the rose arbour where Charles
and Louise walked together. Charles still had his arm
loosely about Louise's waist and they were laughing
easily together, as if sharing some private joke. He could
not believe this was the same Louise he had left earlier
in her room, who had declared her love for him so
passionately and whom he had left with her eyes spitting
fire. And now here she was, laughing as he had never
heard her laugh, and her face was radiant as she looked
up into the darkly handsome face of Charles Stuart. They
looked more like a couple of lovers than two people who
had only just met.

In spite of the deep friendship that existed between
the King and himself, he could not help the rush of
resentment and jealousy rising inside him, but it was gone
almost as soon as it had appeared and he was walking
towards them.

Charles and Louise turned simultaneously when they
heard Francis call from the terrace, and Charles left
Louise standing alone and moved quickly forward, eager
to greet his friend. And then a very strange thing happened, making Louise's heart almost cease to beat, and
she suddenly felt extremely foolish when she realised who
it was whom Francis was greeting. He dropped to one
knee and reverently kissed Charles' hand, before rising

to his feet where the two men embraced warmly. They talked animatedly between themselves for several minutes, almost forgetting Louise's existence, but then they turned and moved towards her.

She was half-dazed, staring with huge eyes, now fully aware that the man who had so fascinated her for the past half-hour with his irresistible charm and deep understanding, which was so strong it was like some deep, physical force, was Charles Stuart—rightful Monarch of England, Ireland and Scotland.

When he stood before her, his black eyes full of unconcealed amusement, a wave of colour mounted her cheeks and she sank into a deep faultless curtsy, lowering her eyes.

'Sire,' she said softly but with a hint of reproach. 'You should have made it known who you were.'

'It's not often I have to,' he replied, laughing lightly, and reaching out took her hand, raising her to her feet. 'But I sincerely ask your pardon. It's a rare pleasure to have someone speak to me as a person and not as Charles Stuart. Since my arrival in Scotland I've been surrounded only by pious, miserable faces, and believe me it was a delight to find you alone so I could make your acquaintance.' He raised her hand to his lips and kissed it lightly, letting his dark, brooding eyes linger once more on her face.

Once again Francis felt the rush of resentment at the familiarity Charles was showing towards Louise. The King was quite obviously enchanted by her, and the way he looked at her was full of unmistakable admiration. Francis noticed the rose resting between Louise's breasts in the bodice of her gown and, knowing only too well of the King's reputation with beautiful women and that they held a fatal attraction for him, he was in no doubt as to how it had got there. Charles released Louise's hand and turned to Francis.

'Buckingham informed me of your arrival in Scotland and that you were here at Kilcrae. I had the devil of a time getting away, I can tell you. Argyll and these Scottish Politicians watch over me like gaolers.'

'I had intended riding to Perth to see you later, but you beat me to it,' said Francis.

'I'm glad I did because apart from my companions it was a most enjoyable ride, and it also gave me the opportunity to meet Mistress Cranwell,' he said, smiling once again at Louise. But then his expression became serious and he looked once more at his friend. 'She has told me of what happened to your family in Ireland, Francis. I can only offer you my deepest, heartfelt sympathy.'

'Thank you, sire,' said Francis, his eyes clouding. 'Although I fear it will not be over for either Louise or myself until we find Christopher and Clara, and Louise's sister Elizabeth.'

'Have you any idea where they were sent?'

'The West Indies. Barbados, I think, but I cannot be certain. I'm here in Scotland not only to offer my services to yourself but also to find the perpetrator of that terrible deed.'

Charles nodded sympathetically. 'Then I wish you luck, Francis. Do you intend joining David Leslie?'

'Yes.'

Charles sighed deeply. 'Then I wish you luck there also. As you will know he is in the south, positioned around Dunbar, and from what I hear all is not well with the troops. Those meddling ministers of the Kirk have purged the Scottish ranks of all men who had shown themselves to be ungodly, even though most of them are experienced soldiers—able men and true Royalists like yourself. They treat the whole affair like a religious war rather than a military campaign.'

He spoke with much bitterness, and Francis considered him with concern. The change in him since their last meeting at The Hague seven months ago was obvious. After what Charles considered to be the judicial murder of his father, Charles I, he had emerged with his spirit unbroken, a cynic, who observed the world about him with a sceptical eye. Francis suspected that signing the Covenant would be his first step towards vengeance. There was no doubt that he was burdened by a heavy feeling of guilt brought about by his compliance with the Scots, which had caused widespread condemnation and outrage among the Anglican Royalists. His first weeks in Scotland had also been full of gloom and despondency. The all-too powerful Politicians and the Marquess of Argyll—who had ambitions that Charles should marry his daughter Anne—kept a strict guard over him, allowing no one into his presence but those who were acceptable to them. His freedom was limited and he had to endure frequent long, boring sermons. Even some of his court attendants had been removed and replaced by dour Presbyterians. It was clear to see that Charles was unhappy, that this land and its people did not endear themselves to him in the least. He had been nurtured at the courts of England and France by his mother, Henrietta Marie, and this had not prepared him for the low-standard harshness of Scottish life.

'When do you hope to leave?' asked Charles.

'I am ready to leave immediately. I'll ride back to Perth with you and go on from there.'

'Then take care of yourself, Francis,' said Charles, his tone grave. 'There are few men I can still call my friends left.'

'I shall,' replied Francis. 'But tell me—what is the situation in Cromwell's army?'

'They fare badly. What with sickness and hunger, they are discouraged. Leslie's forces outnumber them two to one, but so far he has refused to come out intó the open for battle. He has also cut off Cromwell's withdrawal towards England, so his situation is not good.'

At that moment two grim-faced gentlemen who had accompanied Charles to Kilcrae came out on to the terrace, impatient to leave for Perth. He noticed and cursed softly, irritated by their presence.

'It seems I have stayed long enough,' he said, 'but if you are to accompany me back to Perth we will talk on the way.' He turned back to Louise and, taking her hand, again raised it to his lips, his black eyes smouldering under his heavy lids when they looked deep into hers. 'Goodbye, Mistress Cranwell,' he said softly. 'It has been a pleasure making your acquaintance and—perhaps—if I can escape my captors I shall come riding this way again.'

He left her alone with Francis, who turned and faced her, a scowl on his brow when he noticed her flushed cheeks.

'I apologise for not being here when the King arrived. I was riding with Sandy.'

'Oh—it doesn't matter,' she said, sighing. 'Although I do wish he'd told me who he was.' Absently she removed the rose from her bodice, holding it to her nose and smelling its sweet perfume. She seemed unaware of Francis' presence. Her cheeks were flushed a delicate pink, and a half-smile played on her lips. There was a dreamy, faraway look in her eyes as she watched Charles' tall figure disappear into the house. Such was the impact he had made on her. She sighed and looked up at Francis. 'I like your King, Francis, and I think I now understand why you serve him with such blind devotion.'

His face stiffened at her words. 'So,' he said. 'I thought you were indifferent to him.'

'That was before I met him. Now I think he's perhaps the most charming man I have ever met and—perhaps—the most lonely,' she finished softly.

'Be careful, Louise,' said Francis, a warning note in his voice. 'Charles has a love of a pretty face.'

'Yes—I'm sure he has,' she replied flippantly. 'And now—if you'll excuse me——'

'Louise, wait,' he said, reaching out and grasping her arm as she was about to move away. By bringing her to Kilcrae he had believed she would be safe while he went in search of Robert Grey. But now, after her meeting with Charles, he wasn't so sure any more. He recognised the imminent danger of leaving her here alone with Charles so close at Perth. She was so vulnerable, and he found himself wishing she had never met the King.

She paused, and looked at his hand on her arm and then up into his troubled eyes, waiting for him to speak.

'I hope you won't do anything foolish while I'm away.'

'Foolish? Why—what do you mean?'

'You know perfectly well what I mean,' he said, his face taut and his eyes burning down into hers. 'I saw the way Charles looked at you. I've seen him look at women that way before, and the next minute they were sharing his bed.'

The delicate flush that had mantled Louise's cheeks a moment earlier disappeared, leaving her deathly pale when realisation of what he was implying hit her. 'How dare you?' she whispered. 'You have no right to suggest such a thing.'

'No—maybe not,' he said. 'But don't forget that I know him. I know what he is capable of where women are concerned. You will be nothing more than a dis-traction while he is here in Scotland—a passing fancy, that is all—soon to be forgotten when next he sees a pretty face.'

She became indignant. 'I have only just met him, yet you speak as if we were already lovers.'

'That is what I'm afraid of,' he said, his grip tightening on her arm. 'I also saw the way you looked at him, giving him smiles and glances. Have you set out to entrap him?'

Louise looked at him incredulously, hardly able to believe this was Francis saying these terrible things to her. 'No, I have not,' she flared. 'But if I had, it would have nothing whatsoever to do with you.' She saw the pain enter his eyes at her words, and laughed mirthlessly. 'Why, Francis—I do believe you're jealous.'

'I have no time for petty jealousy.'

'Then what is it? If you don't want me yourself, surely you cannot object when someone else does.'

'No,' he said, his voice shaking with a quiet anger, his eyes darkening. His fingers were like a vice on her arm, biting cruelly into her soft flesh. He pulled her menacingly towards him, gripping her other arm. 'That's not true and you damn well know it, so don't play games with me, Louise. I want you so much I believe I would kill any other man who so much as laid a finger on you.'

'Even the King?' she spat, trying to taunt him.

He didn't answer her question but merely pulled her closer to him, his face not far from hers. 'Promise me,' he said through gritted teeth. 'Promise me that while I'm away you will not go to the King as his mistress. Believe me, Louise, Charles has all the practised arts of a seducer, and if he has a mind for you to be his mistress then you will find it extremely difficult to refuse. So—promise me you won't go to him.'

'No,' she fumed. 'I promise you nothing.'

'Then, by God,' he said, inflamed by her defiance and sheer beauty, 'I swear I'll make you remember me so you'll not want to go to him,' and he caught her to him.

Angrily she tried to pull away, but his arms tightened about her and she shuddered when she felt his strong, muscular body, so warm and vital beneath his clothes. She tried to struggle, but it was useless. He bent his face to hers, his eyes dark and glowing, and covered her mouth with his own. Her lips were like ice, forming angry words, but they did not stay that way. They became soft and moist and she began to kiss him hungrily, as a starving child craves for food. Her arms stole upwards, her fingers fastening themselves about his neck, and all the pleasurable sensations she had despaired of ever feeling again flooded her whole being. She closed her eyes, feeling his lips leave hers and move to her throat, where he kissed the soft hollow of her neck before returning once again to her eager lips, where he kissed her long and deep, the sensations inside her exploding in a fountain of pleasure.

It was only after what seemed to be an eternity that they pulled apart, once again both shaken by the depth of feeling they had awoken in each other. But the passion on his face was replaced by the hard mask of a stranger, his eyes expressionless, and an eerie silence stretched between them until he spoke.

'Try and forget me if you want, Louise, but I don't think you'll succeed.'

And then he left her. She had her back to him and didn't even turn to watch him go. It was not until he had left with the King that she turned and walked slowly back to the house. Her heart was filled with pain and so heavy she had forgotten all about the rose the King had given her earlier, which now lay crumpled and broken on the ground.

CHAPTER SIX

THE days after Francis' departure were filled with emptiness. Louise thought of him every minute of every hour and missed him dreadfully. That last fierce kiss he had given her still burned on her lips, sending a tremor through her, and she wondered how she was possibly going to endure the long days of waiting for him to return.

She busied herself helping Mary—who was more than glad of her company—about the house, and when there was a let-up in the rain, which seemed to pour down constantly, she went riding with Sandy through the green, open spaces along the banks of the Tay and up into the wooded hills where, in the distance, she had a wonderful, wide-ranging, panoramic view of the majestic peaks of the Scottish Highlands.

It was on another miserable, wet afternoon when King Charles next came to Kilcrae. Louise was taken completely by surprise, truly believing she would never see him again. Not only because of the strict guard kept over him by the Covenanters and his total lack of freedom, but also because she thought he would have forgotten all about her.

He was shown into a small reception-room off the great hall where a welcoming log fire blazed merrily in the huge fireplace. He was not so immaculately dressed as he had been the last time he had come to Kilcrae, and his clothes were spattered with mud. He was with a small hunting party which he had left in the courtyard, where Mary was supplying them with refreshments. When

Louise entered the room he was standing in front of the
fire, staring into the flames, his hands joined loosely
behind his back, and once again she was struck by the
strong resemblance he bore to Francis. Her heart sank
when she thought how much she wished it were he alone
in this room with her and not the King.

At her entrance he turned, his black eyes brooding
and thoughtful, but then he smiled and moved towards
her. She sank into a deep curtsy, her eyes lowered and
her dark-fringed lashes shadowing the exquisitely pale
skin of her cheeks. He reached out and took her hand
and slowly she rose to her feet, her beautiful, liquid-
brown eyes looking into his, and as before he was enchanted by her. Since their last meeting he had found
himself thinking of her often. Since coming to Scotland
there had been a lack of pretty faces at court, and if he
was caught dallying with any woman by a member of
the Kirk then he was severely chastised over his indecent,
sinful behaviour and threatened with being handed over
to the English. But meeting Mistress Cranwell, with her
refreshing innocence, had been like a salve to his body,
starved of the attentions of a beautiful woman, and she
had aroused a desire in him he had not felt since coming
to Scotland. He had a mind to have her near him at
court, if it could be contrived.

He still held her hand in his, his fingers warm and
firm, but he found hers cold. He raised them to his lips
and placed a lingering kiss on them. She flushed slightly
and looked him full in the eyes, and what she saw there
made her suddenly afraid and she knew already why he
had come. But then she remembered Francis and what
he had said about the King's reputation with women,
and how she had foolishly provoked his anger by leading
him to believe she might go to the King as his mistress
in Francis' absence. But she now knew beyond doubt

that she could never love another as she loved Francis.
No, not even the King, and she must not give him cause
to think otherwise—that she could offer him anything
but friendship. Although she was not so insensible to
the fact that he was a very attractive man, in a sensual
way, and that any woman would be flattered by his
attentions.

'Sire,' she murmured. 'Can I offer you some
refreshment?'

'No—thank you. I'm only here for a short while.
Come—let us sit by the fire. You feel cold.'

He led her to a sofa beside the fire, where she sat with
her hands folded demurely in her lap, trying to still the
wild beating of her heart and not to show the turmoil
taking place inside her. He stood with his back to the
fire studying her face closely, one of his sleek black brows
raised and a half-smile curving his lips.

'I trust you have not forgotten our last meeting?'

'I'm hardly likely to,' she replied, smiling softly. 'I
only hope I'm forgiven for not recognising you.'

'Yes—but only on one condition.'

'Oh? And that is?'

'I will tell you later,' he said, a secretive smile playing
on his lips. He moved over to the latticed window overlooking the terrace. 'Are you to remain here at Kilcrae
until Francis returns?'

'Yes.'

'I can't say that I blame you. It's very peaceful.'

'Yes, it is,' she replied, sighing deeply. 'Although I
cannot deny that it gets on my nerves at times. I'd give
anything to be with Francis, searching for the man who
sent his brother and sister and Elizabeth to the Indies.
But I must remain here until he returns—although that
might not be for months.'

'I too have a sister called Elizabeth,' said Charles sadly. 'She also is a prisoner with my young brother Henry in Carisbrooke Castle on the Isle of Wight. She is so young, and by rights should be with our mother in France. Her health has always been delicate, and I pray it will not be long before they will be allowed to go to the Queen. Children should be with their mother.'

Louise noted the deep sadness in his voice and she rose slowly, filled with pity and tenderness for him. She moved towards him as he silently stood looking out of the window, lost in thought. He was so still and brooding, he might have been alone. She reached out and gently touched his arm, causing him to turn and look at her, and for a brief moment all the hurt and humiliations he had been forced to suffer since coming to Scotland were mirrored in his eyes. She felt a poignant tenderness for him welling up inside her, and she understood how he must miss his family and how much he was suffering here, in a country which had so joyfully acclaimed him King, and yet here he now was, kept a virtual prisoner of the religiously fanatical Covenanters, ruled over by the ever-watchful eye of the Marquess of Argyll. Where he was merely a puppet in the hands of these people, who would use him to gain their own ends.

'I'm sorry,' said Louise sympathetically. 'It cannot be easy for you here in Scotland.'

'No,' he replied, a cynical twist on his lips. 'It isn't.'

'You must miss your family very much and want to be with them.'

'Yes,' he sighed. 'But life rarely gives us what we want and I tell you, Louise, these Scots have dealt ill with me—very ill. But come,' he said suddenly, his expression relaxing and a smile breaking on his lips. 'This is not the time for gloom and despondency. There is enough of that at court—believe me.'

'What—what's it like at court?' asked Louise tentatively. 'Is it very grand?'

Charles' eyes opened wide and he looked at her incredulously, as if she had said something remarkably funny, and then he threw back his head and laughed, his black eyes dancing gaily.

'Grand? Oh, Louise, it is anything but grand. There is certainly no pomp or luxuries at the court in Perth, I can tell you. I am completely in the hands of the elders of the Kirk, and that should speak for itself. And indeed we seem to have been in the most wretched straits for so long, I cannot remember its being otherwise, and money has always been and continues to be a grave problem. So—grand it certainly is not.'

At his laughter colour had flooded Louise's cheeks, but then the laughter died on his lips and he looked at her, suddenly serious.

'And now,' he said, 'coming back to my condition.'

At his words she felt a sudden unease, but at the same time she was curious as to what his condition could be. 'And that is?'

'That you join the court,' he said, watching her face intently.

She stared at him in amazement, wondering if she could have heard correctly. 'Oh, but—but I cannot possibly,' she gasped. 'And besides—I don't know anyone at court.'

'That can soon be remedied,' he said softly. 'I find it damnably difficult escaping my captors to ride all this way to Kilcrae to see you, but not only that—we have to leave for Dunfermline during the next day or so and I would consider it an honour if you would accompany us.'

Louise turned away from him in confusion, her cheeks burning and her heart racing madly as she tried to make

up her mind about what she must do. What he had asked
her was so unexpected. She didn't want to risk his displeasure by refusing to go—but then, it would be exciting
if she did. Preferable to remaining in total seclusion at
Kilcrae while she waited for Francis to return. At the
thought of him her heart sank, and she knew how angry
he would be to discover that she had left Kilcrae at the
request of the King, and in his anger would draw only
one conclusion as to why she had done so: to become
the King's mistress. Well, she thought, coming to a
decision. She would show him just how wrong he could
be, because she had no intention of becoming the King's
mistress. She turned and looked directly into Charles'
eyes, her mind made up.

'Very well,' she said, taking a deep breath. 'I will join
the court, but I must tell you that I promised Francis to
remain here until he returns. He'll be angry to find me
gone.'

At the mention of his friend's name and the softness
that came into her voice when she spoke of him, Charles
scowled, the first hint of suspicion forming in his mind.

'Francis will know where to find you,' he said, his
voice hardening slightly. 'Tell me about you and Francis.'

Louise averted her eyes, trying, unsuccessfully, to hide
the truth and her pain when she spoke of him. 'There
is nothing to tell. You already know how we met in
Ireland. How he found me and brought me back to
England. We are just two people thrown together by circumstances—that is all.'

'I see,' said Charles quietly, but he was not convinced
and sensed that it went much deeper than that. 'Louise—
there is something I must ask you, and I want you to
be truthful. Have you and Francis ever been lovers?'

Her eyes opened wide in genuine amazement at the
bluntness of his question.

'Forgive me,' he went on, quickly, 'but I have to know. You see, Francis is my friend—one of the few remaining friends I have in Scotland. In fact, when I had to leave England for The Hague he was by my side constantly. I can always depend on his loyalty, and I know he would never betray me. We have shared good times together and—some sad. Indeed, he was more like an older brother than a friend, so you see—I would not like to do anything that would hurt him in any way. Do you understand what I am saying?'

Louise fixed him with a steady gaze. 'Yes, sire—I do understand what you're saying, and I too have no wish to hurt Francis. Indeed, I owe him a great deal—perhaps my life. I have been totally dependant on him since leaving London—for food and even the clothes I wear. I can only hope you will believe me when I say we have never been lovers—or are ever likely to be,' she finished quietly, lowering her eyes.

Charles stared hard at her for several moments and could almost swear that what she said was the truth, but he had to be sure. Reaching out, he placed his fingers gently beneath her chin, tilting her head so that she was forced to look up at him.

'So—I suspect you would have it otherwise. And can you look into my eyes and say truthfully that there is no emotional entanglement between you two?'

Louise shook her head. 'No—I cannot. But he is betrothed, sire—to Mistress Sinclair—and they are to wed when he returns to Holland.'

'I am acquainted with Mistress Sinclair. A delightful young woman, but I am somewhat curious as to why Francis has delayed the marriage for so long. Can it be that she no longer holds his heart?'

'Oh, I believe he loves her, and whatever his feelings are concerning me he is still determined to marry her.

He has known her a long time—her father also—and he has made it quite plain that there can never be any future for us together,' she finished softly—but she could not hide the hurt and bitterness in her voice.

There was a silence between them as Charles considered what she had told him, aware of her misery. Thoughtfully he moved slowly back to the fire, where he turned and looked at her. She was staring disconsolately out at the rain washing the window-panes, and he knew that regardless of what lay between her and Francis he still wanted her to be near him. Perhaps he could make her forget.

'Will you still come with us when we leave?' he asked.

She turned and looked at him, the firelight dancing on his luxuriant, wavy, thick black hair. 'Of course—if you still want me to.'

'Good. Then that's settled—although it's not going to be easy explaining you to certain people. The majority of my attendants who accompanied me from The Hague have been dismissed. They were considered altogether unsuitable,' he said sourly. 'But some refuse to leave Scotland and follow the court. They always stay in lodgings close by. I shall inform my Lord Buckingham to arrange for you to stay with Lord and Lady Brett. You will like them, I know.'

It was at this moment that a knock came on the door and George Villiers, the Duke of Buckingham himself, came to tell the King that they were about to leave for Perth. He was a fair, handsome young man with a certain arrogance and with bold, searching eyes. Perhaps too bold, thought Louise crossly, as they swept appraisingly over her curvaceous form, and there was something insolent about his manner.

George Villiers was twenty-two years old and had been brought up with Charles in the Royal household and, because of their shared childhood memories, they had become close friends and a deep bond existed between them. But Louise had no way of knowing that it was said of George Villiers that he had been the one responsible for leading Charles along the path of dissipation several years ago when they had been in Paris, that city of gaiety which had so appealed to Charles—and he had by no means been an unwilling pupil, and ever since had sought the company and amusement of beautiful women.

'Mistress Cranwell is to join us when we leave Perth, George. Will you arrange for her to meet and share lodgings with Lord and Lady Brett?'

'It will be my pleasure,' said the Duke smoothly, thinking to himself that her appearance would create a sensation. Not only within court circles but also among the Covenanters, who would be angered beyond words if Charles dared to make her his mistress. There was nothing better than an unknown beauty hanging on to the arm of the King to make the tongues wag and create a scandal. Perhaps life would not be quite so dull in Scotland after all.

It was only after the King and the Duke of Buckingham had left the castle, and the clatter of horses' hoofs on the cobblestones of the courtyard could be heard no more, that Louise put her hands to her burning cheeks and had deep misgivings about what she had done, wondering if she had done the right thing. But then she felt a strange excitement coursing through her veins, as if she was on the brink of some whole new experience.

When she told Mary of her plans and the King's request that she join the court, she wasn't nearly so enthusiastic as Louise had hoped she would be. At first her face had registered shock and then dismay. It was late and the two women were alone in the hall, just about to go to bed, but at Louise's words Mary paused and went to stand in front of her. For the short time Louise had been at Kilcrae, Mary had grown very fond of her, and was not unaware of the feelings she had for Francis—or his for Louise, no matter how hard he was trying to fight them. Mary had eyes and ears and could see that the love Louise bore him, while knowing he was betrothed to another, was tearing her apart, but she couldn't let her seek refuge in the arms of the King. Her kindly face was full of concern when she spoke.

'Child—stay here with us. You can't go to the King.'

'Why not?'

'Because you promised Francis to remain here. Have you not thought what he will say when he returns and finds you gone?'

'Francis. What does he care where I am? I mean nothing to him,' she said coldly.

'Of course he cares. He brought you here so that you would be safe. And do you realise what it will mean if you join the court? What the King will expect of you?'

Louise lowered her eyes and had the grace to blush slightly. She did not reply.

'Louise—how can you go to the King, loving Francis as you do?'

Her eyes flew open in alarm. 'You know?'

'Of course I know. I'm not blind. Anyone would have to be a fool not to notice how things are between you two.'

'Well, he doesn't want me. He made that quite clear before he went away.'

'Oh—and the King does? But for how long, Louise? How long? And what will happen when he tires of you— when you have lived openly in a state of sin? What will

you do then with your reputation in ruins? Kings do not
marry their mistresses.'

'But I have no intention of becoming his mistress.'

'No—not now, perhaps, but you will, once you leave
Kilcrae and join the court with all its intrigues. You will
become the subject of all kinds of malicious gossip, and
by the time they have finished with you it will not make
the slightest difference whether you slept with the King
or not, because you will be ruined just the same. Not
even Francis will want you then.'

Mary's harsh reminder of what her position could be
struck Louise like a blow. She became angry and refused
to be deterred. 'But he doesn't want me,' she cried. 'At
least, not as his wife. Can't you see that what he feels
for me is exactly the same as what the King feels? He
too would take me into his bed, so whichever one I go
to the sin would be just as great. Oh, Mary—I want to
see him. I want to be with him, but my mind is made
up. When he returns he will know where to find me. I
am leaving for Dunfermline in two days' time.'

Mary sighed and nodded her head, knowing that
nothing she could say would make Louise change her
mind. 'Very well, Louise, if you must—but please
remember that the doors of Kilcrae are always open.
Promise me that you will come back if you feel you have
made a mistake.'

'Oh, yes—yes, Mary—I will,' said Louise, and
reaching out embraced her gratefully, her eyes full of
tears. 'If the court returns to Perth, then I promise I
shall come back.'

When Louise left Kilcrae it was with some regret—but
regret only at leaving her new-found friends and, once
in Dunfermline, where she took up residence with Lord

and Lady Brett, she put Kilcrae behind her and was swept along on a new wave of excitement.

Lord Buckingham had been right. She certainly did set the tongues wagging, and created a sensation among court circles. The Royalists who had remained loyal to Charles and refused to leave Scotland were glad of the diversion her appearance among them created. They were bored and tired of looking at the same old faces, and she made many admiring acquaintances among the men, who flirted with her outrageously. However, many of their wives and other ladies were not quite so generously receptive; in fact, many made no attempt to hide their hostility towards her.

For a few days no one was able to talk of anything else but Mistress Cranwell, and they were puzzled as to who she was and where she had come from. Louise was so deeply embarrassed by all the attention she received and the enormous fuss she had created that she tried, with great difficulty, not to draw unnecessary attention to herself and to keep a low profile, but it proved to be virtually impossible with people calling at all hours of the day. Only the elderly, good-natured Lord and Lady Brett, in whose charge Charles had placed her, remained unmoved by it all.

Louise saw little of the King while in Dunfermline. The Covenanters rarely let him out of their sight for a moment, but they were not unaware of Mistress Cranwell's appearance within their midst or at whose invitation, and it was not the first time the King had defied them in this manner and had had to be severely chastised for it.

Louise had seen the immensely powerful Marquess of Argyll on several occasions and didn't like him at all. The withering, disapproving looks he cast her with his fox-like eyes—one of which seemed to wander so that

you never knew quite where he was looking—made her
cringe. He was tall and thin with red hair and sly lips.
He was the most powerful man in the Kingdom and
ardently religious. He was the head of a mighty clan—
the Campbells—and had vast domains in the west of
Scotland. He had cause, on several occasions, to speak
to Charles about Louise, calling her a temptress and
wanting her banished—not only from court but from
Scotland altogether—but Charles would have none of
it. It was one of the few things which made him stubbornly stick his toes in, for he was becoming increasingly annoyed by Argyll and his bullying.

Life at this time was a miserable existence for Charles,
and he was obliged to sign a declaration denouncing both
his father and mother, acknowledging his own and his
father's sins—one being that he had married into an
idolatrous family. This, to the King, was the final humiliation, but he signed it nevertheless, complying with
their demands for the sake of his crown.

Most of Charles' supporters were not allowed into his
presence, and it was only with the connivance of Lord
Buckingham and Lord Seymour—two of the nine
Englishmen who had been allowed to remain with him
because they were considered by the Covenanters to be
a good influence upon him—that they were received pri-
vately at the palace, and Charles would seek out Louise
and lead her away from the chattering throng to a quiet
corner where they could be alone. But this did not stop
the eyes of the curious following them, or the gossips
laying bets that she would be the King's mistress before
they left Dunfermline. Some had it that she already was.

By the time of the battle of Dunbar on September the
third, 1650, when Cromwell and his generals inflicted

an overwhelming defeat on the Scottish army against all
the odds, the court had moved back to Perth.

Francis was south of Edinburgh with David Leslie and
the Scottish army, and it was only now, when he was
away from Louise, that he was able to think clearly. After
all the time he had known her he could no longer close
his heart to the fact that he loved her. He wanted her
so much that it was like a deep, physical pain. How could
he possibly marry Anne now? Every time he kissed and
embraced her he would see Louise. She had been right
when she had said he would never be able to forget her,
because he now knew beyond doubt that he never
would—not if he lived to be a hundred. He would be
tortured with desire for her to such an extent that he
would more than likely go insane.

No, he thought, at long last coming to a decision. He
could not do that to Anne. Anne—so pure and gentle.
He could never make her happy—not now. She deserved
someone better. At the first opportunity he would go to
her in Holland and explain. But, he thought wistfully,
picturing her lovely face framed by her fair hair, there
had been a time when he had loved her, had loved the
sweet gentleness and innocence of her youth. But with
Louise it was something different—wild and passionate
and primitive—consuming him completely. It was her
he would make his wife, and he was able to savour the
joy of their sharing a lifetime together. Now his mind
was made up he was impatient to be back with her at
Kilcrae—once he had caught up with Robert Grey.

The English, constantly harried by the Scots, had
withdrawn to the coast, more than likely to ship large
numbers of their soldiers home. Hunger and sickness
had certainly taken its toll of the English troops, along
with the appalling wet weather they had been forced to
endure for so long without tents. Morale in the Scottish

ranks, which numbered something like twenty-three thousand men and outnumbered the English two to one, was high. They had the English hemmed in, apart from the cold North Sea on one side, and also the Scots occupied a position of strategic importance—Doon Hill of the beautiful Lammermuirs—which towered menacingly over the sick and weary English troops.

Before darkness descended on them, Francis had stood on the escarpment watching the English troops through some strong glasses, knowing that somewhere down below was Robert Grey. At the realisation that after all these months he was probably within sight of the bloody butcher who had been responsible for all the unspeakable horrors inflicted upon the innocent people of his home village in Ireland and upon his family, it had renewed all the hatred he felt for the man which, with the passing of time, had increased a thousandfold. He had been calm as he'd trained the glasses on the small moving figures below, and he'd known that very soon they might come face to face on the field of battle, and he'd sworn he would make Grey pay for what he had done.

That night the Scots began their fatal descent from Doon Hill and spread their line in a great arc, closing in on the English. But, overconfident, perhaps because of their superior numbers and strategic advantages, and knowing of their foes' weakness, they complacently lay down in the fields to sleep and wait for the dawn before attacking, foolishly unsaddling their horses and becoming separated from their commanders. But they had grossly underestimated the well-trained, superb fighting skills of the English army under the military leadership of Oliver Cromwell, who had become aware of what the Scots were planning to do and was not prepared to wait until the dawn for them to attack.

It was still dark when the English silently manoeuvred themselves and prepared their assault lines, and then made their surprise attack on the unsuspecting Scots. As dawn was breaking, the fighting became fierce and Francis found himself in the thick of it. With his sturdy horse between his knees, swinging his sword with all the practised art of a seasoned soldier, all his years of fighting during the Civil War having given him a sharp, analytical mind, he displayed a skill which, to anyone watching him on that field of battle, made him seem almost invincible, as if he fought under divine protection. He fought like a man possessed, and this time it was not for Charles Stuart or for England but, as he slashed away at each face that appeared before him, it was to assuage his own vengeance as he sought the face of Robert Grey, dimmed as it was by the passing of the years.

And then, like a miracle, out of a sea of faces and blood he saw him. He had made several enquiries regarding Cromwell's troops, and had discovered that Colonel Robert Grey was head of a cavalry regiment and that his troop could be distinguished by the orange sashes they wore. He was not close enough to see the man's features clearly, and the triple-barred helmet he was wearing made it more difficult, but Francis knew, instinctively, that this was Robert Grey. He was beginning a charge against a company of Scottish Lances, and somehow Francis acquired a superhuman strength and rode full-tilt towards him, cutting down those who got in his way. Fierce fighting was taking place all around him and he plunged into the terrifying mêlée, where frightened horses reared and squealed, many unseating their riders to be trampled on the ground.

When in front of Robert Grey, Francis saw he had not been mistaken. The thin face with the long, straight nose and cold, colourless eyes stirred vague memories of his childhood. He was the same but older, this killer of his family. Visions of that night, of tortured and burned bodies and mutilated children, flashed before his eyes and something like madness exploded inside his head now that he was confronted by the monster who had ordered that terrible deed to be done.

'Robert Grey!' he shouted. 'Prepare to meet your maker, for I'll show you no quarter!'

Momentary surprise registered on Robert Grey's face when confronted by this dark-haired man with intense, angry blue eyes, and he wondered fleetingly why he had sought him out from the rest and how he came to know his name. He examined the stranger's features attentively.

'I ask for none and I'll give none,' he replied. 'Who are you? I can almost swear I have never seen you before, and yet—there is something about your face that is not unfamiliar.'

'Think back, Robert Grey. I was little more than a boy when we last met. My name is Francis Slade. So,' he said with icy contempt, 'before you prepare to defend yourself, know first why you die, because by the memory of my mother and father—William Slade—whom you murdered, and my brother and sister whom you sold into slavery, I swear I shall kill you. You shall not live to see another dawn.'

At the mention of his father's name, Francis had the satisfaction of seeing all the blood drain out of Robert Grey's face and his thin lips twisted in an evil sneer.

'So,' he hissed. 'You are his son. Then you shall suffer the same fate.' His face became contorted out of all recognition and he was like some demon cast up from hell itself. He raised his sword and it came crashing down on Francis.

All the hurt and rage that Francis had felt disappeared, and in its place came the well-trained mind and body of an experienced soldier. Their swords clashed and they began the fight on equal terms, and it soon became evident to each of them that the other had studied his weapon thoroughly. But it also became clear that, whereas both men were experts, Francis was a master. He dodged his opponent's thrusts easily enough, and Robert Grey became more enraged when he could find no opening in Francis' unwavering guard.

Francis had the satisfaction of feeling his blade sink into his opponent's flesh, drawing blood, but because of his breastplate the injury was only superficial. Grimly the fight went on, the exertion reddening the face of Robert Grey who, finding himself at a disadvantage, began to thrust wildly—but now, with his age against him, he was beginning to tire and make mistakes. Francis saw this and when the time was right lunged forward, thrusting the point of his tempered blade beneath Grey's breastplate and, with a cry of triumph, driving it home.

Robert Grey's eyes opened wide with a look of enormous surprise, and then he flopped forward on his horse and, like an axed tree, went crashing to the ground. Francis jumped down and knelt beside the body of his fallen foe, who was barely alive. Blood was pumping from beneath his armour, soaking into the ground. Francis reached out and, placing his hands firmly on his shoulders, shook him violently until he opened his eyes and fixed Francis with a frozen stare.

'Where are my brother and sister? Where did you send them?'

Robert Grey's mouth cracked into some semblance of a smile and he laughed—a low, evil sound. 'You don't know?' he gasped.

'No—damn you. Where are they?'

Robert Grey looked at him hard for a moment longer, and 'Barbados' was all he managed to say before blood began to bubble from between his lips and his head rolled back. He was dead.

Francis left the body of his most hated enemy lying there, the black hatred and rage having left his heart at long last. He hurriedly climbed back on to his horse and rejoined the fighting before he should be dragged down beside Grey.

It was six o'clock when the sun rose over the North Sea and the battle, which had lasted for just over an hour, was almost over. The Scots already knew that they had suffered a most humiliating defeat. After being thrown from his horse, Francis looked about him at the hundreds of bodies of dead and dying Scots and he was filled with the urgency to escape from the battlefield at all costs, before he was discovered and either run through or taken prisoner.

And so it was that he joined the large number of Scots fleeing for their lives, and it was with an immense stroke of luck that he found a stray horse and, after jumping into its saddle, pointed it in the direction of Stirling where he again joined David Leslie, who had also escaped from Dunbar. It was also in Stirling that he at last heard the rumour of the King's new mistress, and that her name was Louise Cranwell.

CHAPTER SEVEN

WHEN news of the battle of Dunbar and the Covenanters' defeat reached Perth, Charles received it with mixed feelings. Part of him rejoiced, and he secretly delighted at their defeat because of the treatment he had received at their hands since coming to Scotland, which had made him feel an acute resentment and dislike for them. But there were those who blamed Charles' presence among them for their defeat at Dunbar, accusing him of hypocrisy, saying that he only signed the Covenant out of self-interest, complying with their demands for the sake of his crown.

But the defeat proved advantageous to Charles even though it weakened Argyll and the Covenanters, and he became increasingly determined to rally the Scottish Royalists to his side, especially those in the Highlands, and create a national Scottish army to resume the fight against the English. But then, perhaps there would have been no humiliating defeat at Dunbar if the Scottish army had not been purged and decimated of all its experienced fighting soldiers.

It was at this time that the sad news reached Charles of the death of his sister Elizabeth, still held captive in Carisbrooke Castle. She had died of consumption and he was devastated by the news—and more so when he was told that, with their brother Henry, at long last they were to have been allowed to go to their mother in France two days later.

After Dunbar, the King attempted to escape his captors by riding north with three companions to raise the

Highland Royalists—at which he was unsuccessful—and when he had gone just forty miles he was recaptured and taken back to Perth. But this episode made it plain to Argyll and his adherents that they needed the King if they were to unite Scotland, which they now realised was the only way they could ever hope to beat the English. He was therefore given more freedom and some of his attendants returned to his side. He was even allowed to address Parliament. Preparations were also set in motion for his coronation at Scone.

Louise divided her time between Kilcrae and the court, and now saw more of the King. Mary was overjoyed to see her back at Kilcrae, although here sadness prevailed. Two of her sons, Stewart and John, had returned from Dunbar but the youngest, James, had been killed. His brothers, lucky to escape with their lives, had been forced to leave him where he had fallen, because if they had been caught they would have been taken prisoner and shipped off to the West Indies with hundreds more. As many as three thousand Scots had been killed at Dunbar, while the English casualties had been a mere twenty dead and fifty-eight wounded.

Stewart and John brought Louise eagerly awaited news of Francis—that he had escaped uninjured from the battle and was now at Stirling with David Leslie. At this she said a silent prayer, thanking God with all her heart that Francis was safe.

Contrary to all the rumours which seemed to have spread far and wide in Scotland, Louise had not succumbed to the King's charms and become his mistress, although there had been times when she had found it difficult to resist him, especially when a few new gowns and small presents had begun to appear. This had embarrassed her, knowing how scarce money was. She had tried to return them, but Charles had laughingly told her that, if she was to remain at court, then he would not have her dressed in miserable, dour clothes like the Scottish women.

Francis returned to Perth before the King's coronation, and as much as Louise longed to see him she had no way of knowing how hard he was avoiding coming into contact with her. If she was at Kilcrae then he was in Perth, and when she returned to Perth it was only to find he had left for Kilcrae. He had too much anger in his heart to set eyes upon her soft, sweet face just yet, or look into those beautiful eyes of hers in which a man could lose all reason. To Francis, in his hurt and anger, it was all false, a façade which hid a calculating, deceitful heart, and he would never be able to forgive her for becoming the King's mistress.

But it was inevitable that their paths should cross, and it was in a crowded room. Louise was with Charles. She saw Francis before he saw her, his tall, powerful frame with his proud, handsome face and deep blue eyes, and her heart nearly burst with joy. He irradiated her whole being with love. Her fingers, resting lightly on the King's arm, trembled slightly and he looked down at her, at the joy shining from her eyes. He followed their direction until his too came to rest upon Francis, and sadness crept into his heart.

Suddenly, Francis looked in their direction, his eyes drawn to hers like a magnet, and they rested on her face, feasting upon her loveliness and at the brilliance shining from her eyes as they locked on his, and he experienced a fierce joy, but it was only fleeting and disappeared when he noticed her fingers resting on the arm of the King.

Louise excused herself and moved towards him. His face became a hard mask when she paused in front of him, and he looked at her with the cold eyes of a stranger. She looked at him uncomprehendingly; all the joy she'd felt a moment before had gone and the light had vanished from her eyes, and she wondered what could have happened to make him look at her as he did. When he spoke his tone was mercilessly cutting.

'Louise—I trust you are well?'

'Yes—thank you,' she murmured, flushing slightly as his eyes travelled contemptuously ove. her beautiful deep pink silk dress, with its low décolletage, which Charles had given her. He carefully took in every detail, knowing where it had come from, and when his eyes settled on hers they were hard and accusing.

'You look lovely, Louise,' he said, but in no way did he make it sound like a compliment. 'You seem to have come up in the world since I last saw you. I trust you like being at court?'

'Of course,' she replied coolly, pride coming to her rescue when she realised why he was behaving like this. That he believed she could become the King's mistress while loving him as she did ... She felt a growing anger.

'You have certainly acquired a reputation for yourself—although perhaps not the kind of reputation for a respectable young lady,' he said with crushing scorn. 'Why, everywhere I go people are talking about the lovely Mistress Cranwell, at her unrivalled beauty and how she has captivated the heart of the King.'

Louise's cheeks flamed. 'And you, Francis? Do you believe what they are saying?'

He shrugged carelessly, as if it were a matter of no importance to him. 'Who am I to judge, Louise? What you do is really of no concern to me any longer. Little did I know when I brought you to Scotland that you would turn out to be the most true Royalist of us all.'

Discover Masquerade

WITH 2 FREE BOOKS

Masquerade historical romances bring the past alive with splendour, excitement and romance. As a special introductory offer we will send you 2 Masquerade romances together with a cuddly teddy bear and a surprise mystery gift - completely FREE.

We will also reserve a subscription for you which means you could go on to enjoy four more exciting new books, delivered to your door before they're available in the shops, every two months for just £1.75 each - postage and packing FREE. Plus a FREE newsletter giving you information on the top authors, competitions, (our last lucky winner won £600!), and much more.

What's more there are no strings attached, you can stop receiving books at any time, so don't delay, complete and return this card NOW!

Complete the coupon overleaf.

FREE BOOKS COUPON

Fill in the coupon now!

Yes! Please send me 2 FREE Masquerade romances together with my FREE teddy and mystery gift and reserve a subscription for me. If I decide to subscribe I shall receive 4 new Masquerade titles every two months for £7.00, postage and packing FREE. If I decide not to subscribe I shall write to you within 10 days. The FREE books and gifts are mine to keep in any case. I understand that I can cancel or suspend my subscription at any time simply by writing to you. I am over 18 years of age.

Free Gift

Mystery Gift

Name _____ 6AOM

Address _____

_____ Postcode _____

Signature _____
(I am over 18 years age.)

Send no money now - take no risks

She lowered her eyes so that he would not see the tears in them or the hurt his words had caused. Not only to her pride but also to her love.

'And now, if you will excuse me, there is a matter I must discuss with His Majesty,' and with a curt bow he was gone, leaving her in a room full of people but in which she felt so alone. She felt as if her whole world were crumbling to pieces around her. How would she ever be able to convince him now that she loved him with all her heart and soul?

Somehow she managed to escape to another room where she could be alone with her thoughts, away from all the prying eyes, and it was here, some time later, that Charles found her. Her lovely face was smudged with tears and a wave of tenderness swept over him. At that moment he would have given anything to know that the tears had been shed for him.

He sighed and moved towards her. Her depth of understanding and intelligent deep brown eyes, along with her irresistible charm and gracious beauty, made her different to any other woman he had ever known. For the short time he had known her he had hoped she would come to him. His body had ached with desire for her, longing for fulfilment. She had the seemingly rare capacity which inspired love, and he had known from the beginning that if he was not careful she would possess his whole heart. But as for hers...alas, he was not blind. By the way she had looked and let her eyes linger on Lord Slade, it was no longer hers to give.

'My dear,' he said softly. 'You have been crying.'

She smiled, a pitiful little smile. 'Just a little. It was silly of me—but I'm all right now.'

Reaching out, he took both her hands in his, where they fluttered like captive birds. He looked down at her seriously. 'Louise—let me tell you something. Since I have come to know you I have valued your friendship a great deal. Since the first time I saw you in the garden that day at Kilcrae I have wanted you—like a fool, patiently waiting for you to come to me, while knowing all along how you felt about Francis.'

She opened her mouth to protest but he placed his fingers gently on her lips, silencing her.

'No—wait—let me finish. It wasn't your fault. You were honest with me and told me how you felt, but I had hoped I could make you forget him—knowing how he had refused your love because of his impending marriage to Anne Sinclair. But I realise now that Francis is also a fool. If he marries her then he will be doing so out of duty and honour and for no other reason, and these two things can be a heavy burden to bear.' He looked down at her from his superior height with those seductive, lazy black eyes under their heavy lids, and it was not the first time that Louise had felt the power of his gaze. 'Tell me, Louise, if it were not for Francis— if you did not feel as you do for him—would you have come to me, and loved me?'

'Oh, yes—yes, I would,' she said without any hesitation, and looking up at him sideways she suddenly smiled teasingly. 'But perhaps you should not have been so patient with me, sire.'

He raised his black brows in mock amusement. 'You mean I should have forced my attentions on you?' He laughed softly, his white teeth gleaming in his swarthy face. 'No, Louise—it is not my way to take a woman against her will.'

'But I do love you, sire. I love you truly—but as a friend. Please don't be angry with me.'

'Angry? I could never be angry with you, Louise. You really are the most adorable patriot I have ever known.

Ah, Louise,' he said sighing deeply and tucking her hand into the crook of his arm. 'What am I to do with you?'

She smiled wistfully. 'As to that, I think I have already decided.'

'Oh?'

'Yes. I shall see Francis and ask him if he's found Robert Grey, and if he knows where Elizabeth was sent. When I discover this, however difficult it may be I shall go and look for her. Even if it means going to the ends of the earth.'

'So—you will leave Scotland?'

'Yes, but I shall always be grateful to you for your friendship.'

A deep sadness entered his eyes. 'And I yours. I think—perhaps—we have helped each other over these past weeks more than either of us realises. I shall miss you—you know that.'

She nodded, feeling the tears pricking the backs of her eyes again, but she managed to laugh softly, trying to make light of the situation. 'I know someone who won't. Someone who will be more than glad to see the back of me.'

'And who might that be?'

'The Marquess of Argyll.'

Charles smiled ruefully. 'I'm sure you're right. There are times when I do believe he would be glad to be rid of me also. By the way, did you know he has a mind for me to marry his eldest daughter, Anne?'

'Yes, I have heard a rumour, and I have also heard she is quite lovely. What will you do?'

He sighed deeply. 'Nothing for the moment. I shall consider it, of course, and then—when the time comes— I shall do what I think best and consult my mother the Queen, and no doubt take her advice. Now—let us get back to the others. I am sure we will have been missed.'

He was right. Francis had noticed that they were both absent, and when they entered together neither saw the deep hurt in his eyes before he turned abruptly and left the room.

It was after she had taken supper with Lord and Lady Brett that Louise sneaked out of the house to go to the inn where George Villiers had told her Francis was staying. She had to see him, perhaps for the last time, and as she fastened her cloak she became determined not to think of that. But a flush of anger swept over her cheeks when she remembered their last meeting that afternoon, when he had unjustly accused her of sleeping with the King without giving her a chance to explain— and even if she had he would never have believed her. There were some things a man as inflexible as Francis would not forgive. But she must discover if he had found Robert Grey, however much he despised her at this moment. When he had told her what she wanted to know, then she would leave Scotland at once for Worcester and from there go to wherever she would find Elizabeth.

Francis had made it quite plain that he no longer wanted her with him, so it seemed pointless staying in Scotland any longer. She had very little money, but she did have a few small trinkets given to her by the King which she would sell—however callous this was, and however much she would hate parting with them, but she must put sentiment behind her now. It seemed she really had lost everything—even, she thought ironically, her reputation—but she did still have her pride, and that was one thing she was determined to keep.

The night was cold and a wind had risen, howling up and down the narrow vennels and passageways of Perth, driving the rain into Louise's face so that it stung her cheeks. She knew it was foolish and dangerous to go about the streets unprotected after dark, but thankfully, on a night such as this, there were few people about and besides, the inn where Francis was staying was only a few streets away from where she was lodged with the Bretts.

She hurried along, her cloak drawn tightly about her now almost saturated, and in the dark her feet kept disappearing into deep puddles, and she shuddered when she felt the freezing water come over the tops of her shoes. It was so dark she could hardly see where she was going, but suddenly the ghostly battlemented tower and short spire of St John's Church loomed before her above the rooftops and she sighed with relief, knowing that the inn wasn't far away now. On any other night she would never had possessed the courage to enter it alone, but now she was so wet and cold and so desperate to see and speak to Francis that she didn't give it a second thought and entered quickly, blinking her eyes as they adjusted to the light.

A big log-fire burned in a large fireplace and she had the urge to go over to it and warm herself, but she must find Francis first. All about the room men and women were drinking and eating. She searched the faces first on one table and then the next, hoping to see him, but he wasn't there. Despair was beginning to creep into her heart when a young serving-girl, bearing a tray loaded with food, stopped in front of her, eyeing her curiously.

'Can I get something for you?' she asked.

'Yes. I—I'm looking for someone. I've been told he's staying here.'

'What's his name.'

'Francis Slade.'

'Oh, yes—he's upstairs. Just a minute and I'll get someone to see if he'll come down.' She turned towards the stairs as a youth was going up. 'Billy—tell His Lordship there's someone to see him, will you?'

He nodded and went on up the stairs, and after knocking on a closed door disappeared inside. After several moments, which to Louise, waiting conspicuously in the tavern doorway, dripping wet and with what seemed to be a hundred pairs of eyes all staring at her, was like an age, Francis finally appeared and for an instant her heart almost stopped beating. He seemed taller than ever. His loose-fitting white linen shirt was unfastened, revealing a mat of thick black hair on his chest.

At first his blue eyes wandered lazily over the people in the tavern, but then he saw and recognised Louise standing in the doorway, so still she might have been a statue. She clutched her cloak tightly beneath her chin and her head was partly covered by her hood. Her eyes were huge, staring out of her face, which was deathly white. Their eyes met and locked and for a brief moment time seemed to stand still, but then his face darkened with anger. He leaned over and quietly spoke to the youth who had told him he had a visitor and, suspecting he was ordering him to send her away, Louise's body suddenly came to life and she hurried up the stairs until she stood in front of him.

'Please, Francis—don't send me away. I must talk to you.'

His eyes swept contemptuously over her and then over the upturned, curious faces of the people below and he turned sharply. 'Come in,' he growled and she followed him inside.

Closing the door behind her, she leaned against the hard wood. The room was warm with the glowing embers of a fire in the grate. A few candles burned, sending gloomy shadows dancing on the walls, and a large, unmade bed occupied the centre of the room. A table with an almost empty wine decanter surrounded by dirty glasses stood in front of the fire, with two shabby chairs on either side.

Francis surveyed her coldly, his hands on his hips and his eyes holding a deadly glitter. There was something in their inner depths that Louise could not read. Something that went deeper than anger.

'Well, to what do I owe the honour?' he drawled, his lips twisting with sarcasm. 'I must say that you are the last person I expected to see.'

The tone of his voice sent a thrill of fear down Louise's spine and she shrank back against the door as he moved slowly, menacingly towards her. She could tell that he had been drinking heavily. His eyes were bloodshot and there was a strong odour of wine about him.

'Well—what do you want? Who told you where to find me?'

'I—I asked George Villiers. He told me.'

Francis nodded and his lips twisted in a sneer. 'I bet he did, and no doubt everyone at court will know by now that the King's favourite is visiting me in my rooms. You should have known better than to ask him.'

'I—I'm sorry—I never thought,' she stammered. She should have remembered that Francis and the Duke of Buckingham had no liking for one another and she cursed herself for her blunder, praying that she had caused the King no embarrassment. But when she remembered the knowing smirk and mocking gleam in the Duke's eyes when she had asked him, she knew Francis was probably right. She had neither liked nor trusted George Villiers, believing him to be both devious and dangerous, and he was one person along with the Marquess of Argyll that she would certainly not miss seeing again. But then, what did it all matter to her now? Tomorrow she would be gone.

'Well, now you're here, what do you want? Perhaps you didn't understand me when I said that what you do no longer concerns me.'

His voice was filled with cold contempt, and anger suddenly welled up in Louise's heart.

'Oh, yes—I understand, Francis, but what I don't understand is why. I have done nothing that I'm ashamed of. Nothing to deserve this kind of treatment from you of all people. How could you assume that what the gossips said about myself and the King was true? I thought you had more faith in me than that. How could you even think me capable of such conduct?'

'You lie,' he snarled, bringing his face closer to hers, contorted with blazing fury. She turned her face away from his, but he reached out and caught her chin in his hand, forcing her to look into his rage-filled eyes. 'You dirty little whore. And just to think I loved you. That I was so besotted by you that you took over my mind so that I could think of nothing else. While I was at Dunbar I could think of nothing else but you, and only you. I placed you above all other women. But then I found out that you're just like all the rest. How many more men have there been, Louise, before the King? Answer me—that is, if you can. What a fool I was to love you—to be taken in by you. What could I ever hope to offer you that could match that of a King?'

'I have never belonged to the King,' she cried desperately, 'or any other man. Please—you must believe me.'

'Don't take me for a fool. You forget that I know Charles and his ways with women better than most. Can't you understand the torment I went through every time I imagined you in his arms? Kissing him? Smiling at him? Sharing his bed? Oh, Louise—every time I thought of you and him together it was like having a knife thrust into my heart.' His fingers still held her chin but they had slackened, and she raised her hand to remove them. He only lowered his head to hers. The look on his face had changed. His eyes had darkened and his voice became thick with passion. 'Perhaps I should have made you mine, Louise. Perhaps then you wouldn't have wanted to go to the King.' He let his gaze wander hungrily over the strained beauty of her face which emphasised the largeness of her eyes, flecked with gold, and the long, slender column of her neck. 'May God forgive me, but I still desire you. Whatever you are guilty of, I still have the misfortune to desire your body.'

'Oh, Francis—whatever you have been told, the King has never been my lover. Ask him if you don't believe me. But please believe me when I say that I have never belonged to Charles or any other man. I couldn't. As God is my witness I swear I love you and only you.'

He looked hard at her for a long moment. She had spoken with such an intensity of feeling that somehow it had penetrated his angry mind and, however much he tried to doubt her, he could no longer deny the truth staring out of her eyes. He sighed deeply, and reaching out slowly pushed the hood from her head, and for the first time he became aware of how wet and cold she was. Slowly he removed her cloak and threw it over a chair.

'I'm sorry,' he said huskily. 'Please—come over to the fire. You're wet through.' He took her cold hand and led her to the fire, where he poured her some wine. 'Here—drink this. It should warm you a little, if nothing else.'

She took it in her trembling fingers and sipped it gratefully, feeling its warmth course through her veins and the heat from the fire on her back.

'Why did you come here, Louise?'

She looked up at him, trying to recollect why she had come, having forgotten for the moment, and then she remembered. 'I came to ask if you'd encountered Robert Grey.'

At her words his lips twisted ironically, and he ran his fingers tiredly through his untidy hair. 'I might have known—and for a moment I was beginning to believe you might have come to see me. But since you ask, the answer to your question is yes. I did encounter Robert Grey. I killed him at Dunbar,' he finished quietly.

At this revelation Louise stared at him, hardly able to believe that what he had said was true, and then she closed her eyes and lowered her head and turned, staring into the fire, her hands clasped in front of her. She felt a bitter satisfaction and a fierce joy that Robert Grey was dead at last. That the monster who had almost destroyed her life was gone forever, and she found herself wondering if he had ever repented of the evil he had done in Ireland. But she doubted it very much. She had nursed a burning hatred for the man in her heart for so long for the cruel savagery he had invoked that now he was dead she felt a strange, hollow emptiness. She gazed into the glowing embers through a mist of tears, his death at last releasing her from her hatred, and she felt an enormous relief.

'I'm glad he's dead,' she whispered. 'And I thank God. But it was more than he deserved—to die a soldier's death on the field of battle. He will be remembered with honour, while all those he murdered so callously will be forgotten. Did you find out about Elizabeth and Clara and Christopher? Did you discover for certain where they were sent?'

'Yes. It was as I thought. They were shipped to Barbados.'

She nodded slowly, too full of emotion to speak. Francis stood behind her, looking at her, at the sad droop of her shoulders, realising what a culmination of feelings were going through her mind. She was such a tragic figure. Reaching out, he placed his hands on her shoulders.

'Louise—it's over. Come—don't upset yourself. Look at me,' and he turned her to face him. Her cheeks were awash with tears and she made no move to stop them. He was deeply affected by her anguish and he did the thing which at that moment seemed so natural. He folded her in his arms, her head cradled against his breast, while she cried brokenly. A surge of deep compassion swept through him and all the jealousies and rancour he had felt earlier were washed away with her tears. He held her tenderly, as he would a child, murmuring soft words of comfort against her sweet-scented hair.

Slowly her crying ceased and she became calm within the warm circle of his arms. Her despair and anxieties of the past months since leaving Ireland were suddenly lifted from her, leaving her weak and light-headed, and she had an enormous feeling of joy and well-being as Francis held her against him, feeling his warmth, smelling his maleness and taking comfort from his strength.

Slowly and reluctantly, because she did not want to spoil the moment, she raised her head and looked up at him, her eyes shining with her tears, her lips soft and quivering. She trembled slightly at the naked desire in his eyes which their closeness had awakened in him. He reached out and very gently cupped her face in his strong, lean hands.

'How will you ever be able to forgive me for doubting you? I want you, Louise. I want you so much I think I'll go crazy. Will you stay with me—tonight?'

At his words her heart soared. 'Will you think me shameless if I say yes? I think I would die if you sent me away. I never wanted it to be like this, Francis, but if this is the only way it can be between us, then yes.'

He bent his head and placed his mouth on hers and kissed her gently, tasting the sweet wine on her lips. His kiss was so gentle it was like a caress, arousing all the passions inside her with exquisite slowness. He raised his head, his eyes never leaving hers as he slowly removed the pins from her hair, releasing it so that it tumbled about her shoulders. He plunged his hands into the luxuriant, silky mass and kissed her again, finding her lips soft and eager. He began fumbling with the fastenings of her dress until it slipped from her shoulders, settling in shimmering folds at her feet.

When finally she stood naked and trembling within his arms he scooped her up and carried her to the bed, placing her tenderly on the rumpled sheets. Impatient to be with her, he tore his clothes from his strong, muscular body and threw them on to the floor before lying beside her. At first he didn't touch her, he merely looked at her with a kind of wonder, feasting his eyes on her beauty, which was so perfect. Her creamy skin was like silk, glowing as the soft light from the candles washed over her. His eyes darkened and came to rest on her face and the undisguised passion that filled them made her tremble. Very slowly he leaned over and kissed her, first her lips and then her eyes, his hand so surprisingly gentle but firm, caressing her body.

'Say you want me, Louise,' he said huskily, his lips against hers. 'Say this is what you want also.'

'Yes,' she murmured. 'Oh, yes.' She had no thoughts on what was right or wrong any more, nor did she feel any guilt or shame or that what she was doing was classed as a sin. She didn't care any more—as long as she had this one night to remember—whatever tomorrow might bring.

He drew her into his arms and they tightened around her, his lips warm and moist, again urgently seeking hers, and they were both seized by a desire so strong they were like two beings possessed. Louise closed her eyes and let all the pleasurable sensations she was experiencing sweep over her. She was only conscious of Francis and how much she wanted him and had done for so long and now, at last, he was about to be hers.

Passion had suddenly driven him beyond all reason, and now there was no tenderness in his kisses that had become hard and almost violent. He could not have stopped if he'd tried and, sensing this, for a brief moment Louise knew fear and panic gripped her, but then his lips left hers and he bent his head and placed them on her breast and it disappeared. She clung to him as he expertly rekindled her desire until it grew and spread throughout her body. She moaned softly and no longer had any control over her actions. Her arms wound themselves about Francis, pulling him closer and closer until he was crushing her. She clung to him in pure, undisguised passion and unashamedly gave herself to him in a way that Francis had never experienced with any other woman in his whole life. He filled and controlled every part and fibre of her body and Louise felt a sense of such exceptional fulfilment as she had never known or even dreamed of, and as the night closed over them nothing could be heard but the contented sighs of a woman in love.

When Francis awoke the following morning he turned, expecting to find Louise still beside him, but she had gone and all that remained of her was her delicate perfume on the rumpled sheets. It was only later, after making extensive enquiries, that he finally learned from Charles that she had left Scotland and himself for ever.

CHAPTER EIGHT

SINCE leaving Perth, Louise had tried to put all thoughts of Francis from her mind, but never would she be able to forget him or their night of wild and wonderful love—wonderful beyond belief—so wonderful that she had almost forgotten to be brave and the promise she had made to herself before seeking him out at the inn: that whatever happened she would leave him forever. When she had looked down at his naked, sleeping form her tears had almost blinded her. 'Goodbye, my darling,' she had whispered brokenly, and with a terrible effort had turned from him and stumbled out of the room, which was the most difficult thing she had done in her whole life. She wondered wretchedly, and with self-pity, what was to become of her. And now she had an added worry: that because of her selfishness in wanting that one night of love to remember, surrendering herself to him so completely, she might find herself with child. At any other time, to bear Francis's child would have made her deliriously happy—but not now, and she reproached herself angrily. How could she have been so stupid—so irresponsible? She had nothing, no home, no money—nothing, so how could she possibly support herself and a child?

Her whole future yawned before her, as endless as eternity, and when she thought of her life—to live each long day and not have his love, which she needed so desperately—she wanted to die. It was only the fact that somewhere Elizabeth lived and breathed and needed her that stopped her from ending it all beneath the dark,

swollen waters of the River Tay, and she centred all her
thoughts on travelling south to Worcester and placing
herself at the mercy of Mr Beamish.

There had been widespread interest in the close friendship
between Charles and Mistress Cranwell, and the
knowledge that she had transferred her affections to Lord
Slade when he had returned from Dunbar, right under
Charles' nose, had caused a great deal of gossip. The
kind of gossip Charles did not welcome at this time of
unrest. He was not a man inclined to petty jealousies,
but was hurt and annoyed by the whispers and rumours
spreading through the corridors of his court regarding
this new intrigue. It was common knowledge that
Mistress Cranwell had visited Lord Slade at his lodgings,
not leaving until the following morning. Charles, even
though he both knew and approved of the relationship
between them, nevertheless felt he had been made to
appear a helpless fool by them both, and for the first
time since their friendship began Francis was aware of
his deep displeasure, and this prompted him to search
out the one he knew was responsible for spreading the
rumours.

   He found George Villiers alone in his room writing
on some papers. He looked up when Francis entered and
regarded him with a contemptuous dislike. The enmity
between these two went back years, and Francis had no
illusions about Villiers, knowing him for what he was:
despised and mistrusted by many, and who had no prin-
ciples, no concept of honour or morality and who possessed a streak of vindictive malice, forever devising
schemes to ruin certain people popular with Charles.
There was no one—apart from himself, who had been
a permanent fixture in Charles' life since childhood—
who was more in favour than Francis, and Villiers would

go to almost any lengths to discredit him in the eyes of Charles. Francis had been a thorn in his side for too long and he wanted him out of the way. Perhaps if he could make Charles angry enough he would have him sent from court, and he had seen his chance when the lovely Mistress Cranwell had unwittingly asked him where Lord Slade was lodging.

The Duke had lost no time in putting a word out here and there, planting a seed for the gossips, then sitting back and watching it grow, lighting a fire and fanning the smouldering embers until it blazed. He cared little for the humiliation Charles would feel, his sole purpose being to get rid of Francis. No, Charles would certainly not feel kindly disposed to my Lord Slade for making him look a fool in the eyes of his courtiers.

He leaned back in his chair, a triumphant gleam in his eyes. His handsome, arrogant face wore an expression of hauteur.

'Why, Lord Slade—this is an unexpected surprise. To what do I owe the pleasure?'

Cold anger showed in Francis' eyes as he moved towards Buckingham. He stopped in front of the desk, glaring down at him contemptuously. 'You know perfectly well why I'm here, damn you.'

'What are you talking about?' drawled Buckingham with a lazy insolence.

'I am talking about the vicious rumours you have spread concerning myself and Mistress Cranwell, so don't pretend you don't know. There was only one other person besides myself and her who knew of her visit to my lodgings, and that was you.'

'Oh, that,' he said casually. 'Well—I may have mentioned it to someone in conversation—quite unintentional, I can assure you.'

'Nothing you do is unintentional. You are a villain, Buckingham, an evil, black-hearted villain, and if Charles ever learns of your disloyalty, how truly rotten you are—then he will ask for nothing less than your head.'

'I doubt that,' Villiers replied smugly, malice in his cold blue eyes. 'Charles is fond of me—everyone knows it, and I am his most loyal subject,' he mocked. 'Whatever I do, I always have his best interests at heart.'

'Not quite as much as your own. You do nothing unless it is for your own amusement. What did you hope to achieve by spreading such malicious lies about myself and Mistress Cranwell? My disgrace? Is that more important to you than Charles' happiness? He deserves better from you, Buckingham, but consider yourself lucky he has always been too soft on you—too forgiving. You play on his emotions too often, but be careful, for the day will come when he will see you as you really are.'

Buckingham leaned back in his chair, fixing Francis with a cool, casual stare. 'Lies, you say? Are they lies? If you held Mistress Cranwell's reputation in such high esteem then why did you allow her to leave your lodgings alone at such an early hour for all to witness? But,' he sighed, a bored expression on his face, 'I do believe her reputation was in ruins long before you returned from Dunbar. We all know the effect Charles has on his women—that none can resist him.'

Pure, cold fury filled Francis' eyes and his countenance darkened. He leaned forward, placing his fists on the desk and bringing his face closer to Buckingham's.

'If you were not who you are I would break your neck for that, but just let me say this, Buckingham—either you tell Charles that it was you who started these vicious rumours, or I shall have a thing or two to tell him myself.'

His eyes, narrowed and sparkling with anger, conveyed the threat.

'To what do you refer?'

'To whom, I think. Margaret Law was her name,' he said, coming straight to the point. 'She was at court at The Hague.'

He had the satisfaction of seeing Buckingham's handsome face pale, his eyes staring at him with incredulity, and he knew his words had struck home. He was the one person other than the lady herself and two of her maids to know of Buckingham's affair with her, but had kept it to himself, waiting for just such a time as this to use it against him.

'What of her?'

'Perhaps Charles would be interested in knowing what happened to her. Why, when he was so taken with her, in love with her at the time I believe, you yourself were carrying on an intrigue with her behind his back. If there is one thing Charles will not put up with it is being made a cuckold—especially by someone he believes is his friend.'

'You wouldn't dare tell him,' spat Buckingham.

'Wouldn't I? I know a thing or two about playing your sort of games, Buckingham. I have studied your methods for long enough. But tell me—when you got her with child, where did you send her? Back to England? Back to her father? Or,' he said, his voice low and menacing, 'to save you from any future embarrassment did she meet her fate beneath the blade of a murderer's knife?'

Buckingham's lips were drawn tightly against his teeth in a snarl. 'How do you know of this? Who told you? I thought no one knew.'

Francis raised himself to his full height, looking down at him with loathing, nodding slowly. 'So—I was right. It was the latter. Is there nothing that you are incapable of? What a low, despicable creature you are, Buckingham.'

'You have no proof. Charles will never believe you.'

'Oh, he will. Let me speak plain to you. I have some letters in my possession. How I came by them is my business, but they are letters written by you to her. Love letters, in which you also attempt to discredit Charles. I'm sure he will be more than interested to read their contents. So—either you tell him you are the one responsible for spreading the rumours and bringing about his displeasure, or I will make sure he sees them.'

Pure madness flamed in Buckingham's eyes and he rose from the desk, trembling with the anger that forced its way through him, knowing he was beaten, and he cursed himself for his own stupidity, for putting his thoughts on to paper. He knew not how Francis Slade had come by the letters, but the one thing he was certain of was that if Charles read them then Slade was right. He would ask for nothing less than his head.

'Damn you to hell, Slade. Very well—I will do as you ask, but only if you return them—all of them—to me, so making sure you will not be able to use them against me in the future.'

Francis nodded but had no time to reply, for at that moment they both spun round in astonishment when, before either of them had had time to compose themselves, Charles came into the room. His black eyes shifted from one to the other and his mouth tightened. He stopped in front of them, taking in the situation at once. The look of open contempt his two friends felt for each other had not gone unnoticed by him.

'Enough, gentlemen,' he commanded. 'I will not have my friends quarrelling like this. I leave that to the Covenanters. Lord knows there are few enough of you left. Now, would either of you be so good as to tell me what you were quarrelling about before I came in?'

'I believe Lord Buckingham will do that, sire,' said Francis, throwing Buckingham a meaningful look.

'Well, George—what have you to say?'

Villiers took a deep breath, cursing Francis with every fibre of his being for forcing him to humble himself in this manner before Charles, before them both—but he would, knowing that it was expedient for him to do so.

'Only that I must ask your pardon, sire, for any embarrassment my careless words have caused you. I am the one responsible for the rumours circulating the court concerning Mistress Cranwell's visit to Lord Slade in his rooms. I did not realise it would upset you. It was thoughtless of me, and I beg your forgiveness. You know I would die rather than offend you in any way.'

Charles looked Buckingham in the eyes, his dark face etched with stern lines. He lifted one quizzical eyebrow and considered what he had said thoughtfully. He had no illusions about George Villiers—they had been together for too long, and he had always suspected that the Duke only showed him one side of his character. The one he wanted him to see. But he believed that Villiers' nature was too frivolous for him to be of any great danger to anyone but himself. He knew he was forever scheming and plotting against someone and that this time it was Francis, but he had never had cause to doubt his sincerity, his loyalty, where he himself was concerned. But, contrary to what Francis and many others might think, he was no fool. Perhaps he did allow George to get away with too much. Perhaps he was too forgiving where he was concerned, but he knew him so well and, looking at the two men before him, aware of the hatred that existed between them, he felt a deep sadness. He had always considered himself fortunate in having two such loyal friends, but how he wished they could reconcile their differences.

He looked at Francis. 'There is no one in this world more happy than I that you have found happiness with Mistress Cranwell, Francis, but did you have to do it quite so openly? Some of my courtiers have gone to great pains to let me know of the affair and for some days now I have suffered the indignity and embarrassment of being laughed at, being made to look a fool. However,' he said, fixing Buckingham with a sombre stare, a hint of sarcasm in his tone when he spoke, 'it seems that I have George to thank for that. One day that tongue of yours will get you into trouble,' he reprimanded. 'You must learn to put a curb on it. You will also see that a stop is put to the silly rumours, and quickly. Not only has it damaged my reputation but also Mistress Cranwell's, and she did not deserve that.'

He sighed, suddenly feeling very tired, feeling his anger and annoyance over the affair seep from him. He was glad George had seen fit to confess and apologise for his indiscretion, but he was also convinced he had been pressured into it by Francis. He was also certain that this was the reason for their quarrel. Still—what did it matter now? The one person who would have been hurt by all the vindictive gossip and would no doubt have been branded a harlot was Louise, and she was no longer in Scotland.

Francis noted the weariness on Charles' face and he knew the gloom and despondency was brought about not only by the rumours. They were trivial compared to what he was having to endure at the hands of the Covenanters.

Charles placed a hand on either of their shoulders, looking from one to the other. 'I hold you both in the greatest esteem and affection—you know that, so let us end this affair here and now. We will not give the Covenanters the satisfaction of letting them see that we quarrel among ourselves. There are more pressing matters here in Scotland which concern me, for us to allow court intrigues to interfere with them. My coronation is imminent, as well you know, so there is much to do. But Francis—I hear you are to leave us.'

'Yes, only for a short time. I am going to Holland to see Mistress Sinclair and—to tell her that I can no longer let her go on hoping that one day we will be married.'

Charles nodded, understanding. 'I'm glad to hear it. You are doing the right thing, but it is with regret that I see you go. Don't be absent from my side for too long.'

'I'll be back before your coronation in the New Year, sire. Nothing will keep me from that.'

Charles smiled gratefully and nodded slowly, a faraway look coming into his dark eyes. 'Perhaps then we will be able to leave for England. Oh, what I'd give to be rid of this land.'

While Louise was travelling to Worcester, Francis set sail on a ship bound for The Hague to see Anne. He had no intention of being absent from Scotland and Charles for longer than was necessary. When he thought of Buckingham he smiled to himself, satisfied that he would have no further trouble from him. He had kept his part of the bargain and returned the letters, but Buckingham would never be quite certain that he had returned them all. He would think again the next time he chose to cross him. More than anything else he had wanted to follow Louise when he'd discovered she had boarded a coach for England, and he was certain she had gone to Worcester to see Mr Beamish. But before he could think of going to her he had to see Anne, however much he would hate telling her about Louise, knowing how much

pain the knowledge that he loved another would cause
her. It was something he had to do, now more than ever.
If Louise was to have his child then he must be with her.

From The Hague he travelled north to the beautiful
old town of Leyden, six miles from the sea, where Anne
and her father were living with her brother George and
his wife. Whenever Francis had been in Holland he had
never ceased to be amazed by this artificial land below
the level of the sea, its ancient cities full of people from
all over Europe fleeing from religious persecution. In
early times it had been a swamp, buried from time to
time beneath the North Sea, but its people had beaten
back the ocean, keeping the waters of the sea in their
place by building great dykes of stone and earth along
the coast. Canals and waterways wove their way through
the country and drained the land, which was rich and
fertile, dotted with windmills and covered with gardens,
orchards and fields which gave its people an abundant
harvest.

Leyden, encircled by a moat, was the seat of one of
Europe's oldest universities and had a host of canals and
narrow, twisting streets flanked by elegant, gabled
houses.

When Francis came to the house where Anne and her
father were staying, he paused before going up the steps
to the door, hearing female laughter coming from the
garden behind the house. It was familiar laughter, and
he knew it was Anne. He went straight to her. She was
in a garden surrounded by flowers, all the colours of the
rainbow, and his heart lurched when he saw how pretty
she was in her pale blue dress. He loathed himself for
what he was about to do to her. He was just in time to
see a smiling young man go through a gate at the bottom
of the garden, where he turned and waved back at her
before disappearing along the moss-covered banks of the

canal. And then Anne turned and saw Francis, and suddenly he was walking towards her through the garden. She gave a start of surprise, her face radiant, a smile curving her soft lips. But it wasn't until later that he was to ask himself if he was the cause of her pleasure or the fair-haired young man he had seen disappearing through the gate.

'Francis.'

Laughing, Anne flung herself into his arms, which wrapped themselves around her until gently he pushed her from him, no real gladness in his expression. It was not the welcome she had hoped for. She wanted to tell him how glad she was to see him, how much she had missed him, but the words froze on her lips. She stood back in his arms and looked up at him, sensing a change. He looked the same, still tall and handsome, the same face and features imprinted on her heart, and yet—there was something different, something had changed. It was as if she were looking at someone else—a stranger. There was something distant about him, something which removed itself from her.

'Why, Francis, this is an unexpected surprise,' she said, gazing at him intently, her eyes questioning. 'We've all worried about you so much—especially when we heard of the battle at Dunbar. Were you there?'

'Yes, I was, but—but it isn't that I've come to see you about, Anne,' he said, knowing that telling her about Louise was going to be no easy task, but he must get it over with. 'It's so good to see you,' he said, but sounded so formal.

'Father will be pleased that you've come. I think he finds things pretty dull over here. A little news about what's happening in England and Scotland does manage to filter through to us, but now you're here you'll be able to tell him everything. He's inside—would you like to see him?'

'No—at least, not yet. I—I wanted to see you first, Anne. There is something I have to say.'

His voice was calm, but she sensed some tension inside him. She neither moved nor spoke but looked up at him steadily, knowing he was leading up to something. He had something to tell her, something awful that he knew would hurt her, and he could do nothing about it. But she already knew what it was. It was a fact that she hadn't wanted to believe, had refused to believe until she had come to Holland. She had loved him for so long that she could not remember a time when she hadn't, but for months now she had felt things had changed.

She swallowed hard. 'I think I know why you've come, Francis. I think I knew when you didn't come with us to Holland. It—it's because of Louise, isn't it?'

He nodded. 'Yes, it's Louise. I love her, Anne. At first I tried to fight it. You have no idea how much, or how wretched it made me. How I despised myself when I thought of what it would do to you. I do love you, Anne, but——'

'But you love her more,' she said quietly, and he would have been a fool not to notice the bitterness in her tone, which was a feeling she had never shown in all the years he had known her, but it was soon gone.

'Tell me, Francis, when did you realise you loved her and not me? Was it on board the ship that brought you both from Ireland or when you discovered that she'd run away from you in London? When you thought you might never see her again?'

He sighed and shook his head dejectedly. 'I don't know. I only know that I do and always will. But—what does it matter, anyway? I know I have hurt you, and for that I am deeply sorry. I never intended to—please believe me.'

She knew he spoke the truth. He really hadn't meant to hurt her. She listened to him silently, calmly, realising that he meant every word he had said, but now what did he expect of her? How did he expect her to react now he had told her he no longer loved her? Did he expect her to break into tears? Appeal to his honour, his emotions? Well, she would do none of these, because now that he had told her, now that she had heard the truth from his own lips, this man who had been a part of her life for so long, loving her, understanding her, somehow the knowledge did not hurt.

'I do understand,' she said, her eyes very clear, but she gave a sad little smile that tore at Francis' heart. She knew she should be angry with him, feel resentment towards both him and Louise, but she didn't.

'I'm sorry I've let you down.'

'You haven't let me down, Francis—never think that, and if it had to be anyone then I'm glad it was Louise. She is so beautiful.' And, she thought, hadn't she run away from them in London to spare her pain? 'But I cannot deny that I am not sad that it's all over between us. I'm glad you found her again before she went to the Indies. I worried about her so much being alone in London. Anything might have happened to her.'

'I know. I found her working in a tavern trying to save enough money to buy her passage.'

'Oh, dear God—poor Louise,' said Anne, horrified.

'She went with me to Scotland to find our mutual enemy, Robert Grey. He was with Cromwell when he invaded Scotland.'

'And did you find him?'

He nodded. 'At Dunbar. I killed him,' he said quietly.
'I had left Louise at Kilcrae—you remember—I believe
I have told you of Sandy and his wife Mary.'

She nodded. Yes, she remembered, but she didn't want
to dwell on it now. She didn't want to remember how
he had promised to take her there one day as his wife
to stay with them.

'We do get news here in Holland from time to time,
Francis, and I am not unaware that Louise has been in
Scotland these many months. Is she not the same Mistress
Cranwell they say is close to the King?'

She had said this without malice, no hurt intended,
but was sorry to see that her words had wounded him
deeply. He blanched visibly and his eyes filled with pain.
She reached out her hand to him. 'Forgive me,' she said
quietly. 'I didn't mean to hurt you.'

'None of the rumours are true, Anne—you must
believe that. I heard them myself after Dunbar and in
my anger I was ready to believe them, but they were just
the result of cruel, vindictive tongues, bored with nothing
better to do. It is true that Charles was quite enamoured
by her—and who could blame him? She was like a bright
light in that miserable land, but it went no further than
friendship.'

'Is she still in Scotland?'

'No,' and he gave a wry smile. 'Once again she has
run from me and has no idea that I am here now.'

'Then where is she?'

'I believe she has gone to Worcester to see Mr Beamish,
her aunt's trustee, and from there she will go to Barbados
to look for her sister. She is still under the impression
that I am to marry you.'

Anne's blue eyes widened in amazement. 'You mean
you haven't told her? She doesn't know?'

'No, she left Perth suddenly—no doubt thinking she was doing the honourable thing by running away. The last thing she wanted was to come between us. She both liked and respected you so much, Anne.'

'Then I think you should go and find her before it's too late. But—will you not stay with us a few days?'

'No, I cannot. I must sail back to Scotland immediately. Charles has need of his friends around him at this time. His coronation is imminent,' and taking her hands in his own he stood looking down into her oval face, so unworldly and full of goodness. There had been no accusations or reproaches from her as he had feared there might be, and he was filled with remorse and felt an acute pain somewhere in the region of his heart, because everything was over between them. But it was only now, when he was about to leave her, that he eyed her curiously. So wrapped up had he been with what he had to say to her that not once had it crossed his mind that she might not still feel the same for him, and he found himself wondering if the young man he had seen earlier had anything to do with the calm way she had reacted to the knowledge that he no longer loved her. Could it be that she too had found someone else?

'Thank you, Anne, for understanding,' he said quietly. 'I'll go in and see your father. Are you coming?'

'In a while. You go. I'll be there in a moment.'

She watched him go out of the garden and out of her life, and tried to remember the times when the mere thought of him or the mention of his very name had evoked such joy inside her, such delirium that even in the throes of war she had been so happy. She tried to remember those days, expecting to feel a sad, aching hunger at the memories, at their loss, but there was nothing. Only an emptiness in her heart. Could it be that her love for him was also dying? Was that why it didn't hurt and why she no longer saw him as her shining knight? She had expected pain, heartbreak and sorrow, but it was strange—there was none. She would always feel a deep tenderness and affection for him, but without the passion of love. That had gone. It had passed and she knew in her heart that it was all because of Peter Edwards, and at the thought of this handsome young man who had come into her life so suddenly, at the time when she and her father had come to Holland, a soft glow shone from her eyes and a secretive smile parted her lips. A deep affection had grown between them, but she had kept him at arm's length because of the ties that still bound her to Francis. The ties were broken now, and she would reject him no longer.

CHAPTER NINE

THE days of Louise's journey to Worcester were long and arduous, and it was late afternoon when she finally paused in the broken gateway of Bessington Hall, tired and exhausted. She peered into the gathering gloom, feeling the stillness all around her, and up the dark tunnel made by the avenue of stately elms which led to the house. Out of the last gathering rays of the afternoon sun, she allowed her eyes to travel up that avenue and they became misted with tears, and a hard lump appeared in her throat when they settled on the blackened and ruined shell which bore no resemblance to what had been the well-remembered, noble and dignified home of her mother's family for over a hundred years.

Carrying her few belongings, she moved slowly towards the silent, ghostly ruin, those once beautiful walls of mellowed brick now blackened by the fire. No light shone from the gaping, blind windows and there were no servants or Aunt Katherine standing in the doorway to bid her welcome. She walked on, past the trees which cast giant shadows in her path and were like huge sentinels on either side, and all around her the air was filled with a haunted desolation. Even the black crows perched silent and still on the almost leafless branches of the trees, watching threateningly as she moved closer to the house.

When she stood in the circle of what had once been the gardens, the hideous destruction caused by the fire struck straight at her heart. She found it difficult to believe that this sad pile of ashes was where she had

visited as a child, where she and Elizabeth had played
so happily, and that it had been the house where her
mother had been born. She thanked God she wasn't here
now to see this. It would have broken her heart.

Wretchedly she turned away, realising there was
nothing for her here any more. She must make her way
to the town and find lodgings, and tomorrow she would
go and see Mr Beamish. Out of the corner of her eye
she thought she saw a movement among the trees. She
stopped, hearing a gentle rustling, and then the shadowy
figure of a woman emerged from the undergrowth, a
woollen shawl hanging loose about her shoulders. Louise
stood quite still until the woman had come close. She
was perhaps in her early fifties, small and plump with
a kindly, familiar face, but there was an air of sadness
about her. It was Lucy Proctor. She had been her aunt's
housekeeper and her husband the gardener for a number
of years. Louise remembered her so well. She had always
treated herself and Elizabeth with extraordinary
kindness. Louise smiled softly, glad to see someone she
knew.

'Hello, Lucy.'

The woman peered closely at Louise and on recognition her face broke into a smile. 'Why, if it isn't Miss
Louise—all the way from Ireland.'

'Yes—it is me,' said Louise, reaching out and grasping
Lucy's hands in her own. 'Oh, Lucy—you don't know
how good it is to see someone I know. I thought—
perhaps—everyone had perished in the fire.'

'No—not me or Ben. We still live in our cottage on
the edge of the wood. But what are you doing here—
and all by yourself?'

Louise sighed and turned and stared once again at the
ruin. 'It's a long story, Lucy—and a sad one—but after
hearing of my aunt's death I have come to see Mr

Beamish. My mother is also dead and I believe—apart from Elizabeth—that I am my Aunt Katherine's closest living relative.'

'Where is Miss Elizabeth? Why is she not here with you?'

Louise took a deep breath and looked again at Lucy. 'She was captured by Cromwell's army when they invaded Ireland. No doubt you will have heard of the terrible massacres that took place. She was sent to Barbados to work on the plantations. But—that was months ago now and I pray to God that she is still alive.'

She lowered her eyes and waited for Lucy to speak. The older woman seemed to sense Louise's inner sadness and heavy heart, but also that she was fighting to keep control over her feelings, and so she offered no sympathy. For this Louise was grateful, because it would only have made her cry, and she didn't want to.

When Lucy spoke her tone was kind. 'There is nothing I can say that will make you feel better, Louise, but some day I hope you will find her.'

'Tell me what happened here, Lucy. How did the fire start?'

She shook her head sadly. 'It was a sad business, the house going up as it did. Some said it had been started deliberately and others that your aunt might have accidentally knocked over a candle—but, well, I don't suppose we'll ever really know.'

'But you knew her better than most, Lucy. What do you think happened?'

'It's not for me to say, but I don't believe it was an accident. Your aunt was many things but she wasn't careless.'

'Then do you think it was deliberate?'

Lucy nodded. 'Yes. I've always kept my suspicions to myself—let the others think what they like—but on the night of the fire your aunt told me she wanted to be left alone in the house. I didn't want to leave her but she was adamant—and you know how stubborn she could be.'

'Yes, I do,' said Louise, remembering the small, frail-looking woman, but also remembering how stubborn she could be and that she had an indomitable will of iron. 'But where were the servants?'

'There were none—only a young girl to help with the housework, but she was staying with her family that night. You see, your aunt had closed most of the house. After Parliament took the land, she became almost fanatical about the Royalist cause, and gave them almost all her money and sold a great number of expensive items from the house. She used to say, what is the use of all these pictures and expensive furniture standing idle when the King is in need of money to regain his throne? She became almost penniless, and just before the night of the fire she was informed that the house was to be taken over as well. You can imagine what that did to her. She hated the Parliamentarians. They were her enemies, and she would not allow them to desecrate the precious rooms of her house.'

'So—she set fire to it herself,' whispered Louise, and her heart swelled with pride when she thought of the gallant sacrifice her aunt had made. At last it became clear to her to what lengths people like her aunt and Francis and others—all over England—were prepared to go in to support of the King and the Royalist cause. She was deeply ashamed of the way she had so foolishly chided Francis for putting his loyalty to England and Charles Stuart before the finding of his brother and sister. But they and Elizabeth were young and strong and, God willing, should survive...

'Where are you staying?' asked Lucy, breaking into
her thoughts.

'I don't know. I'll have to find somewhere before it
gets dark.'

'Then come back to the cottage and stay with us. For
tonight, anyway. It's not very big, but you'll be more
than welcome.'

Louise smiled at her gratefully. 'Yes—thank you. I'd
like that. I must admit I don't feel much like walking to
the town and trying to find lodgings at this time, and
besides,' she said, slipping her arm through Lucy's and
turning to walk along the path towards her cottage, 'it
will be nice to see Ben again.'

The following day found Louise in Worcester, a city
fiercely proud of its loyalty to the Royal House. Perhaps
it could claim to be the most Royalist city in England.
The narrow streets, with their black and white timber-
framed houses, were congested with wagons and horses
and, after a bumpy ride on Ben's cart, he left Louise
outside the house of Mr Beamish, promising to call back
for her later.

Mr James Beamish lived in a large, medieval old house
overlooking the College Green, close to the cathedral
which towered over the wooded banks and graceful sweep
of the broad River Severn, where it flowed down towards
Bristol. He had been a good friend of her aunt's, and
Louise had met him on several occasions when she had
visited Bessington Hall. She remembered him as being
tall and dark-haired, but now he was lean and bent with
age, though somehow he still managed to move with
dignity. His eyes were pale with a sharp intelligence, his
hair sparse and white, but he shunned the artifice of a
wig.

He couldn't recollect who she was at first, not having seen her for several years, but as soon as she mentioned her name his face flushed with pleasure, which filled his old grey eyes. He ushered her quickly into the warm parlour, where his wife brought them some tea and fussed about like a mother hen before disappearing into the kitchen.

It was when they were settled comfortably and a few pleasantries had been exchanged that Mr Beamish told her of her aunt's death. She told him she was already aware of this, and quickly gave him an account of her circumstances. He expressed great concern, especially when he learned of her mother's death and Elizabeth's capture.

'But why did you not come here instead of going to Scotland?'

'I couldn't—not right away. I—I went with a friend—Lord Francis Slade, whose brother and sister were taken along with Elizabeth. You see, after my mother died we went to stay with his family. At that time he was in Holland with the King, but he returned to Ireland on the day after the massacre. Because of the uprisings, they were about to leave Ireland and we were to travel with them to England. On our arrival we were coming here to stay with Aunt Katherine. There was nowhere else we could go.'

'I see. But when you did arrive in England, why did you not come to Worcester right away?'

Louise smiled a little sadly. 'Because it was only then that I learned—through enquiries made by Lord Slade—what had happened to my aunt and Bessington Hall. There seemed little point after that. Mr Beamish—you have no idea how desperate I was at that time. All I could think of was Elizabeth and what she might be suffering. I would have done almost anything—even sold

my soul to the Devil—in order to board a ship bound
for the Indies, because that is where I thought she'd gone.
But I had no money—nothing. All that my parents had
left Elizabeth and myself was destroyed in the fire which
followed the massacre.'

Mr Beamish looked at her with deep sympathy, at the
sadness and pain brought on by her vivid memories of
that awful time. Her face was pinched and there was a
strained, pathetic look in her eyes.

'My dear, there is nothing I can say that will ever be
able to erase what you went through. Could you not
have borrowed money from your friend? Was he not as
eager to find his own brother and sister?'

'Yes, but he had done so much for me and I was
already deeply in his debt. Besides, neither of us knew
for certain where they'd been sent. For all we knew they
could still have been in Ireland—or even dead,' she finished quietly.

'Then why did you go to Scotland?'

'Because when Cromwell moved north to invade
Scotland, with him was Colonel Robert Grey. He was
the man responsible for the massacre in our village and
he was the only man we knew who could tell us where
they were.'

'And you found him in Scotland?'

'Yes,' she said quietly, lowering her eyes. 'At least,
Francis did. He killed him at Dunbar, but before he died
he told him what we wanted to know. They were shipped
to Barbados.'

'I see. And where is your friend now?'

She paused a moment before continuing. 'I—I left him
in Scotland. There are reasons—personal reasons why I
am here alone. I came to see you because I knew you
were my aunt's trustee and—to be honest—I had
nowhere else to go.'

Mr Beamish looked at her thoughtfully, wondering what her feelings were concerning this Lord Slade. That she cared a great deal for him he could see in her troubled eyes, and he wasn't unaware of who he was: that he was close to the young King, who valued his loyalty and friendship highly. But that was her affair, and he had no right to question her about it.

'You did quite right to come here, Louise, but you do know that your aunt died leaving no money or property?'

'Yes. I met Lucy yesterday. She used to be my aunt's housekeeper. I stayed the night at her cottage. She told me how Parliament had taken the house as well as the land, and how Aunt had gradually sold off everything of value, donating all the money to the King's cause.'

'That's right. But there is one thing she did not sell— her jewels, although,' he said, sighing deeply and shaking his head, 'I do believe she would have got round to that in time. They are worth a small fortune, my dear, and perhaps after all you have been through they might be your salvation.'

At this disclosure Louise's eyes opened wide in surprise, which caused Mr Beamish to smile.

'As you know, your aunt died a spinster, although in her day she was a very beautiful woman and—if I may say so—you bear a great resemblance to her. She had more than her share of young men calling. But she was so intelligent and strong-willed, it would have had to be a man of exceptional qualities for her ever to have considered marriage. I know your mother was her only sister and, if she is dead, then you are your aunt's rightful heir.'

Louise was staring at him incredulously, trying to digest his words, and suddenly she was filled with a sense of freedom and at last hope began to course through her veins, making her curiously light-headed. For the first time since that terrible night when Elizabeth had been abducted, the future had taken on a whole bright new meaning.

'Would you like me to arrange for you to see them?'

'No,' said Louise quickly, an almost feverish look in her eyes. 'If they are indeed mine, then sell them. Sell them all. What use have I for fine jewels? But, with the money they will fetch, at last I shall be able to buy my passage to Barbados.'

'But it would be sheer madness to embark on such a perilous journey alone, and if you did have you given a thought to what you will do when you get there? Do you know anyone or anything about the island? About the heat and the conditions the labourers are forced to live under?'

'No.'

'Then please think again. And supposing you did find your sister on an island which already has a population of well over thirty thousand white people—you wouldn't be able to just take her away. You would have to buy her freedom.'

Louise felt the euphoria she had experienced a moment before ebbing away. 'Then what can I do?' she asked dully.

'Wait, and I shall try and establish some connections for you over there. You must have somewhere to go. I have a friend who went out there with his wife and son six years ago to escape the political controversies here at home. I don't hear from him very often, but I do know he bought a considerable amount of land and now plants sugar. I shall write to him.'

'And do people like my sister provide the labour for the running of these plantations?'

'Yes,' he said, with a trace of bitterness in his voice. 'And one cannot escape the fact that the selling of these white prisoners taken in war is dishonourable and a disgrace to the English name. How can we call ourselves a civilised society when we sell and enslave our fellow countrymen? But,' he sighed, shrugging his shoulders and shaking his head slowly, 'it happens. They have to work alongside negroes from Africa and the other kind of labourers—the indentured servants. These are men and women who want to emigrate to Barbados but cannot afford to do so by themselves. They sign an agreement to serve on a plantation for a number of years, and in return their passage is paid and they are also maintained by the planters. Those who survive their term of indenture are given a sum of money and about five acres of land.'

Louise paled and lowered her gaze, keeping the fact that she had once considered going there as an indentured servant to herself.

'There is also the other kind of indentured servant, Louise,' went on Mr Beamish, wanting to make her understand what it was like. 'These are the ones sent there on a kind of compulsory transportation. People forcibly gathered up from the streets of London and other places, especially vagrants and the destitute—men, women and even children. They are shipped out to the plantations, where they have no choice but to serve a period of up to ten years. Then there are the convicts, violent criminals from prisons all over London, who prefer to serve out their time there than be hanged.'

'Elizabeth was none of these,' whispered Louise, horrified.

'I know. To transport people to the Indies was one of Cromwell's odious ways of getting rid of his opponents. But, however the white labour is acquired for the plantations, once there the picture is indeed grim—but the treatment they receive is not the same for them all. They can be bought and sold from one planter to another.'

Louise wanted to ask him about the work they had to do and what kind of treatment they received from their masters, but somehow she didn't want to know. While she remained ignorant as to what Elizabeth might be going through, she could bear it, so she didn't ask. She pondered over his words and had to admit they made sense. It would be better if she had someone she could stay with in Barbados while she made enquiries about Elizabeth and Francis' brother and sister. After all, she had already waited many months trying unsuccessfully to find the means of getting there, so a few more weeks might not make any difference. Her eyes met those of Mr Beamish.

'Very well,' she said, resignedly. 'I shall do as you suggest and wait until I have somewhere to stay.'

'Good—then that is settled, and believe me, my dear, you'll not regret it. And in the meantime,' he said, rising to his feet, 'you must stay here with Mrs Beamish and myself. When Ben returns I shall have him go back to the cottage for your things.'

'Oh—but—but I can't impose on you,' she protested.

'Nonsense, and no buts,' he said gently but firmly. 'It will be a pleasure to have you stay with us. Now come along—let us go and tell Mrs Beamish the good news. It will make her day having someone to fuss over.'

Louise settled down to life with Mr and Mrs Beamish and the weeks slipped by. Weeks which turned into months as she anxiously waited for a reply to the letter Mr Beamish had sent to his friend in Barbados. After four months and no word, she became convinced that the ship must either have gone down in a storm or been set upon by pirates, preventing the letter from ever getting there, and at times it was all Mr Beamish could do to prevent her from rushing off to Bristol and boarding the first ship bound for Barbados, especially after her aunt's jewels were sold, fetching her a small fortune. This brought her an immense feeling of security and relief such as she had not felt since her mother's death. Relief at being able to buy her own clothes at last and, hopefully, under no obligation to borrow anything from anyone ever again.

No matter how much she tried not to let her thoughts dwell on Francis, it became impossible. He filled every part of her, her dreams, her heart and indeed her very soul. The pain she felt almost tore her apart and she was seized with a fierce longing to run back to Scotland to be with him. How well she remembered what it was like to be with him, for him to hold her, to love her, to feel his lips on hers, the smell of him and the way his hands had so lovingly caressed her naked body, setting it on fire, and how her own had responded so readily and shamelessly. His memory was not dimmed by the passing of time but only intensified, so it almost drove her mad.

She listened avidly to the news which filtered out of Scotland, and how she rejoiced when she learned of Charles' coronation on New Year's day at the Cathedral of Scone. How she would have loved to have been there to see it. All the pomp and ceremony and elaborate celebrations. At last the Scots were being drawn to him, this young King they had dealt so ill with when he had first set foot upon their soil. He now generated a new national loyalty in Scotland and also a rising authority over that of the detestable Marquess of Argyll, whose power over him diminished greatly as the months passed. So much so that the gentleman moodily retired from the scene to his home in the Western Highlands.

Charles' spirits were high as he rode at the head of his forces, proudly inspecting the lines of troops, but he could not escape the fact that as yet they did not have the military might to engage Cromwell's Roundheads, situated in Edinburgh and scattered about the border lands.

The question arose as to what they should do next, and after many deliberations and listening to his advisers, and intent on being restored to the throne of England—also the fact that Charles' dislike for the Scots was as great as ever and he had no wish to remain in their country for longer than was necessary—instead of riding north to rally the Royalists in the Highlands to his side, at the end of July, 1651, he chose to ride south in the hope of rising the English Royalists, taking the western route towards the Royalist areas around Wales where there had been stirrings in his favour.

The march was doomed from the start, for although Charles was proclaimed King of England at Penrith, many of his Scottish troops deserted him and retreated back over the border the further south they progressed, and, sadly, no English Royalists came to join his standard.

Such was the contempt the northern Royalists held for the Presbyterian Scots who had invaded them so many times in the past and who now followed Charles into England. There were many passionate displays of anti-Scottish feeling, and there were still those Monarchists who could neither forget nor forgive Charles his betrayal in signing the Covenant.

The further south this demoralised army of sixteen thousand men marched, things did not improve. They were constantly harried from the rear by Commonwealth troops and finally, exhausted and ragged and lacking arms, they arrived at Worcester over three hundred miles

and three weeks after leaving Scotland. This was where
Cromwell, marching from the north and choosing a route
which ran parallel to the one Charles had taken, his
troops totalling more than thirty thousand seasoned men
and with more promised him, hoped to besiege him.

The Scottish troops were exhausted and walked with
their heads bent, worn out and hungry after the long
march. Many, having no boots, walked with rags tied
around their feet, and others were barefoot, their dirty,
bleeding feet painfully treading over the cobblestones.

The walled city of Worcester occupied a defensive
position, although building outside the walls had ex-
panded considerably during the last hundred years. The
wall extended to a height of fifty feet and was bordered
by a deep ditch. From Sidbury Gate in the south to Fore
Gate in the north was a distance of no more than three-
quarters of a mile. With most of the Royalist troops
concentrated within these walls, the Parliamentary garrison having withdrawn, the narrow streets and alleyways became crammed with so many horses and wagons
and men that there was utter confusion, and some houses
were taken over for the billeting of officers and troops.

But it had been two weeks before the King reached
Worcester that Mr Beamish had at long last received a
reply to his letter from his friend John Carstairs in
Barbados, saying he and his wife would be delighted to
have Louise stay with them while she searched for her
sister. Louise had been overjoyed, and Mr Beamish had
immediately booked her a passage on a ship that had
been due to leave Bristol for the West Indies a month
and a week hence.

Louise couldn't believe that at long last she was going,
and she began preparing for the journey. But little did
she know as she folded and packed her belongings of
the terrible turn of events which was to take place before

her departure, and which was to result in the ruin of the
Royalist cause.

As soon as she heard of the King's approach it meant
only one thing to her—that Francis would be with him.
She was right. She had just come in from the garden
when Mr Beamish, his face full of concern, met her in
the hall to tell her she had a visitor. Her heart leapt in
her breast. She knew instinctively who it was and mechanically followed Mr Beamish to the parlour, where he
ushered her inside, leaving her alone with her visitor.

It was Francis. He was shrouded in a long black cloak,
making him look unapproachable and forbidding. The
parlour was quite small, and his tall, broad-shouldered
frame seemed even taller so that he appeared to fill the
whole room. He stood quite still and watched her enter,
his face expressionless, his eyes blue and so bright, fixed
intently on her face. She closed the door behind her and
stood leaning on it for support. It was ten months since
she had last seen him, but he was just the same. She had
a weak, tremulous feeling inside her and her legs felt like
jelly. All these months she had tried not to think about
him, to wipe him and that one glorious night they had
spent together from her mind—but for what? It had all
been useless and she could not deny her feelings because,
faced with him now, all the love she felt for him which
she had locked deep in her heart came back to over-
whelm her. Oh, why had he come? screamed a voice
inside her head. Why had he come when she was just
beginning to live without him?

He still didn't move, and the muscles of his darkly
handsome face and his blue eyes hardened, but his voice
was calm, too calm, thought Louise when he spoke.

'Why did you run away from me in Scotland, Louise?'

She stared at him, riveted by the brightness of his eyes. The question he asked was a simple one, but oh—how hard it was for her to answer.

'I—I had to,' she whispered. 'I couldn't stay with you. How did you find me? Did you have me followed?' .

'No. I suspected where you were all along. As soon as I learned you had left Scotland I felt this was where you would come. If I remember correctly, you had nowhere else.'

'Then why are you here?'

'To ask you to leave this house and Worcester altogether.'

'Leave? But why?'

'Because it's not safe. Very soon we will be under Commonwealth attack. Cromwell is marching on the city with an army of thirty thousand men—almost twice our number. It is probably the only chance you will have to escape before his troops surround the city.'

'And is this the only reason why you have come here?'

'No,' he said, his control crumbling, and he took a step towards her, his eyes flashing with anger and his lips curling cruelly. 'I think you owe me an explanation as to why—at our last meeting—you went sneaking off like a thief in the night. Couldn't you have waited to say goodbye?'

'No—no, I couldn't,' she cried brokenly, hot tears burning the backs of her eyes. 'Don't you realise how difficult it was for me—knowing there was no future for us together? Do I have to spell it out? If I had waited I would not have had the strength to leave you. Oh, why have you come here now?' she cried wretchedly, her eyes full of anguish and pain and brilliant with tears. 'For pity's sake, Francis—if you have any love for me at all, why can't you leave me in peace? Can't you see what you're doing to me? That you're breaking my heart?'

Drawn by the deep misery in her eyes, which looked enormous in her white face, all his anger drained away. Slowly he moved towards her, and there was a look in his eyes she had despaired of ever seeing again. The cold anger and hardness had been replaced by all the love and passion that burned in his heart for her.

'I never meant to hurt you, Louise. Please believe me when I say that was never my intention. I love you. I love you in every possible way. When I woke and found you gone after what we had shared, I believed I had lost you forever. I can't begin to tell you of the torment and the hell I went through.'

'I know,' she said, tears spilling over her lashes. 'Oh, I do know because I too went through hell. But—but what about Anne?'

'Things have changed. I am no longer betrothed to Anne. Oh, my love—why do you think I did not come after you right away? I went instead to Holland to see her—to tell her. That night when you came to the inn I already knew I could never marry her. It would have been unforgivable of me. I had made up my mind at Dunbar that it was you I wanted to be with for the rest of my life, but later—when I heard the rumours about you and Charles, that you had become his mistress— oh, Louise, I could have killed you.'

'But why didn't you tell me?'

'I would have, but how was I to know you were going to leave before I awoke?'

They stood motionless, gazing at each other, devouring each other with their eyes, Francis' blue ones burning with all the passion he felt for her, and she glowed with happiness. Suddenly his arms were wrapped around her and he was crushing her to him fiercely, kissing her tear-washed face, her eyes, her hair and then he found her lips, soft and tender, and he held her prisoner with a deep, burning kiss. He could feel her shuddering as she clung to him. Reluctantly his mouth left hers and he looked down at her face, her moist lips quivering. All the loveliness in the world was mirrored in her face, and his body ached with longing for her.

'I love you, Louise. I love you so very much.'

She sighed, thrilling at his words and so blissfully happy. She nestled her head against his chest, smelling his maleness and feeling his heart beating rapidly beneath his jacket. She could scarcely believe this was happening. Never had she been so happy, and she felt a great joy and an overwhelming feeling of well-being.

'You'll never know how much I've wanted to hear you say that, but I thought I would never see you again.'

'Did you really believe I would let you go and not come looking for you?' he said, his lips against her hair.

'I didn't know what to think,' she whispered. 'But when we had news that the King was marching towards Worcester with his Scottish troops, I knew you'd be with him. Oh, Francis,' she said, drawing back in his arms, her eyes flying to his in alarm, and for the first time since those exhausted troops had poured through the gates of the town she felt afraid. 'What will happen, do you think? Will there be fighting?'

'Yes. It cannot be avoided,' he replied gravely. 'Already we have begun strengthening the fortifications. We had hoped to advance towards London, but because of the gathering Commonwealth forces we must stay here. This may be the last time I shall be able to see you before we are surrounded and attacked, so please leave the city before it is too late. I must know that you're safe.'

'Leave? No—I won't leave. I cannot leave now.'

'But you must. Before you came in, Mr Beamish was telling me that he and his wife are leaving to stay with relatives in Bromsgrove, and that you have a passage booked on a ship leaving Bristol for the West Indies.'

'Yes,' she said. 'But there will be others. I shall not leave Worcester until we are able to leave together.'

'Then go to Bristol and wait for me there.'

'No,' she said, with that stubborn tilt to her chin that he was beginning to know so well. 'Even should the King himself command me to, I will not leave. We will leave Worcester together—or not at all,' she finished quietly but firmly.

Francis looked at her upturned face, strained and white, for a long time, and said nothing else to try and persuade her to leave. Her mind was made up, he could see that. Gently he took both her hands in his, his dark brows drawn together in a frown.

'You do understand that I cannot leave Charles now? That I must serve him to the end?'

'I would not want you to leave and neither will I,' she answered softly, knowing as she said these words that even if she had wanted to she couldn't. She now realised that she had become a victim of the Royalist cause. That Charles Stuart was a man who had put inspiration into her heart as well as into all those loyal to the Crown. He was the heart and hope of England. The shame of those cruel, unforgivable words she had flung at Francis when he had told her he was going to Scotland to be with the King—that she doubted the gallant sacrifice he was making was worth it—came flooding back, but that had been a long time ago, before she knew Charles. Now she remembered him with warmth, and treasured the all too brief but close friendship that had grown between them in Scotland. She remembered his strong, magnetic personality and his unusual dark, foreign looks, the richness of his voice and the deep warmth of his eyes, and she wondered fleetingly, if it had not been for the love she bore Francis, whether she would have gone to him as his mistress. Oh, well, she thought wistfully, it was something she would never know. But now she was as sincere and true a Royalist as Francis, and would no more think of deserting the King than he would. She sighed as Francis broke into her thoughts.

'You do realise that, when we are attacked, the fighting will be bloody and vicious—that many will be killed?'

She nodded. 'Yes.'

'We will fight desperately to defend the city and the King—to the death, if need be.'

'Then we will die together,' she whispered, trying to ignore the sound of urgent knocking on the door which led to the street.

'Let's hope it doesn't come to that, but keep to the house, and if the worst happens and we are defeated then I shall do all in my power to get to you. But whatever happens the King must escape. When it comes to his life, my own matters very little. He must not be captured, whatever the cost.'

It was at that moment that Mr Beamish came to tell him that someone was asking for him in the hall, and Francis immediately gripped Louise's hands and looked earnestly into her eyes.

'I must go, my love. If possible I shall come again, but if I can't, please keep to the house and be brave.'

He gathered her into his arms and they clung to each other tightly.

'Take care,' she whispered, oblivious to Mr Beamish hovering behind her. 'Please take care. I could not bear it if anything happened to you.'

'I will,' he said fiercely. 'Never fear that we will be together when this is over, Louise—I swear it,' and he placed his mouth on hers in a last burning kiss, infusing her with all his love, and with a final, terrible effort he released her quickly and was gone.

CHAPTER TEN

WHEN the Commonwealth troops were sighted the exodus of civilians, mainly Puritans, began from the city, as many of their possessions crammed into wagons and carts as they could muster. Even Mr and Mrs Beamish left to stay with his sister fifteen miles to the north in Bromsgrove, and no amount of persuasion could make Louise go with them. She had made her decision to stay close to Francis and the King, and she would not be shaken.

Cromwell's troops encircled Worcester and for the second time in five years this city, so fiercely loyal to the Crown, was under siege, its thick, ancient walls and narrow streets providing a defensive fortification. It was on the King's orders that the four key bridges over the River Severn guarding access to the town were blown up, although one bridge, ten miles south, was unsuccessfully destroyed and eventually recaptured by the Commonwealth, and repaired sufficiently to be used to their advantage.

For almost six days Cromwell's guns pounded the thick walls from the east, but it was not until the third of September—exactly one year to the day since the Battle of Dunbar—that he attacked. Charles had situated three of his Scottish regiments below the city in fields to the south to prevent the Roundheads crossing the River Teme, where it flowed into the Severn and where the vital but now captured bridge was situated, while the majority of his troops were concentrated within the walls.

Although action began at daybreak it was not until the afternoon that Cromwell finally attacked the town from the west, having towed boats used for carrying heavy loads upstream and making a bridge with them so that his troops could cross the river. Charles, with some of his chief officers, had climbed the endless flight of steps to the square tower of Worcester Cathedral and was using it as an observation post. It provided an excellent vantage point, with a splendid view of the two rivers spread out below, and for watching the Cromwellian troops and their tactics.

Alone in the house, Louise became restless. She watched the scenes in the streets that were seething with activity out of an upstairs window, fear growing in her heart, and she was almost frantic with anxiety over Francis and prayed to God to keep him safe until this was all over and they could be together. Since daybreak on that fateful day she had stood by the window, her tension and nervousness increasing by the minute, starting at every nerve-shattering explosion from Cromwell's cannon as they constantly pounded away at the walls. Long processions of troops marched by with their colourful standards waving in the breeze, but later, when the battle began to take its toll, she saw the first of the wounded. The columns of troops which had so bravely marched by to defend the city earlier became columns of wounded with shattered limbs and dripping blood, and her heart contracted with pity when she saw the grey and blackened faces of men staring mutely ahead, some little more than boys, supporting those of their comrades who were unable to walk unaided. Then came the wagons carrying the wounded, and Louise's heart ached with helpless pity for them when she heard their moans

and cries of pain as they were jostled over the rough
cobblestones.

The boom of the cannon became so loud that she was
almost convinced they were within the city walls, and
she felt as if she were locked in some kind of hideous
nightmare world where chaos and noise reigned supreme,
and suddenly the house became stifling and she wanted
to get out. She covered her ears with her hands as another earth-shattering explosion hit the town and she
sank down on to the bed trembling, but after a while,
unable to stand being cooped up a moment longer and
forgetting Francis' words—that she must keep to the
house—she ran down the stairs and out into the street.

The grey sky was veiled in black smoke, which swirled
upwards as cannon balls cleared the walls and landed
on buildings, splintering the wooden structures.

Louise paused and looked about her, feeling so useless.
Surely there was something she could do to help? She
began pushing her way forward, but the narrow streets
were so crammed with wagons and men on horses it was
difficult. When near the garrison at the heavily defended
east wall she halted and looked dazedly about her, confronted by a hideous spectacle, finding herself in an in-
ferno of noise and smoke and chaos. Through the clouds
of black, suffocating smoke belched out by the cannon
she watched young boys carrying earth and stones, in
an attempt to strengthen the battered walls, and powder
to supply the garrison. She shrank back, her eyes
smarting and beginning to stream with the effects of the
smoke, covering her mouth with her hand to stop herself
from choking. After a moment she pulled herself together and made her way to where a group of women
were tending the wounded. Their faces were strained and
white and their clothes dirty and bloodied. They were
trying to dress the wounds and ease the suffering of the

soldiers, but for many it was too late. She found herself
working alongside them, helping the doctors while they
worked frantically to repair shattered and broken bodies,
cutting away at the mortifying flesh. Some soldiers had
lost arms and legs, which had been blown away by the
cannon, and it was almost impossible to do anything for
them.

Never had Louise seen anything like it. She was engulfed in a world of blood and pain and her ears were
filled with the soul-destroying screams of men. She
worked on, doing what she had to do, forever conscious
of the boom of the cannon and the pile of dead which
was mounting up at an alarming rate.

It was later in the afternoon when she looked up from
trying to staunch the flow of blood from a gaping wound
in a man's side that she saw the King. He presented a
strange, unreal picture in the midst of the mêlée and she
thought she must he suffering from some kind of delusion, but no—he was real enough. Royalist horse was
pouring out of St Martin's gate to the east and Sidbury
Gate to the south-east of the city, Charles gallantly
leading the charge. He was dressed in his now familiar
uniform of buff coat and boots with a bright red sash
and the precious George around his neck. This was the
insignia of the Garter, a jewel made of a single onyx
passed on to him by his father Charles I before his
execution.

From his observation post the King had seen the fierce
fighting taking place on the west bank and Cromwell's
move to join them from the east across the River Severn,
over the bridge of boats. Believing the Commonwealth
forces to be somewhat weakened to the south-east he
had quickly and desperately decided to take advantage
of this and attack them out of the Sidbury Gate.

With undaunted courage he and his troops surged forward, driving the Roundheads back up the hill and overrunning some of their guns. For the next three hours some of the fiercest and bloodiest fighting of the battle took place. At first the Royalists were successful, covered by their own thundering guns from the great Fort Royal which stood close to the south-east of the town on Castle Hill, but seeing what was happening Cromwell brought his troops back from the west to strengthen those in the east, outnumbering the Royalists by more than two to one.

Without any further support the wretched Royalists were pushed back, and Fort Royal was captured and its guns turned on the city. On foot the King, careless of his own safety, fought valiantly, side by side with the brave Highlanders, displaying an incomparable courage. Their ammunition now exhausted, they fought on with pike and musket butts, but gradually they were driven back through the Sidbury Gate.

Many Royalists, discouraged and feeling the enemy was too numerous and that the battle was lost, were beginning to throw down their arms, but Charles, riding among them on a fresh horse, tried to rally them, furious with them, commanding them to fight. But it was in vain. No amount of urging and entreaties would make them fight on.

Seeing the utter confusion and believing the end of the battle was near, Louise left what she was doing and turned in the direction of the house. If Francis came for her she must be there. She refused to let herself think that he might be wounded, lying unattended and in pain somewhere in the streets or on the battlefield, or even worse—killed. She had to go on believing he was safe and that he would come for her.

She was unprepared for the carnage that met her eyes. Of streets and alleyways blocked with hundreds of corpses, not only of men but also those of horses. Death was everywhere. At the end of the day they would number almost half the King's army. The air was foul and thick with swarms of flies, feeding on blood-soaked bodies, and she turned away in disgust, nausea rising inside her. She pulled herself together quickly, taking deep, gulping breaths, and began climbing over the corpses that littered her path, trying not to let her eyes linger on the frozen, wax-like features and cold, sightless, staring eyes.

When she at last managed to reach the house, amazingly it hadn't been broken into like many others. She fled up the stairs to her room, tearing the revolting blood-soaked clothes from her body before washing herself all over. It was only when she had scrubbed herself clean that she tried to settle down and wait for Francis, the battle continuing to rage all around her, closing in all the time. Fear gripped at her heart like an ice-cold hand. Fear at what would happen if desperate soldiers broke into the house, and fear at what she would do if Francis didn't come—or perhaps he had come earlier, finding the house empty.

So many incoherent thoughts ran amok inside her head that she thought she was going mad, and it was only when the light was fading that she braced her shoulders and wrapped her cloak about her, having decided to go in search of him.

Eventually she found herself outside a small house which she had been told was where the King had been lodging before the battle. She saw a group of officers talking animatedly to each other, their tunics battle-torn and dirty. She looked at each in turn for the familiar,

well-loved face of Francis. She moved closer, recognising the arrogant profile and fair features of the Duke
of Buckingham and then, just a few feet away from her,
stood a man so tall and broad-shouldered, with the
blackest hair curling to his shoulders, that her heart
swelled with love and she moved towards him, his name
on her lips. In her joy at finding him so soon she forgot
everything, and her face shone with happiness. The
officers standing around him parted to let her pass,
staring at her with undisguised amazement, looking at
her admiringly as her hood fell away to reveal all the
loveliness of her face and her rich chestnut hair, coiled
in a glossy snake about her head. Several remembered
her and how she had so mysteriously vanished from the
court in Scotland.

Before Louise could speak Francis' name, he turned
and, once again, as had happened before in the garden
at Kilcrae Castle, she was mistaken. It was the King who
turned and looked at her, and her heart plummeted like
a stone and the light went from her eyes. She stopped,
speechless, so much had she wanted it to be Francis.
Quickly she recollected herself and sank in a deep curtsy,
lowering her eyes, but not before he had seen the pain
and disappointment in them, and he sighed.

'Sire—forgive me, only I—I thought——'

'That I was Francis?' and taking her hands in his he
raised her to her feet. She appeared more beautiful than
he remembered and even now he felt the familiar ache
of desire and remembered how much he had longed to
possess her but, he thought regretfully, now was not the
time to let his thoughts dwell on what might have been.
Not now when he was planning his escape from
Worcester. Francis had told him she was here, but he
had hoped she would have got out of the city before the
battle.

'Oh, sire—have you seen him?'

He shook his head. 'No. He went to defend the bridge south of the city. I saw him earlier when I visited the troops—but not since.' He turned to his officers. 'Have any of you seen Lord Slade?'

They all shook their heads, but it was George Villiers who spoke.

'I do know he was in the thick of the fighting on the west bank,' he said with a malicious gleam in his eye, still finding it difficult to conceal his dislike for Lord Slade.

At his words Louise paled and she looked back at the King. 'I must find him,' she whispered.

Seeing the stricken look on her face and still holding her hands in his, Charles pulled her a little to one side, away from the others, and looked down at her gravely, his sleek black brows drawn together.

'Louise, listen to me,' he said earnestly. 'You must escape from the city before it's too late. In a short time those who do not escape will either be killed or taken prisoner. I am leaving now—I have to, although I would gladly have laid down my life today. I fought for the future of my realm knowing that my blood would have been well spent, that the succession doesn't end with me, that there are still my brothers James and Henry. But it was not to be. Death eluded me and now, as the Sovereign of England, I know where my duty lies. I cannot risk being captured and used as a pawn by Cromwell and perhaps—eventually—executed like my father. I must get away, although as long as I live I shall remember the past twenty-four hours and I know that my enemies will continue to hunt me down. The nightmare of this day will shadow me for a long time to come, Louise,' he said sadly. 'I fear our cause is in ruins.'

'No—you mustn't say that,' she said passionately, gripping his hands. 'While ever you are alive it will never

be in ruins. There will always be those who will strive
to help you regain your throne.'

Charles smiled down at her, a softness in the quiet
depths of his velvety black eyes. 'Bless you for that, my
dear—and you—why not come with us?'

'No—no, I couldn't. I must try and find Francis—but
I thank you. I shall go back to the house and wait.
Perhaps he will come and we can escape together.'

'That won't be easy,' said Charles gravely. 'Think of
him, Louise. How he looks. We are so alike, Francis and
I—why, even you have been mistaken at times, and there
will be many more who will mistake him for me. It will
be harder for him to disguise himself and escape than
most.'

George Villiers had come to stand beside them and
Charles looked at him.

'I'm sorry, Charles, but we must leave,' he said
urgently. 'Word has it that the Parliamentarians are
searching everywhere for you.'

Charles nodded, understanding the need for haste, and
looked down at Louise. 'We must go.'

She nodded, tears almost blinding her. 'Yes—you must
hurry before it's too late.'

'Farewell, my dear,' he said hoarsely, bending down
and placing his lips tenderly on her cold, wet cheek.
'When you find Francis tell him—tell him I shall miss
him and hope we will meet in better times.'

'I hope so, sire. Indeed I hope so. May God go with
you.'

He released her hands and she watched him disappear
into the little house from which he would escape through
a back door, closely followed by his friends, and she
thought fleetingly what a valuable prize that group of
some of the most notable gentlemen in England would
be if captured by the Commonwealth. After a while she

dashed away the tears and turned and hurried back to the house, her heart beating rapidly.

It was all she could do to get back. The streets were chaotic, full of men desperately trying to find a way out of the city to escape the Roundheads. The city, which the Royalists had hoped would protect them from Cromwell's army, had now become their prison. Louise had to fight her way through, and only when she had closed the door behind her did she breathe more easily.

She moved wearily towards the parlour door but suddenly stopped, certain she'd heard a sound from inside. It was true—there it was again. Someone was moving about. Her first terrified impulse was to turn and run out of the house, but she took hold of herself and gingerly moved towards the door, hardly daring to breathe, and with trembling fingers reached out her hand and shoved it open.

At first she couldn't believe her eyes. She stood rooted to the spot, one hand rose and froze at her throat. Francis stood in the centre of the room holding on to the back of a chair. On seeing his towering frame, all the colour drained out of her face and her lips formed his name but no sound came and then, with a small cry, she crossed the short space that divided them, hurling herself into his arms, almost knocking him off balance.

His arms were around her, holding her while she cried, tears of relief that he had come at last and tears which washed away the dreadful fear and anguish she had carried in her heart but had refused to think about— that he was dead.

'Oh, Francis, God be praised—at last. I was beginning to think you wouldn't come.'

'Hush, my love,' he whispered, his lips against her hair. 'There is not a power on earth that could have prevented me from getting to you. No—not even Cromwell's Ironsides.'

He swayed slightly. Louise looked up at him in alarm, standing back in his arms, the tears frozen on her cheeks. A dark red stain marked his coat from a wound in his shoulder, and she gasped. So great had been her joy at seeing him again that she hadn't noticed he was wounded.

'Oh—why, you're hurt!'

At her alarm he managed to smile weakly, but even in the gathering gloom she could see the pain etched on his smoke-grimed face, and the deep lines and dark shadows circling his eyes that had not been there before the battle.

'It's nothing, Louise. Please don't worry.'

She looked at him aghast. How could he tell her not to worry when he looked as if he would collapse at her feet at any minute. 'But you must let me see.'

'No,' he said sharply, gripping her shoulders. 'There isn't time. We cannot afford to wait any longer. We must get out of the city and the sooner the better. I only pray Charles is safe.'

'Yes, he is. I've seen him. He was just leaving.'

'Thank God. Let us pray he isn't captured—that Cromwell doesn't get his murdering hands on him. Now come—we must leave—at once.'

'But you are wounded,' she argued. 'How far do you think you'll get when you look as if you'll collapse at any minute?'

'I don't know,' he replied, wiping the perspiration from his brow with the back of his hand. 'But I must try. We must get as far away from Worcester as we can before daybreak.'

Louise looked at him for a long moment, understanding the urgency. He was right. If he remained inside the city he would most certainly be captured and killed.

'You are right, Francis,' she said steadily. 'At least away from the town we might stand a chance.'

They lost no more time on conversation—time was too precious. The town was full of confusion and seething with activity. The noise of shouts and cries and the crackle of musket-fire was deafening. Royalists were fleeing in every direction, running for their lives. Most would be captured before dawn and who knew what dreadful fate awaited them?

Louise and Francis made their way through countless winding alleyways heading towards the north gate, which was not as heavily defended as the south, and out of it poured the wretched Royalist fugitives. Louise could see that Francis was in great pain and weakening rapidly, and knew they wouldn't get very far on foot. They looked for a horse but there wasn't one anywhere with an empty saddle.

By the time they had left the town behind Louise desperately tried to keep Francis moving, but he kept stumbling and falling from fatigue and loss of blood, and each time it became harder for him to get up. He was more seriously hurt than he had led her to believe and began mumbling incoherently, and she noticed with a deathly chill that the dark stain on his coat was spreading. Thankfully the countryside was now shrouded in darkness, the trees standing out like big black ghostly shapes against the night sky. Within the city fighting still raged, and they could hear the shots and pitiful screams as some wretched soul was run to ground by the enemy.

When Francis fell for what seemed like the hundredth time Louise crouched beside him and lowered her head, biting her trembling lip to stop the tears of helplessness from running down her face. A terrible despair took hold of her at her own inadequacy, and she wondered how on earth they were going to escape when Francis could barely stand. What could they do? Where could they go? The dark offered them some protection, but when the sun rose there would be no hiding-place for them. The whole district would be crawling with Parliamentarians.

She squared her shoulders, suddenly furious with herself for her weakness, knowing their survival now depended on her and her alone. She must get Francis to safety before he passed out altogether. Somewhere where she could take care of him. She was determined not to give him up to death without a fight.

It was then, like a lightning flash, that she thought of Bessington Hall and Lucy. It wasn't far from here and perhaps they would be able to hide within the ruins until the danger was past. And so, driven on by a compelling need to survive and with renewed hope surging through her veins which seemed to give her added strength, she again helped Francis to struggle to his feet, placing his arm about her shoulders and hers firmly about his waist, taking most of his weight. His steps were slow and heavy and he walked like a man drunk, but she urged him on, giving him soft words of encouragement, taking care to keep to the shadows and off the main highways. She knew they couldn't be far from Bessington Hall, but at the rate they were travelling it could be hours before they got there. There were times when she shuddered, half-crazed with fear, and she would cower with Francis in the shadows as men went by, some on horseback and some on foot like themselves. Whether they were friend or foe she had no way of knowing. They all looked the same in the dark.

She sent up a silent prayer when the dark, familiar ruins of the Hall loomed before her, and it was with great relief that she loosened Francis's arm from about her shoulders and lowered him into the corner of a high stone wall where she sank to her knees beside him, wiping the sweat from his face with the hem of her skirt.

'Francis—Francis,' she whispered anxiously and sighed with relief when his eyes flickered open, although it was with great difficulty that he focused them on her face. 'Oh, thank God. I thought you'd fainted.'

'Where are we?' he mumbled, fighting with himself to keep from falling into oblivion.

'Bessington Hall. Listen to me, Francis. I'm going to leave you here while I get help. My aunt's housekeeper and her husband live close by. Do you understand?'

He nodded, closing his eyes as a fresh tide of pain swept through him. He reached out and gripped her hand hard. 'Yes—I understand—but for God's sake be careful.'

'I will. I promise. I won't be long.'

She tore herself from his side and hurriedly made her way through the trees in the direction of Lucy's cottage. The little house where Lucy and Ben lived was so dark and still she thought no one was there, but she sent up a silent prayer of thankfulness when she saw a faint light shining through a small chink in the wooden shutters. She knocked on the door softly. After a while she heard Lucy's voice on the other side, asking who it was.

'It's me, Lucy—Louise. Please let me in.'

The next moment she was inside the cottage, pouring out her story to a startled Lucy and Ben. They knew of the battle which had taken place in and around Worcester, the distant thundering of the great guns never ceasing. They had watched the gathering of the Parliamentary army for days and some troops had even

camped in the woods around the ruined Hall, but thankfully they had been left alone.

When Louise had finished telling them about her plight
and how Francis was hurt and waiting for her in the
ruins, she looked at them in desperation, anxious to get
back to him quickly.

'I don't wish to endanger either of you, but we must
find somewhere to hide. If Francis is caught they will
kill him.'

'I think I know where you can hide,' said Ben, who
had listened to her intently, seeming to know what had
to be done and quickly. 'The old shed near the orchard
which was used for storing apples. It's small, I know,
but at least it's dry and it escaped the fire. It's so covered
in undergrowth now you'd hardly know it was there.'

'Oh, yes—I remember it,' said Louise, looking into
his wise old eyes with relief and gratitude. 'It should be
perfect. Please come and help me with him, Ben. He's
lost so much blood and he's so weak.'

Francis was still where she had left him, his head back
against the wall. She helped Ben hoist him to his feet
and together they managed to get him to the old shed,
where Lucy had gone on ahead of them and lit a candle
and spread some blankets on the ground. They succeeded in crawling through the hole, which had at one
time housed a door that was long since gone, and was
now mostly blocked by stones and ivy. Casting her eyes
quickly over the small shed, at the dusty, windowless
walls with broken shelves and old woven baskets, Louise
prayed that they would be safe here. From outside it was
almost impossible to believe it could be anything other
than a heap of rubble covered with weeds and thick trails
of ivy.

'We must hurry and dress his wound,' said Lucy quietly, kneeling down beside Francis. 'We daren't keep the candle burning for too long in case the light is seen.'

Together the two women worked frantically to remove the blood-soaked coat, revealing an angry-looking wound in his left shoulder, probably caused by a sword thrust. Blood still trickled out of it and Lucy worked rapidly to staunch it. Louise looked anxiously at Francis, his face so drawn and pale and his bare, powerful chest heaving painfully. His eyes kept flickering open but the effort of doing so proved too much and, after the large amount of blood he had lost and suffering from complete and utter exhaustion, he closed them again and, unable to fight it any longer, fell into a deep sleep.

When the wound was cleaned and bandaged they covered him with blankets, and getting to her feet Lucy looked down at Louise, pale with misery and her heart written all over her face as she stared at Francis.

'He should sleep now, Louise, and you must try and get some rest. It will soon be dawn and soldiers will be all over the place, so you must try and keep quiet. Ben will bring you some food and drink—if and when it's safe—and also one of his shirts. But please stay inside the shed.'

'Yes—yes, I will.' She looked back at Francis, unconscious and with deep purple shadows around his closed eyes. 'Do you think he'll be all right, Lucy? I couldn't bear it if he died.'

'Yes, I think so. The wound is deep but I don't think it's done any serious damage. He's lost a lot of blood but he's strong. He should be all right.'

When she was alone and Ben had placed some stones and more foliage over the small doorway, she lay down beside Francis before snuffing out the candle. She lay with her arm about his waist, staring blindly into the

blackness, the shed filled with the musty smell of tallow,
and listening to the mysterious sounds of the night. The
occasional mortar-fire still rumbling in the distance
brought with it sinister and eerie undertones and she
wondered with fear in her heart what the dawn would
bring. Could it be any worse than the dawn of yesterday,
which had brought with it a day of the most appalling
carnage and death?

Weariness at last overcame her and she drifted into a
troubled sleep. Her subconscious was full of terrible
dreams of death and danger and she slept badly, a suffocating sensation waking her, bathed in sweat, suddenly. The hours during which she lay by Francis were
interminable, and Lucy had been right. With the first
fingers of dawn peeping through the cracks between the
stones came the Parliamentary soldiers, and the ruins
and woods around Bessington Hall were crawling with
them. She lay clutching Francis, frozen with terror, her
heart pounding so hard she was sure they would hear it,
and she had no illusions as to what would happen if they
were discovered. She heard voices close by but mercifully they went on, and as time passed she began to
breathe more easily.

CHAPTER ELEVEN

DURING the morning Francis groaned and, reaching up, Louise placed her hand gently over his mouth lest he betray them. She struggled to sit up, her body stiff and sore, and in the dim light she looked down at Francis, her heart leaping with gladness when she saw his eyes wide open and clear. She placed a finger to her lips, implying he should be quiet, and when he nodded she removed her hand from his mouth. His gaze wandered curiously around the walls of the shed in the semi-darkness.

'Don't worry,' whispered Louise. 'We're safe for now.'

'Where are we?'

'In an old shed in the grounds of Bessington Hall, but it's well hidden. Parliamentary soldiers searched the ruins earlier but I'm afraid they'll probably be back.'

'Yes—it's more than likely,' he said, struggling to sit up, his face creasing with the pain this brought to his injured shoulder, and he cursed softly, propping himself up against the wall. He tried to remember their journey of last night but everything was hazy. He had the impression that he had walked and stumbled and fallen often, only to be pulled to his feet and urged on by Louise's gentle but firm voice, and he realised what a terrifying ordeal he had put her through. The strips of light lit up her pale, drawn face and huge dark eyes with their flecks of gold, and all the love he felt for her moved through his heart. He reached out his arm.

'Come here,' he said softly.

She crept towards him and nestled close, like a child seeking comfort from its mother, while his arm fastened about her shoulders.

'Oh, my love—what an ordeal I caused for you last night. It cannot have been easy for you and you did well to get us as far as you did, although I had intended getting further away from Worcester.'

'I know, but it's too late now. We'll have to stay here— at least until you're well enough to travel and things have quietened down.'

She suddenly started, her nerves taut, and she sat up on hearing a soft rustling in the undergrowth outside the shed and someone pulling away the stones from the doorway. They both held their breath but then uttered a sigh of relief when Ben's round face appeared through the hole, followed by his body pulling a basket behind him, and on seeing Francis sitting up his face broke into a smile.

'So—you're awake. How do you feel?'

'Let's say I've felt better,' replied Francis grimly.

'This is Ben, just in case you can't remember,' said Louise. 'He helped me get you in here last night and Lucy—his wife—dressed your wound. She used to be my aunt's housekeeper.'

'Then it seems I have much to thank you for,' said Francis. 'But tell me, Ben—have you news of what's happening in the city? I had hoped to have put a greater distance between us and Worcester, but I had not reckoned on my wound.'

'The soldiers who came by earlier searched everywhere—including the house. Worcester is in turmoil— dead men all over the place with Royalists fleeing in every direction. Many have been caught and taken prisoner.'

'What news have you of the King?'

'None that I've heard. All I know is that Worcester is so full of confusion no one really knows what's happened, and they're searching for him everywhere. His description has already been put about.'

'Then let us pray he escapes,' said Francis, 'for if he is captured Cromwell will show him no mercy.'

Something of his deep misery transmitted itself to Louise, which only added to her own. 'What will we do now, Francis?'

'If you want my advice you'll stay here until things quieten down,' said Ben. 'You're safe enough for the time being. But the first thing you must do is eat. You'll feel better with food inside you.'

Out of the basket he produced a white cloth, which he spread on the ground followed by some freshly baked, sweet-smelling bread and cheese and cold beef, all prepared by Lucy.

'I'll leave you now but I'll come back later. Perhaps I might be able to find out more about what is happening.'

He left them alone and Louise and Francis fell upon the food, both ravenously hungry, neither having realised until now just how hungry they were. It was twenty-four hours since either of them had eaten and when they finished they sat leaning contentedly against each other, and for a short while the dimly lit shed seemed like paradise. They were oblivious to the dust and dirt, forgetful of all the dangers outside, but later they talked over the events of the battle and Louise's heart contracted at the deep sadness and resignation she saw in Francis' dark blue eyes.

'When I think of yesterday I feel only agony and despair,' he said. 'Despair that the cause is lost and that the King is a hunted man with nothing ahead of him but the dark days of a fugitive. I wonder what will become of him. Eventually I think he will try to get to France—if he can escape Cromwell—and may God help him and go with him.' He sighed deeply. 'Our defeat has been a bitter blow, but we must now think of ourselves, Louise. There's nothing to keep either of us here any longer. Not the cause—not the King—nothing. The fight is over.'

Louise twisted herself round and stared at him, unable to believe it was Francis who spoke these words. What had happened to his indomitable fighting spirit which had sustained him throughout the long, turbulent years of the Civil War? The moroseness into which he had sunk saddened her.

'For now, maybe, but surely it's only temporary. As long as there is a Stuart alive it will never be over. Be it Charles or his brothers, there will always be something to fight for, so enough of this defeatist talk, Francis. The situation will recover.'

He looked down tenderly into her anxious, upturned face and smiled, inspired by her words. 'It will recover and when it does I shall have a part in it, but now what matters most is that from now on we'll be together. We have ourselves to think about and how to get out of the country. We have travelled a long road since Ireland, Louise, and it is far from over. You had a passage booked on a ship for the Indies. When does it sail?'

Once again she looked at him incredulously. 'In—in about two weeks, I think. Why?'

'Because I think we should be on it. It's time we went to look for our families.'

'But is that wise just now, with Parliamentary soldiers everywhere? We have to get to Bristol, which will not be easy.'

'I know, but if we're careful and disguise ourselves we might do it,' he said, tightening his arm about her reassuringly. 'It's a risk we're going to have to take some

time, but we're going to need assistance. Perhaps Ben
will help us. We shall need horses and some clothes.'

And so Francis began to make plans for their escape
and Louise experienced a lightening of her heart, and
for a short time she forgot her terrors and hope took the
place of fear as she put all her trust in him. But parties
of soldiers often came by searching for fugitives, and it
was at these times that she was reminded of the threat
hanging over them. It was only under cover of darkness
that they dared to leave the confines of the shed to
venture outside and walk within the shelter of the trees.

In the days that followed their escape from Worcester,
Francis grew stronger and his wound less painful, but
with his returning strength he became restless and impatient to leave. After more than a week, in order to
find out more about what was happening, Ben took his
cart into the city and returned with news that Mr Beamish
had returned from Bromsgrove to put his house to rights
after it had been broken into by Commonwealth soldiers
searching for hiding Royalists. He was full of concern
over what had happened to Louise, but Ben had reassured him that she was safe. He was eager to aid them
in their escape and was to ride out to Bessington Hall
the following day with clothes for their disguise and a
horse. He agreed that to get out of the country was the
best thing, that the sooner they got to Bristol and
boarded the ship bound for the Indies the better. Ben
also told them that a proclamation had been circulated
seeking the King's capture and a reward of one thousand
pounds for his whereabouts had been offered. Posters
had also been put out seeking a tall dark man over two
yards high.

At this news, all Louise's fears came creeping back.
A thousand pounds, she thought, horrified. Some people

would sell their soul for that much money. She had an impending feeling of doom. It was as if the posters were describing Francis, and because of this the dangers to themselves were greatly increased. She remembered Charles' words with a deathly chill—that Francis would not find it easy to disguise himself, that they were too much alike and mistakes could be made. Oh, yes, she thought, he could dress himself up as anything he chose and crop his black hair and grow a beard if he so wished, but his height was the one thing he could not hide.

It was when Ben had left and they were alone and the shed grew dark, its occupants in shadow, that Francis gathered Louise tenderly into his arms, holding her close, sensing her fear and apprehension.

'Don't be afraid, my love.'

'I'm so afraid for you,' she whispered. 'Afraid you'll be caught and taken away from me. Oh, Francis, I couldn't bear it. I love you so much.'

'And I you,' he said huskily. 'But I want you to promise me something, Louise. Promise me that if I am caught and you are free you will still go to Barbados. That you will do all in your power to find Elizabeth and my brother and sister.'

As his words penetrated her mind he felt her whole body stiffen within his arms and she looked up at him, stupefied.

'How can I do that?' she whispered, horrified by what he had asked of her. 'How could I go away and leave you here? I have no illusions as to what will happen to you if you're caught. Already you are a condemned man—you said so yourself. Oh, Francis—you cannot ask that of me.'

'I can and I must,' he said, gripping her shoulders and looking down at her face, scarcely discernible in the gathering gloom. 'It's no use pretending it can't happen.

We must face facts. If I am taken you must do as we
have planned— Louise, you *must*. God knows I don't
want to leave you, and only death will prevent me from
coming to you again. As long as I live I will never give
you up, but I want you to promise me that you will go
to Barbados and I will do everything I can to meet you
there.'

She nodded dumbly, her throat swollen so much that
it hurt, and tears began to fall down her cheeks. He
gathered her into his arms and kissed them away gently.

'Don't—don't cry, Louise. It may not happen. All is
not lost, and if we are careful then we may outwit
Cromwell and his troops, and by this time next week we
could be on our way to the Indies.'

He felt her shudder within his arms and she clung to
him desperately, her heart hammering in her breast as
their desires for each other were again rekindled as on
that other night in Scotland, which now seemed to belong
to another age. Aware that this might be the last night
they would be together, their love lifted them to heights
beyond which either of them had ever dreamed.

The following morning, Mr Beamish arrived on a sturdy
mill-horse with bags fastened to the saddle. Louise
greeted him joyfully, glad to see his friendly face again,
and smiled at the somewhat comical figure he portrayed
on the little horse. He had come to help them prepare
for their journey, which would have to begin immediately if they wished to be on the ship bound for the
Indies. They had just two days to reach Bristol. He eyed
Francis' tall frame and shook his head slowly.

'I'm sorry, Lord Slade, but you'll have to let Lucy cut
your hair. As it is now, and as tall as you are, you look
too much like His Majesty for comfort. Since the posting
of his description the danger to yourself is more acute

than ever, so we must take care of every minute detail. Now—here,' he said, passing each of them a bundle of clothes. 'Unless you have your own ideas on how you wish to reach Bristol then may I suggest you dress in those country clothes. You'll attract less attention, as the whole countryside is seething with inquisitive Commonwealth soldiers.'

They lost no time in dressing in the clothes he had brought. Louise put on a simple homespun dress and Francis a coarse shirt with a thin, worn leather jacket and breeches and a battered and grimy steeple-crowned hat. After Lucy had shorn his black locks he certainly looked the part he had to play—if a little ridiculous.

Mr Beamish nodded, satisfied with their disguise, but Louise wasn't quite so convinced. Perhaps it was his demeanour or the way he walked, but whichever, he still looked conspicuous.

'You will find a change of clothes more suitable for on board ship in there,' he said, indicating another large bag still fastened to the horse. 'If you are stopped and questioned you must have a convincing story. You could say you are man and wife and are travelling to Bristol to visit a relative. You will also have to assume other names. Perhaps you could call yourselves John and Mary Tanner.'

'How long will it take for us to reach Bristol?' asked Louise.

'You should be able to reach Cirencester by nightfall and spend the night there and, providing all goes well, you should be in Bristol tomorrow afternoon.'

Looking at the horse, Louise wasn't so sure.

'Don't be put off by the horse,' said Mr Beamish, noticing her frown. 'Archie is a strong, reliable animal. You'll have to sell him when you reach Bristol. I'm sorry there's only the one, but it's not uncommon for a woman to ride pillion. I have written a letter for you to give Mr Carstairs on your arrival in Barbados explaining your affairs, and I will have your belongings sent on at a later date.' He handed Francis a small purse. 'There's enough money in there to see you to Bristol and also enough to pay for your passage.'

Francis took it. 'I cannot thank you enough for all you've done.'

'There's no need. Just take care of Louise—that's all I ask. She's become more like a daughter to me over the past months.' He looked at her and pulled her to him, placing a kiss on her forehead. 'May God go with you, my dear,' he said softly, his voice trembling with emotion. 'And now—you must be on your way. There's no time to lose.'

He stood back while Francis handed Louise up on to the horse and, together with Lucy and Ben, he watched them gradually disappear down the road in the direction of Bristol.

It was dusk when they rode into Cirencester, riding down the main thoroughfare to the large, square marketplace, the church with its three-storey porch in the background. The journey had been surprisingly easy, there being few travellers on the road, and the town was relatively quiet. They found a small, rather shabby-looking hostelry, and after stabling Archie they went inside, only to find they had walked straight into a nest of Parliamentary soldiers on their way north.

Louise's heart almost stopped beating but Francis, taking stock of the situation immediately and realising that to turn and walk back outside would only draw attention to themselves, moved towards the old inn-keeper and asked for a room.

'Aye—I've just the one,' he said loudly, being rather deaf. 'Follow me. What's your name?'

'Tanner,' lied Francis. 'John Tanner.'

Louise, following, cringed inwardly, knowing how difficult it was for him to play the part of a common countryman, but when he said his name why, oh, why did he have to say it with the simple pride of a man of nobility? She glanced sideways and noticed with a sinking feeling that the brief exchange between Francis and the innkeeper had not escaped the attention of one of the soldiers seated at a table. He watched them through narrowed eyes, a deep frown puckering his brow as they disappeared up the stairs, but not before he had seen Francis stoop slightly to pass under a beam where a man of ordinary stature would not have done.

Fear sped Louise up the stairs and to the small chamber under the eaves the innkeeper showed them to, and she went cold at the thought that Francis might be discovered. She kept her fears about the soldier to herself. She ate very little of the food they had sent up to them and they spoke little, both being anxious and more than a little weary. Louise refused to get undressed for the night and lay on the bed fully clothed, her mind in a turmoil as she listened to the sounds coming from below, fully expecting the soldiers to come bursting into the room at any moment and take Francis away. With a trembling voice she asked him to hold her, and they lay with their arms about each other in the darkness until at last Louise fell to sleep, and presently Francis did too, and he only awoke with the dawn when she stirred within his arms.

When the sun was up and they had eaten, Francis left her to fetch Archie from the stable, eager for them to be on their way. After a few minutes Louise went outside, expecting to find him waiting for her, but she shrank back into the doorway when she saw the marketplace swarming with soldiers. Something was happening which

had attracted a large crowd. Louise's heart was seized
by sudden terror. A group of soldiers stood at a distance
from her and in their midst stood the tall, unmistakable
figure of Francis. He was without his hat and his black,
short, wavy hair gleamed in the early rays of the morning
sun. She saw Archie standing alone near the crowd where
Francis had left him, and slowly she moved towards him.

'What's happening?' she asked a woman close to her.

She shook her head without taking her eyes from the
scene. 'Don't know, really. I've only just come, but I
have heard it's the young Charles Stuart they've
captured.'

Louise's body suddenly went very weak when she
realised that what she had feared ever since they had left
Worcester—that Francis would be mistaken for the
King—had happened. She felt as if she were dying a
thousand deaths and had to fight to keep her knees from
buckling beneath her. All her life and soul was concentrated in her eyes as they fastened themselves on the man
she loved above all else, about to be taken away by the
soldiers.

However much Francis had tried to protest his
innocence it had been no use. Seeking reward and glory
the young, ambitious soldier who had seen him the night
before at the inn had summoned the militia to arrest
him, having virtually convinced himself and them that
here was the fugitive, Charles Stuart.

A command rang out in the square— 'Take him away.'
At that moment a murmur went rippling through the
crowd and, to Louise's already shattered heart, the sound
of the order was like a death knell. Everything had happened so quickly that she stood as one turned to stone,
unable to take in for the moment the fact that Francis
had been captured and that he was to be taken away to
somewhere he had forbidden her to follow. But when

the crowd parted to make way for him and his captors, who now believed more than ever that they had Charles Stuart within their clutches, she wanted to forget the promise she had made to him. Forget all about Elizabeth and everything else and run to him and share his fate. After all, what was anything to her without Francis? He was her life.

The distance between them was not so far, and as she was about to run to him he saw her and the look he gave her, instantly reminding her of the promise she had made to him, made her shrink against the warm flanks of the horse. She held on to the bridle, all her strength concentrated in her fingers as her eyes clung to the receding group of soldiers surrounding the proud figure of Francis, until she could see them no more.

The crowd slowly began to disperse, odd excited groups lingering to discuss what had just taken place while Louise, her legs finally giving way, sank on to a bench and lowered her head in misery, knowing what she had to do, what Francis had told her she must do if he was captured and she remained free. If she stayed here there was a strong possibility that she too would be captured for aiding him. She must go to Bristol alone but she waited, unable to move, until half an hour later when Francis rode out of the town a prisoner of the Commonwealth soldiers. She knew that when it was discovered that he was not Charles Stuart and he was recognised as Lord Francis Slade, the aforesaid's close friend and confidant, and wanted for his traitorous activities during the Civil War, then he would be executed.

Like a sleep-walker she eventually got up and climbed on to Archie's back, and began to follow the road in the direction of Bristol.

It was late afternoon when she made her way through the often steep, narrow and dirty streets of Bristol, teeming with people, her horse moving tiredly over the rough blocks of stone. She stared straight ahead, her lovely eyes devoid of any kind of emotion. Her grief and despair she had left somewhere along the road to Bristol, a never-ending, weary road she seemed to have been travelling ever since she had left Ireland, and now she felt nothing. She would never see Francis again. She wished she were dead, and until that day came her heart would know no peace.

She was unaware of the high timber buildings, their upper storeys jutting out so much that they blocked out most of the light. Horse-drawn sledges were everywhere, some piled high with merchandise from ships in the harbour. No wheeled traffic was allowed in the town, for fear of weakening the structures of the honeycomb of wealthy merchants' cellars beneath the streets, which were used as warehouses for their goods.

She stopped when she came to the harbour, and not even the sight of the busy quay lined with houses and the river so full of masts and sails, the wharves piled high with casks filled with rum and drums of tobacco, moved her. Her eyes were searching for one ship only— the *Western Star*, and when she found her, and after selling Archie at a nearby hostelry, without any hesitation at all she went on board.

It was while Francis was being taken to London to stand trial that he found the opportunity to escape. Unknown to his escort, who stopped for the night at an inn, the innkeeper was a strong loyalist. The soldiers were drinking to their good fortune, although it had not taken them long to discover that it was not the fugitive Charles Stuart they had captured but his good friend Lord Slade, who was perhaps a little less important but a valuable prize just the same. When Francis found the guard outside his room slumped against the wall in a drunken stupor, having been kept well supplied with ale by the innkeeper's wife, he made good his escape out of an unguarded back door and, after many days' hiding and sleeping in fields and hedgerows, succeeded in getting to Portsmouth where he boarded a ship bound for Holland.

CHAPTER TWELVE

BENEATH a cloudless sky, Louise stood holding the rails on the upper deck of the *Western Star*, her eyes fixed on the south coast of the coral island of Barbados spread out before her in the sun, and which had appeared through a shimmering mist fringed with white foam and rising like a jewel out of an azure sea. The gentle wind was hot and the harsh tropical sun scorched her face but she paid no heed to it, so intent was her gaze on the port of Bridgetown, hemmed in by low hills, as the ship edged its way closer through the calm waters of the bay.

What a long time it had taken them to reach Barbados. For the past few weeks the ship had been forced to put in at Antigua after the captain had discovered that Barbados was having problems of her own and was under siege, no ships being allowed near the island. It was now over and peace of a sort had been restored.

Throughout the long years of the Civil War, England had been distracted by her own internal struggle from what had been taking place in the Colonies. Barbados had virtually become an independent state, governed by a powerful assembly, most of its representatives being influential planters on the island. The Civil War had turned out to be a blessing in disguise for Barbados. The planters had been able to avail themselves of the trade facilities of the Dutch and other European countries which had offered much cheaper rates than the English traders. With the help of the Dutch the planters—mainly Royalist exiles and also some Roundhead political outcasts—had ceased to grow tobacco and cotton and had turned instead to the more lucrative sugar trade, the cane growing easily in the rich, young soil of Barbados. The Dutch had provided all the necessary stock and negro labour the planters had required on credit, prepared to wait for their returns until the first crop had been grown, gathered and converted into sugar. The cane had been introduced to the island from Brazil by a Dutchman, and it had brought them a period of unrivalled prosperity that was to change the whole character of Barbados.

With the end of the Civil War and the execution of King Charles I, England, after years of neglect, had turned its attention to its Colonies, and the recognition of the economic importance of Barbados had brought dissension to the island. The Colonists had at first trembled at the thought of home rule when Parliament had enforced its authority upon them, passing an Act forbidding all foreign ships from trading with the Colonies of England without special licence. But tempers had become roused and the planters had angrily and openly opposed Parliament, at which a well-equipped fleet had been sent to reduce Barbados to submission.

When the fleet had reached the island it had found it well fortified and it had been refused entry, but when news of the Royalist defeat at Worcester had become known the wisest Royalists on Barbados, realising home rule was inevitable and without the military strength to declare itself a free state, had finally surrendered, accepting the authority of Parliament.

From the ship, Louise let her eyes wander over the low, green, rolling hills, knowing that somewhere among them was Elizabeth. She felt as if she were entering a strange new world and, for the first time since leaving England, her empty heart experienced a stir of excitement. Since her parting with Francis, the days had passed in a haze and time held no meaning. Some would

say that time would heal her shattered heart, but she
knew differently.

How she had prayed during those first weeks of their
separation that a child might be born out of the love
they had shared in the little shed in the grounds of
Bessington Hall, but she now knew it was not to be. As
each new day dawned her grief did not lessen, but she
didn't cry any more. No matter how uncertain the future
looked, somehow she knew she must carry on—to make
some kind of life for herself and to find Elizabeth and
Christopher and Clara. This last thing she must do for
Francis. She had promised him, and she would keep that
promise—whatever the cost. But one thing she was
certain of, and that was that she would never get over
him. She would never love another as she had loved him.

She looked at the cluster of ramshackle taverns and
shops basking in the sun under a sky the colour of indigo,
around the narrow bridge that spanned the sparkling
river which flowed into the bay. She saw the tobacco
sheds and casks of rum and sugar on the wharf, which
was alive with people. Women sheltering beneath gaily
coloured parasols, protecting their delicate complexions
from the harsh glare of the midday sun, were gathered
around, eagerly watching the ship's progress. She saw
negroes in wide-brimmed straw hats and bright cotton
shirts and trousers, their black skin gleaming in the sun
and their bare feet padding unflinchingly over the baking-
hot surface of the ground, all providing a colourful and
noisy spectacle.

The *Western Star* anchored in the shallow waters of
the bay and the passengers were eventually rowed
through the surf to the shore. When Louise had stepped
out of the boat she noticed a man emerge from the throng
of people and walk towards her. He was perhaps twenty-
five years of age, of medium height and good-looking
in a refined, well-bred sort of way, well groomed with

a fine, delicately embroidered blue satin waistcoat and white lace cravat spilling from his throat.

When he stopped in front of her for a moment he was taken aback by her appearance and looked at her with unconcealed admiration. Her beautiful, dark, liquid eyes, the sun picking out golden flecks, were regarding him carefully and her rich chestnut hair was drawn from her face. She wasn't in the least as he'd expected, in her pale pink dress, one of several she had bought in Antigua with the money intended for Francis' passage, and that was more suited to the tropics than the ones Mr Beamish had given her.

Philip knew very little about her, only that she was here to try and find her sister who had been taken prisoner in Ireland and shipped out to Barbados along with many other wretched creatures to work on the plantations. But for the moment he was delighted to find her so attractive and was glad she was to be staying with them, but he wondered at the sadness mirrored in her lovely eyes that bespoke a deep pain inside her. His lips curled up in a smile, revealing even white teeth in his tanned face, and it was such a wonderful smile, a smile set to charm and warm even the coldest heart—but Louise's was in no state to be charmed, although there was something about his manner and the friendliness in his eyes which she liked. Something that made her feel at ease. He removed his wide-brimmed hat with its dancing white plume, uncovering a shock of pale blond hair tied at the nape of his neck with a thin black ribbon. He bowed politely without taking his brown eyes from hers.

'Miss Cranwell—if I'm not mistaken?'

She nodded, returning his smile. 'Yes, I'm Louise Cranwell.'

'Then I have great pleasure in welcoming you to Barbados. I'm Philip Carstairs. My father sent me to meet you.'

'That was very kind of him,' said Louise. 'It's lucky you knew which ship I'd be on.'

'There haven't been many since the siege ended and we thought you'd be on the *Western Star*. You heard all about that, I take it—the siege?' he said, picking up her bags from the sand.

'Yes. We should have come to Barbados weeks ago, but because of the blockade the captain put in at Antigua. He had business there anyway.'

'Come—I have a carriage waiting. Let's get out of this infernal sun. It's the hottest part of the day. We can talk on the way to the house.'

She followed him to a waiting carriage, trying to avoid the curious stares of the people around her and the admiring glances the ladies cast Philip as he handed her inside. Glances which he must have been aware of but chose to ignore, which made it quite clear to her that he was a well-known figure on the island.

It was only after leaving Bridgetown behind, the carriage being driven by one of the Carstairs' indentured Irish servants, that Louise began to relax, but she was uncomfortably hot. The inside of the carriage was stifling. They travelled in an easterly direction towards St George, one of the island's eleven parishes and where the Carstairs had their five-hundred-acre sugar plantation. She pulled back the lace curtain and looked out. There was a wild luxuriance to the land, aflame with many flowers. The gentle, sloping hills with the unworn, rich earth were clothed with terraces of the tall, leafy green sugar-cane which it produced in abundance, topped with a glory of white plumes gently waving in the light breeze. A few remaining tall, ominously dark forests,

full of unseen life that as yet hadn't come under the
planter's axe, could still be seen.

As her eyes feasted on the beauty of the land she could
feel herself coming under its spell, the sheer magic of
the island descending on her. It was a wonderful yet sinister place with a strange secretiveness to the landscape,
but at the back of her mind lurked Mr Beamish's words,
of the evil and ugliness that lay behind the production
of all this wealth and of the high cost in human suffering
by both the negro slaves brought from Africa and the
white labour obtained from several sources in England,
Ireland and Scotland.

She let the curtain fall back into place and looked
across at the handsome countenance of Philip Carstairs.
It bore a soft expression and his eyes had hardly left her
face for a moment since leaving Bridgetown.

'Barbados is very beautiful, Mr Carstairs.'

'My name is Philip,' he said, smiling. 'And yes, it is
beautiful. While you are staying with us I hope you will
allow me to show you more of the island. My father tells
me you are here to look for your sister.'

'Yes, and the son and daughter of some friends of my
family. They were taken at the same time as my sister
Elizabeth in Ireland. It's very kind of your father to allow
me to stay with you.'

'It will be a pleasure—believe me—but if you do find
them, I must tell you that it will be no easy matter pro-
curing their freedom. How long have they been here?'

'Two years.'

Philip nodded, his face suddenly grim. He remembered the hordes of Irish who had been transported to
the island after Cromwell's ruthless suppression of the
Irish rebellion back in '49. On arrival, most of them had
already been half-dead from starvation and the terrible
conditions of the voyage, and many more had died of

their suffering and the harsh treatment meted out to them by cruel masters on the plantations.

'How old were they when they came here?'

'Elizabeth and Clara were fifteen and Christopher seventeen.'

'I see.'

Good Lord, thought Philip, they had been no more than children. It would be a miracle if any one of them had survived. If disease and poor diet hadn't killed them, then digging in the scorched earth or working in the grinding-mills and boiling-houses of the sugar works surely would have. And then there were the constant floggings which some masters inflicted on their servants for the most minor of offences. But not all masters treated their servants and slaves inhumanely—there were exceptions, and perhaps the three whom Louise was seeking might have been fortunate and been placed on a plantation like his father's. There were no floggings at Carstairs Hall, and once a slave was bought he was never resold. His father also tried, as far as possible, to honour his contracts with indentured servants. At the end of their servitude he gave them a sum of money to enable them to take up land in other established British Colonies such as Virginia or Antigua. Small strips of land on Barbados which they used to be given were no longer available—the white smallholder, unable to maintain himself, was fast disappearing, being taken over by the large plantation-owners with capital, riding on the high tide of wealth.

'How long have you lived on Barbados?' asked Louise, her curiosity about him aroused.

'Since '45. When our property in England was sequestrated after the Royalist defeat at Marston Moor, we escaped and came out here with what little we had left.' He glanced out of the window. 'We'll soon be home, and I must tell you that my mother is looking forward to meeting you. She's talked of nothing else for weeks now. You see, apart from the servants she lacks female company so I'll warn you—she'll probably keep you talking all night,' he said, smiling.

They passed a group of little floorless clay huts with palm-thatched roofs, dwellings of the African slaves, and further on the cabins of the indentured servants, before entering the thickly wooded grounds of Carstairs Hall through a gate set in a high wall. On the brow of a hill overlooking the house stood the sugar works, and Louise could see lumbering, heavy carts pulled by oxen and piled high with bundles of cut cane ready to be fed through the grinding rollers in the mill. From there the extracted juice would go through several processes which would finally result in the pure white sugar—the life-blood of Barbados.

The house where the Carstairses lived was perhaps not as large nor as grand as Louise had expected but, as she was to discover, the larger plantation-owners throughout the early years had been too busy establishing their sugar industry to think about the finer things in life, and only now were architects and masons being brought out from England and employed to design and build bigger, grander houses. But Carstairs Hall had a charm and dignity all of its own, a low part-timber, part-stone-built house with a veranda running around the upper storey. It was covered with a profusion of fragrantly flowering climbing creepers—hibiscus and bougainvillaea and all kinds of succulent tropical blossoms—and in the grounds were palmettos and trees with tremendous girths and huge, spreading branches.

John Carstairs was an older replica of his son, but at fifty years of age thick-set and his once blond hair now silver. He received Louise into his home warmly, as did his wife Eve. She was a small woman with a look of frailty about her but, as Louise was soon to discover, she had a steely quality and presided over the household,

supervising the servants and negroes with kindness but
firmness that was never disregarded. She had a soft voice
which was always obeyed instantly, and it was never
heard to be raised in anger to anyone. She was looked
on with reverence and the utmost respect by everyone at
Carstairs Hall. Louise liked them both immediately.

It was after dinner and candles had been lit, the flickering tapers casting their dancing shadows on the white
walls of the dining-room. They were sipping their coffee
at the large pine table and had talked at length of what
was happening in England and also of the recent troubles
in Barbados. Louise was tired and about to excuse herself
when John Carstairs talked of her reason for coming to
the island.

'If it had not been for the troubles we've had on the
island of late, I would have made enquiries concerning
your sister. Philip informs me that there are others you
wish to find.'

'Yes—that's right. The son and daughter of some
friends of my family.'

'What are they called?'

'Christopher and Clara Slade. They were taken with
Elizabeth.'

At the mention of the name, Philip looked at her
curiously.

'Slade?' he asked, frowning thoughtfully as he tried
to remember where he had heard the name. 'It sounds
familiar.'

Louise looked at him sharply. 'It is not uncommon.'

'No—but wasn't there a Lord Slade close to Prince
Charles? I seem to remember him at Marston Moor.
Francis, I think—who looked uncommonly like Charles,
if I remember correctly.'

He noticed how Louise paled significantly, but the
expression on her face never altered as she fixed him
with her steady gaze.

'Yes,' she said quietly. 'Christopher and Clara are his brother and sister.'

Philip seemed to look at her for a long moment before he spoke, saying slowly. 'I see. And do you know what happened to Francis?'

The awkwardness of the question hung in the air and there was silence as Louise thought carefully about how to answer it, finding it extremely painful to speak of Francis. There was no glow or warmth in her eyes, only a profound, haunting melancholy, and as before Philip found himself wondering what could have happened to her to make her look so sad. It wasn't just what had happened in Ireland—that was two years ago now. No, it was something else—something more recent—and when she finally answered his question he was left in no doubt as to the reason.

'No,' she said softly. 'When I left England he had been captured by the Commonwealth and was to stand trial—accused of being a traitor. By now I believe he will have been executed.'

Mrs Carstairs gasped in horror at her words. 'Oh, my dear—how awful.'

'Yes. Perhaps now you will understand how important it is for me to find his brother and sister.'

There was a long pause in the room, the sounds of the tropical night coming to them through the narrow slats of the shutters. The shrill cry of the night birds, the faint, faraway singing of the indentured servants collected together outside their little cabins and the strange, rhythmic pounding of the Negro drums. Philip rose from his chair and walked slowly round the table to where she was sitting.

'We do understand, Louise,' he said kindly, 'and tomorrow we will begin making enquiries. If they are still alive and on this island, then rest assured we will find them.'

*   *   *

During the days that followed Louise's arrival on the
island, when one or the other was not occupied on the
plantation, John Carstairs and his son began making
enquiries for any information regarding the captives.
They searched through endless and often inaccurate
parish registers and past auctions of transported political
offenders going back two years.

The task Louise had set them proved to be so time-
consuming that the days turned into weeks and, doing
her best to hide her disappointment when they found
nothing, she accustomed herself to plantation life, her
day beginning at six in the morning when the plantation
bell was rung, summoning all the workers to assemble
in the yard where they received their instructions for the
day from either Philip or his father. They worked a
twelve-hour day six days a week, with a break of two
hours at midday, the tropical heat becoming too intense
for work. This was when they had their meal, varying
from crushed Indian corn mixed into a paste with
water—loblolly, the slaves called it—to potatoes, yams,
molasses and saltfish. They rested on Sundays.

Louise soon realised how fortunate the indentured
servants and slaves were at Carstairs Hall compared to
others. They were well fed and clothed and the sick taken
care of, but the same could not be said of some of the
wretched human beings she saw on other plantations
which she visited, the scars on their bodies visible evidence of the cruelty of their masters.

Now that the blockade was over and the planters
settled down once again to a near-normal life, dinner
parties and social events, to which Louise was escorted
and introduced by Philip and where only the best food
and wines from Europe were served, were the order of
the day.

It was four weeks before reference to any of the three
captives was found, and this was the name of Christopher

Slade on one of the parish registers of St Thomas, adjoining the parish of St George to the north. He had been bought by a planter by the name of Samuel Coleridge almost two years before, and had to serve a term of ten years. It was at a planter's discretion to set free any of his servants. Philip knew for a fact that many well-off Royalist gentlemen, who had been transported after uprisings in England and especially after the Battle of Dunbar, had bought their freedom and left the island. Some planters could be bribed for a large sum of money, which was the method he was to use with Coleridge. Through his enquiries, Philip had discovered the planter had come to the island ten years previously and lived alone. He was neither well known nor well liked, kept himself to himself and was seldom seen away from his prospering four-hundred-acre plantation except to buy slaves.

Louise was overjoyed at the discovery of Christopher's whereabouts, knowing that maybe she was one step nearer to finding Elizabeth and Clara. She was impatient to leave for the Coleridge plantation right away, but Philip persuaded her to wait until the following day.

They left on horseback early the next morning when the earth was moist and fresh after the cold night and was saturating the fragrant air. When they entered the parish of St Thomas the scenery was of unique beauty, the lush deep green of the remaining tropical rain forests contrasting beautifully with the paler green of the cane fields. To Louise's English eyes Barbados, with its profusion of gaily coloured birds and big, bright butterflies, was a tropical paradise with an underlying wild savagery that she would never understand.

They were soon on to the Coleridge plantation, where there was field after field of cane, some of the finest Louise had seen since coming to Barbados, giving her the impression that this was the property of one of the island's finest planters. But that was soon to change.

A strange, eerie stillness hung over the place and as they passed through the fields they saw no workers. They saw a cluster of buildings in the distance but it wasn't until they were close that they saw how dilapidated they were. They passed a collection of slave cabins first, and neither of them could believe what they saw. The cabins were falling down and squalid to such an extent that they could not believe human beings lived in them. They were scarcely suitable for pigs. The putrid piles of rotting rubbish and excrement at the back of them took their breath away, and a few scrawny hens scratched in the dirt.

There was an air of neglect hanging over the place, and it stank of evil. Icy fingers began to tighten round Louise's heart, and neither of them spoke as they rode slowly up a tree-lined drive that was overrun with weeds. They saw a low timber bungalow at the end, a broken door swinging open. Seeing no larger building, they assumed this to be the owner's house. It looked like a house out of the past, crude like those the early settlers used to build, facing west, sealed from the trade winds blowing from the east but facing the full glare of the sun.

They rode on, their horses' hoofs scarcely making a sound on the soft ground, but suddenly the silence was disturbed by a nerve-shattering crack echoing through the trees, bringing them to a halt. Their eyes met and Philip went very pale, and then they heard another crack and after that they came at regular intervals from somewhere beyond the trees.

Philip said nothing to Louise, but he knew it to be the swish of a whip cutting through the soft flesh of a man's back. It would explain why they had seen no workers in the fields. It was common practice on many plantations when one of the slaves had committed an offence to flog him publicly as a dire example to others. It was a practice Philip abhorred.

They started riding in the direction from where the sound had come. Trees enclosed them and Louise followed Philip through the cool darkness, seeing the muscles of his back tensed beneath his coat, and all the while the cracks were getting louder. She felt a deathly terror steal over her and she stared straight ahead, fixing her eyes on a shaft of sunlight slanting through the branches of the trees, trying to still the trembling in her limbs. She knew, with a terrifying suspicion, what the noise was but she was unprepared for the nightmare scene that met her eyes when they again emerged into the glare of the sun.

She blinked, a peculiar feeling engulfing her. It was as if what she now saw was a scene which had been frozen in time. Nothing moved. They found themselves in a square compound with people standing around, so still they were like statues, negroes on one side and white indentured servants on the other. Overseers with long, curling whips stood menacingly on guard. But black or white, the expressions on their faces were the same with empty eyes and haggard, hollow cheeks. All looked hungry and emaciated and their clothes were dirty and torn. Even the babes held in their mothers' arms and older children standing rigid by their sides were motionless, and Louise followed their eyes to the whipping-post which was the centre of this terrible, macabre picture.

For the first time since coming to Barbados she was faced with the abomination of slavery in all its most brutal, violent realism. A man was tied to the post, a white man, his arms suspended by ropes. He was bare to the waist and blood trickled from the cuts on his back, staining his trousers, and his tortured body writhed in

pain although he had uttered no sound. A giant of a
negro stood beside him and raised his powerful arm, the
swish of the whip through the air putting a fresh slice
on the man's back. At the sound of the impact a cry
escaped Louise's lips.

At the interruption all attention in the compound was
diverted from the wretched man tied to the post, and
the negro's arm wielding the whip paused, poised in mid-
air, but not before Louise had seen the small, fat man
standing at the opposite side of the post to the negro,
taking an immense, sadistic pleasure in the pain being
inflicted upon the man tied to it, his gloating, horrible,
close-set eyes gazing at him. At the disturbance he looked
up quickly, a savage rage twisting his face, but at the
sight of Louise and Philip it disappeared and, after telling
the negro to untie the man, he slowly moved in their
direction.

Louise shuddered when he stood before them, his little
coal-black eyes fixing them with a hostile stare out of a
bloated, red-veined face. He was dirty and unkempt and
sweating profusely, dark patches staining his worn, grey
shirt. His body reeked hideously, making a violent wave
of nausea sweep over Louise, but she swallowed it down.
That he took exception to their presence on his plantation he did not hide, and his eyes travelled insolently
over Louise's slender form before settling on Philip. He
had a malicious, evil disposition. He turned his head to
one side and spat into the dirt before speaking.

'Lost, are you?' he rasped.

'No,' said Philip. 'This is the Coleridge place, isn't it?
We're looking for Samuel Coleridge.'

'I'm Sam Coleridge. What do you want?'

Philip considered the man before him for a moment,
his face impassive, and when he spoke it was with a
brusque civility but behind his words there was a quiet
anger. 'I'm looking for someone—a white servant I know

you purchased at auction in Bridgetown almost two years ago.'

The sun was behind Philip, almost blinding Sam Coleridge, who had to half close one eye and squint up at him.

'Two years? Then whoever he is he's probably been gone from here months since. What's his name?'

Philip sucked in his breath, finding it extremely difficult keeping his temper. He thought the man utterly repugnant. 'Christopher Slade. He was seventeen years old when he came here.'

That he recognised the name Philip knew immediately, but Coleridge was in no hurry to admit it. His eyes suddenly filled with uncertainty for some reason, and Philip had every intention of finding out why. He appeared ill at ease for a moment, and half turned in the direction of the whipping-post where Louise saw the poor creature who had been flogged slumped on the ground, his legs having given way when the thick ropes had been untied. The giant negro was beside him, the whip lying curled up on the ground where he had thrown it.

'Can't say I recall the name,' said Coleridge, looking up at Philip sideways.

'Think again, Mr Coleridge. There is evidence that you bought him.'

He eyed Philip shiftily, suspecting he might be someone from the council who had different ideas from his own regarding the treatment of slaves. They had the crazy notion that to get the best out of them you had to stuff them with food and give them feather mattresses to bed down on.

'Just who are you?'

'My name is Carstairs—Philip Carstairs. My father owns land in St George.'

'And are you from the council?'

'No—but I have friends who are,' replied Philip meaningfully.

'And what will you be wanting with this servant—Slade, you said his name was?'

'That is correct. I have a contract for his release. If he is still here and you sign him over then you will be well compensated, of course.'

At the mention of payment a greedy, calculating gleam entered his eyes. 'How much?'

Philip would have liked to have stated a sum, but he knew that with a man like Sam Coleridge he would have his own price. 'We would have to negotiate a price.'

Coleridge seemed to consider it for a moment longer but then shook his head, seeming impatient for them to be gone from his land, and quickly.

'He isn't here,' he growled, spitting again into the dirt, indicating that the interview was over as far as he was concerned. 'Now if that's all I'd be obliged if you'd get off my land.'

All the while they had been talking, Louise's eyes were drawn irresistibly to the pathetic figure slumped against the whipping-post, the blood on his back already drying in the scorching heat. His feeble groans came to her across the compound. The negro was bent over him, the look on his face surprisingly tender and his hands gentle as he helped the man struggle to his feet, and it was only when he was erect and turned slightly that Louise's eyes became riveted to him in disbelief, and she suddenly experienced a fierce joy. There was something about his tall but thin frame that fixed her attention. It was Christopher. She knew without the shadow of a doubt that it was he. With a supple movement she slid from her horse and, her eyes shining, moved quickly towards him, but before she could reach him he again slumped to the ground. Louise fell to her knees beside him, gently lifting his head and cradling it on her lap, tears of relief beginning to flow uncontrollably down her face as she bent over him, saying his name over and over again. She smoothed his dark, curling hair from his young face, although in the two years since she had last seen him he looked as if he had lived a lifetime. His eyes were closed, his lips slightly parted, and he bore such a strong resemblance to Francis that it tore at her heart.

Somewhere within the deep confines of his mind, Christopher was aware of the stirring of his consciousness and someone calling his name from far away—willing him to wake up—but he fought against it. He didn't want to leave this blessed darkness that engulfed him, this place where pain and hunger couldn't reach him, but it was no use—he couldn't fight it any longer and gradually the swirling dark inside his head got lighter and the pain came back. The voice was soft, a woman's voice, and he could feel her cool hands gently cradling his face. Something wet splashed on to his cheek and he opened his eyes, and if it had not been for the pain from his injured back he would have truly believed he was in heaven and the face gazing down at him the sweet face of an angel. The wetness he had felt was the woman's tears as she wept above him, and it was only as the mist cleared before his eyes that he recognised her.

'Louise?'

'Yes—yes, it is I,' she wept, smiling through her tears.

'I must be dreaming,' he exclaimed. 'Is it really you?'

'Yes, and what a difficult time I've had finding you. But hush—don't try and talk now. I'm with a friend and we're going to take you away from here. Thank God we came in time.'

At that moment the shadows of Philip and Sam Coleridge fell across them and she lifted her face, all the anger and disgust she felt for the owner of this miserable plantation mirrored in her dark eyes, the golden flecks spitting fire.

'So,' she fumed. 'Do you still say he isn't here? Do you still deny hearing the name of Christopher Slade?'

Sam Coleridge's face became purple with rage, which he vented on Philip, disregarding Louise. 'Now look here, Carstairs, what I do around here is my business, right? It's got nothing to do with you or anyone else. If I choose to sell one of my slaves, that's my affair, and if I flog 'em—that's my affair too. So clear off before I have you run off my land.'

Philip ignored the menacing threat of some of the overseers, who had moved a little closer. He wanted to reach out and throttle this monster before him who derived such an unholy pleasure in the suffering he inflicted on his slaves, but he knew it was wiser to conceal his own feelings—at least until he had succeeded in getting him to sign the contract.

'I have no intention of leaving here without this man,' he said with an icy contempt, his face darkening. He took an official-looking document from inside his jacket and held it in front of Sam Coleridge. 'Sign this contract which will give him his freedom, and I will give you the sum of twenty pounds. I think the time for negotiating a settlement is past—don't you? If you refuse then I can promise you that what I have seen here today will come to the attention of not only the council but also the Governor—who, I might add, is a personal friend of mine. You do realise that the law of this island affords a certain degree of protection to both servant and slave, and from what I have seen of the disgraceful conditions of their living quarters and the violence and inhumanity with which you treat them—I could ruin you,' he finished quietly.

Outraged, Sam Coleridge's eyes bulged in their sockets and the veins of his face stood out. He was so angry he looked like a bloated frog about to burst. He clenched his fists tightly and for one horrifying moment Louise thought he was going to strike Philip, but suddenly his gaze faltered beneath the younger man's cold, hard stare.

'How dare you threaten me——?'

'I'm not threatening you, I'm telling you. Now—sign this,' he ordered, thrusting the document into his hand. 'I've no wish to remain here longer than I have to.'

Coleridge hesitated for just a moment before turning angrily and storming across the compound to find a quill with which to sign his name. He knew it was the only thing he could do if he wanted to avoid the council coming and snooping about.

Philip looked down at Christopher, who still had his head cradled in Louise's lap. 'Well, Christopher,' he said softly, 'you are about to become a free man. It seems we came just in time.'

He managed a weak smile. 'I can't believe it. I think I shall wake up in a minute and find it's all a dream.' He held out his hand. 'Please—help me to stand.'

They managed to get him to his feet where he stood, swaying beside them, holding on to Philip's arm for support.

'Listen, Christopher—I want us to leave here as quickly as possible. We've a long ride ahead of us and unfortunately it's the hottest part of the day. We're going down to St George, to my home, where you'll be well taken care of. Do you think you'll be able to ride on my horse in front of me? I had thought to ask Coleridge to lend us one, but I'd rather not. I don't wish to be indebted to him in any way.'

Weak and exhausted though he was, Christopher nodded. 'I'll manage anything if it gets me away from here.'

'Before we go can you—can you tell me about Elizabeth—and—and Clara?' asked Louise tentatively. 'Do you know where they are?' She waited for his reply expectantly, her heart beating quickly. Please, God, she prayed silently, don't let him tell me they're here in this awful place. Let them be somewhere where people are kind and caring.

A sadness seemed to descend on Christopher and at her question his shoulders slumped and he shook his head dejectedly. 'Clara is dead, Louise. She died on the ship that brought us out here. She wasn't strong enough to take it.'

'Oh, dear God, no,' whispered Louise, her face going white with shock. 'Poor Clara.' A vision of the lovely, blonde-haired Clara flashed before her eyes and a terrible pain wrenched her heart. It was with dread that she again asked him about her own sister. 'But—Elizabeth. Where is she?'

'I don't know. She was here but she ran away a year ago. We escaped together but I was caught. You see, I'd hurt my leg and couldn't run fast enough. I—I suspect she's with other runaways somewhere in St Andrew or St Joseph. That's where most of them go. They hide in the caves.'

'Oh—but she's alive. At least she's alive.'

There was a movement beside the whipping-post, and for the first time in minutes all three of them became aware of the negro, who was still there. Louise looked at him, her eyes wide, as if seeing him for the first time. He was tall and as black as ebony, his smooth skin glistening with small beads of perspiration. There was a smoky blue haze in his black eyes and in a strange way he possessed a noble, savage beauty which had been handed down to him by his African ancestors. He held himself straight and proud with an air of defiance. There was nothing servile about him, and she knew that no matter how many fetters were used to enslave him no man would ever be his master. There was that about him which would always be free. He would die free, delivered up from all that was evil in this white man's land.

He held Christopher's shirt in his hands and slowly moved towards him, tenderly pulling it into place over the young man's wasted body, covering the cruel, bloody welts on his back, and only when he had finished did Christopher take his big black hands in his own and clasp them tightly, looking into his eyes that were filled with a sadness which seemed to come from his very soul. The negro had understood what had taken place even though he could not understand the language, but he didn't need words to tell him that this white friend was leaving. His heart was heavy with sorrow.

At the obvious deep affection the two men felt for each other Louise looked on with a mixture of curiosity and bewilderment.

'But—but Christopher—he was the one who——'

'Who flogged me,' he said fiercely, tears welling up in his blue eyes. 'But it was only because he is my friend that Coleridge made him do it. That was part of my punishment.'

Louise stared at him, horrified. Was there to be no end to the cruelties this man inflicted on his servants? 'What did you do to make him punish you like that?'

'I tried to run away. Since Elizabeth went I've tried so often to escape—to go and find her. After Clara died she became like a sister to me. But each time I ran away he caught me and each time the punishment was the same—with the exception that the number of lashes increased.'

Louise gently took his hand in her own. 'You needn't worry any more, Christopher. We'll go and find Elizabeth together. But come—try and get on the horse. Let us be gone from this place.'

With the help of his negro friend they managed to get him on to the horse, and at that moment Sam Coleridge came striding back across the compound. He thrust the signed document at Philip.

'Here—take it, and I'm not sorry to be rid of him. He's been nothing but trouble since the day I bought him. Should have got rid of him sooner.' He snatched the purse of money from Philip's hand and watched them mount their horses, Philip behind Christopher, but as they were about to ride away he halted them. 'Remember your promise. I want no council snooping about here.'

Philip turned and looked at him for one last time. 'I promised you nothing, Coleridge,' and then he urged his sturdy horse on and hastily followed Louise out of the compound the way they had come, leaving the black and white slaves still and silent but watchful, some beginning to tremble at the rage on their master's face, knowing they would suffer for this strange episode which had taken place.

Sam Coleridge stared after the riders, thinking over Philip's parting words, and the rage drained out of him. For the first time in years fear filled his eyes, which would have increased a thousandfold if he had turned then and seen the eyes of the negro fixed on him, full of a blinding, murderous hatred.

It was two days later in the cane fields as Sam Coleridge watched the negroes toiling beneath the sweltering sun which beat down on them mercilessly that his fears were realised, but they came to him in a different form. It was too late for him to do anything but register surprise when he looked up and saw the machete, wielded by the powerful negro, coming down on to his head, a second later splitting it in two like a coconut.

CHAPTER THIRTEEN

IT WAS thanks to the devoted and tender ministrations of Louise and Eve Carstairs and the many salves that were applied to his wounds that Christopher recovered, although some of the scars on his back would always remain as a constant reminder of what he'd suffered at the cruel hands of Samuel Coleridge. With proper nourishment his fleshless body soon began to fill out and he lost that lean, hungry look, although there was a deep, haunting emptiness in his eyes.

He and Louise spent many hours together talking. They had so much to tell each other and Christopher had so many questions to ask about that last night in Ireland. He knew his father was dead—he had seen him hanged before being dragged away. The picture in his mind would haunt him forever, but when she told him about his mother he bowed his head to hide his deep sorrow and also a terrible anger. She told him about Francis, whom—although Christopher had seen little of him while he had been growing up because he had been away fighting in the Civil War—he had always worshipped, and to be told he too might be dead was almost too much for him to bear.

Immediately they had got back to Carstairs Hall with Christopher, plans had been made to find Elizabeth. Louise had objected strongly when Philip had told her it was impractical for her to go searching for her sister. He'd said it wasn't the same situation as when they had gone for Christopher. Then they had known where he was, but Elizabeth could be anywhere. It might take days

or even weeks to find her. He had tried to make her see
that it just wasn't safe for her to go searching those parts
of the island that were still wild and uninhabited. The
forests and hills were full of runaway slaves, desperate
men who would think nothing of committing murder if
they felt threatened in any way, and besides, she must
remember that runaway servants did not want to be
found and had a way of losing themselves in Barbados.
It was only after much persuasion that she agreed to
employ someone to go and find Elizabeth. Someone who
knew the island and where these people were living.

He finally introduced her to Jake Fox, who had come
to Barbados as an indentured servant to escape being
caught and hanged for killing a man who had taken his
wife. It was only later that he had regretted not killing
them both—after all, he could only hang once. He had
served out his time and now spent his days wandering
the island, just himself and his old horse, his few
necessary possessions packed on its back. Philip had got
to know him on his visits to Bridgetown when he'd often
met him in one of the many taverns by the wharf, and
he'd agreed to try and find Elizabeth for the price of
another horse.

When Philip brought him to the plantation and Louise
first set eyes on him she wasn't at all sure she wanted
him to go and look for Elizabeth. He was so dirty he
resembled a desperado himself, but she was soon to
change her mind. Although she was never able to like
the man she soon learnt to respect him and would have
trusted him with her life, and she realised that if anyone
could find her sister it was he.

It was hard to judge how old he was. His lined face
beneath his battered old hat and multicoloured whiskers
was brown and craggy, his eyes unblinking, pale and cold
with contempt—as if he hated the whole of mankind.
His body was lean and sinewy and he moved with the

stealth of a snake. Jake Fox was a man of few words—
his own man who kept his own counsel and possessed
a fierce pride.

Louise told him all he needed to know about Elizabeth
while he sat on a step on the porch, leaning lazily against
a post and whittling away at a small piece of wood with
his knife, which he always kept shoved down the top of
his boot. All the time she was speaking she thought he
wasn't listening, but when she'd finished he repeated
everything she'd said in his deep guttural voice, word
for word.

He'd been gone two days when news reached them at
Carstairs Hall about what had happened to Sam
Coleridge. The negro responsible for his death had already been caught and hanged, and the four-hundred-
acre plantation was up for sale.

When Louise had overcome the initial shock of what
had happened she fought a decisive battle inside herself,
eventually coming to a decision. It was probably the
biggest and most important decision of her life. She
would buy the Coleridge place. With the money she had
inherited from the sale of her aunt's jewels she should
be able to afford it and if not she would borrow the rest,
and besides, since coming to Barbados she had had
plenty of time to think about her future and Elizabeth's,
asking herself repeatedly what was to become of them.
When her sister was found they couldn't go on staying
with the Carstairs indefinitely, and as things were in
England under the Commonwealth she had no wish to
return there.

But this was not the only reason she wanted to leave
Carstairs Hall. The other was Philip. Although he had
made no advances towards her, she was in no doubt as
to what his feelings were. Perhaps it was the way his eyes
would linger on hers or the gentle squeeze of his hand
as he handed her into the carriage or bade her good-

night, but whichever it was, and no matter how much she enjoyed his company and valued his friendship, she had neither the inclination nor the desire to become romantically involved with him or anyone else. She felt a deep, fond affection for him, this she could not deny, but she didn't love him. The pain of her parting with Francis was still too acute, and besides, she secretly nursed the hope—however forlorn it might be—that he might still be alive and would come to her in Barbados.

The more she thought of buying the Coleridge plantation the more she realised how much she wanted to, how much she needed to. Not since Ireland had she known what it was like to have a home of her own. She knew nothing about Barbados or planting sugar, but she was determined to learn. For two years she had been travelling a long, weary road, terrorised by war and death—well, no more. After all she had been through she had nothing else to fear, and besides, the peace of the island had given her comfort and she had basked in its heat and found compassion in its unique beauty and freedom. After all, what had she to lose? And so, with her mind made up, she went in search of Philip and Christopher.

She found them outside the house sitting at a table in the cool shade of a giant cabbage palm. Philip had just returned from Bridgetown and was sipping cold lemonade. His handsome face looked troubled, a frown puckering his brow, but when he saw her walking towards them it disappeared and he smiled, pouring her some lemonade. She sank into an empty chair.

'You're looking well pleased with yourself, Louise,' said Christopher, as she smoothed her skirts.

'Am I?' she replied, a little secretive smile playing about her lips and an unusual sparkle in her eyes. She raised the glass to her lips, taking a sip of the delicious liquid before placing it on the table. 'Perhaps it's because

I have something to tell you both—especially you, Philip, because I'm going to need your help—and your father's.'

'Oh?' chorused the two men together, studying her with ardent curiosity.

'Yes,' she said, taking a deep breath and looking from one to the other. 'I've decided to buy the Coleridge plantation.'

'What?' they both gasped in shocked amazement, sitting forward in their seats.

'Yes, and before either of you says anything I'd like you to know that I've thought about it a great deal.'

'Louise—have you taken leave of your senses?' asked Philip.

She laughed lightly. 'No—I can assure you I'm quite sane.'

'But—but you can't,' gasped Philip.

'Why not?'

'Well—because—because it might already have been sold.'

'Then I'll look for another,' she replied firmly, fixing him with a level stare. 'I have money, Philip, and from the way I see it buying a sugar plantation—especially one that is already established—would be a good investment.'

'But you know nothing about growing sugar,' said Christopher.

'No—but you do, and I'm counting upon your coming with me. You can teach me. Oh, Christopher,' she said, reaching out and gripping his hand. 'Don't you see what this could mean for me, you and Elizabeth? It's like grasping a lifeline.' She didn't see the pain her words caused Philip or the way he paled. She went on, 'We all lost everything in Ireland—including our families. We have nothing there any more or in England. Don't you see this is a chance for us? We must take it.'

•

'But that place. Oh, Louise—it would be hard going back there.'

'I know and I do understand, but it will be different now. We'll build a new house and cabins for the workers. Oh, Christopher—I have so many plans.'

'But you'll become a slave-owner, and you know how you feel about that.'

'I know,' she said, the sparkle leaving her eyes. 'That's the part I don't like. Perhaps we could employ more white labour—more indentured servants.'

At her words Philip shook his head slowly. 'You really do have a lot to learn, Louise,' he said, not unkindly. 'The sad reality of the fact is that we need slaves for our economic success. Without them we are doomed. It is also much cheaper to buy black slaves than white. The money you pay for one white servant for ten years will buy one negro for life. They have also proved to be more efficient and work well in this tropical climate, which is very similar to their own in Africa. So you see without them there would be destruction and ruin for us all. I can't say that I agree with it, but if I wish to stay here then I must accept it—and if you're serious about wanting to buy the Coleridge place then that is what you'll have to do. Otherwise you might just as well forget it.'

Louise looked at him for a long moment before replying. He spoke the truth, she knew that, but she had made her decision and she would not change her mind. She nodded slowly. 'I don't think I'll ever be able to accept slavery, Philip, but I still want to buy the plantation. At least I shall see to it that they're properly treated, and who knows what may happen in the future?' She looked again at Christopher. 'You will come with me, won't you, Christopher?'

'You know I will, but—well—I would like to find out what happened to Francis. Even if it means going to England.'

'Then perhaps I can help you there, and I don't think you will need to go back to England,' said Philip, suddenly getting to his feet and looking down at them, watching Louise's face closely, and when he spoke she realised what had been troubling him earlier. 'I made enquiries while I was in Bridgetown of an English captain whose ship had just come in. The latest news is that Charles Stuart escaped safely to France and your brother escaped his captors before reaching London. His whereabouts are not known but it is suspected that he also escaped across the Channel.'

Louise stared at him uncomprehendingly and silent for what seemed an age. Many jumbled thoughts raced round her mind, but at last the distinct knowledge of what Philip had said—that Francis was alive, that he'd escaped the executioner—became clear, and all the joy of their love engulfed her. At last the fire that had been lit between them, that had lain dormant inside her for so long—all these months when she thought he was gone from her forever—began to smoulder, and she knew she would only have to see him again, to feel the delight and beauty of the touch of his lips on hers, for it to burst into flames and engulf her completely.

At the relief, all her restrained grief came pouring out of her. Her whole body was shaken by her tearing sobs, the tears at last bursting from her. Christopher wrapped his arms comfortingly about her as she wept, and so blinded was she by the tears streaming down her face that she didn't see the hurt and misery in Philip's eyes nor feel the gentle pressure of his hand squeezing her shoulder before he turned and walked towards the house, knowing that he had been right not to declare his feelings for her. Perhaps if Francis Slade had died then even-

tually she would have got over him, but he knew it was
only a matter of time before they would be reunited.

Louise became a familiar figure in Bridgetown when she
came to collect supplies for Carstairs Hall, being driven
in the carriage by two of the indentured servants, and
it was on one of her visits that she first saw the Dutch
trader with its white topsail drawing into the bay. At
first she paid no heed to it and went to collect some
material she was to make into dresses for Elizabeth when
she was found. Handing the package up to the servants,
she turned and looked again out into the bay and at the
usual crowd of people which always gathered to watch
a strange ship's arrival. She squinted into the sun, the
hot wind caressing her face and, reluctant to enter the
stuffy confines of the carriage just yet, she moved
towards the shimmering, sun-scorched sand to watch the
ship with the rest.

   She saw the heavy vessel gradually steer round the
point under a cloudless sky, her white sails billowing out
as they caught the wind. Somewhere up above came the
persistent screeching of the gulls and she glanced up, but
only fleetingly before she again looked at the ship and
saw the white foam of sea as it broke over her bows.
She anchored in the shallows and people could be seen
moving about on the deck, seamen clambering barefoot
among the rigging. A longboat was lowered over the
gunwale and began rowing passengers to the shore.
Louise detached herself from the crowd and moved away
from them to watch the boat. She had seen the passengers climb into it from the swaying rope ladder and
her eyes were drawn by an irresistible impulse to one in
particular. From where she stood he appeared tall, taller
than the rest, and beneath his wide-brimmed hat his hair
was black, curling to his broad shoulders.

Her heart leaped in her breast, but then seemed to stop altogether. She stared at him as he sat in the boat looking straight ahead. It was Francis. She took a step forward but then checked herself. No—it couldn't possibly be him. She must be mistaken. But as the boat came closer and his features were more defined she saw that it was him, and observed joyously that he had not changed. He was still the same with his handsome, proud, clear-cut features. He removed his hat, revealing hair of sable blackness, shining like silk in the sun. The bottom of the boat scraped on the shore and she stood rooted to the spot as he rose and strode over the vessel's side, his long, booted legs splashing in the surf as it broke over the sand.

A gust of wind took hold of Louise's hat, blowing it away, but she didn't care. Like the wind her heart soared, and her face glowed with rapture, her eyes filled with an unearthly brilliance as she watched him. He hadn't seen the lone woman standing just a few yards from him. He had his back to her and was conversing with a fellow passenger, but then he suddenly turned and saw her, a soft smile parting her lovely lips and her beautiful mane of deep brown hair blowing wildly behind her, the sun picking out the golden lights.

Their eyes locked and held and for a moment everything and everyone around them ceased to exist, all but the glow of their love. And then, with an ecstatic cry, she was in his arms, the arms of the man she loved above all else, the man she had thought was dead and then found was alive.

People around them watched in astonishment as he swung her off the ground and carried her away and only when they were alone did he put her down, covering her face and mouth with kisses like a starving man, kissing away her tears of sheer happiness, and only when their

passion was exhausted did he take his lips from hers and
look down into her eyes.

'Oh, Louise—if only you knew how much I've craved
for this moment—to see you—to hold you in my arms.
But how did you know I'd be here—on this ship?'

'I didn't. It's sheer coincidence—or fate—that I'm here
in Bridgetown today. Oh, Francis—I've missed you so
much. So much has happened and I've so much to tell
you. But—but when you were captured I—I thought you
were sure to die,' and once again she was in his arms,
fresh tears flowing down her cheeks. 'It was only later—
here on Barbados—that I heard you'd escaped.'

'Yes. I went to Holland but I couldn't wait to come
to you.'

She stood back in his arms and looked up at him
questioningly. 'Holland? Did—did you see Anne?'

'Yes—I stayed with her brother. Her father is well
and,' he said, 'you'll be pleased to learn that Anne is
married—to a young man she met in Holland. She is
very happy and wishes us well.' He smiled at the relief
in her eyes. 'I boarded a ship just as quickly as I could.
Oh, my love, after I was captured you have no idea how
I was tormented with thoughts of you, knowing you were
frightened and alone and—perhaps, carrying my child.'

'There was no child, Francis, but I wanted one so
much. Your child would have brought me such joy. But
tell me—what of the King?' she asked, looking up at
him through her tears. 'Is he safe?'

'Yes, he's safe, but I haven't seen him. He's in France
waiting for the time when he will be restored to his
throne.'

'Poor Charles,' she whispered, knowing how he must
be suffering.

'I know—but it will come—you'll see. England will
tire of Oliver Cromwell and his military rule and want
a King again. But what of you, Louise, and Christopher

and Clara and Elizabeth? Tell me—have you found them, and if so how are they?'

She looked up at him, knowing she would have to tell him about Clara. 'I have found Christopher and we have someone looking for Elizabeth up north on the island, but—but Clara—I have sad news regarding her, Francis. She—she died on the ship bringing them here. Oh, Francis—I'm so sorry,' she whispered, seeing the sadness fill his eyes.

He nodded, swallowing hard. 'It is as I expected, but I always hoped I might be wrong. Clara was never very strong. It does not surprise me to learn that she did not survive the voyage. How is Christopher?'

'He's fine now. You'll be so proud of him. I bought his freedom and at the moment we're trying to buy a plantation. Of course we shall have to borrow half the money to buy it, and I have thought of asking Mr Beamish to lend it to us. Land prices have soared since everyone started growing sugar, but we'll be able to pay him back after the first harvest. You see, Francis, when my Aunt Katherine died there was no estate, no property left. Everything had gone towards funding the King's cause. Everything, that is, but her jewels. If she had lived, no doubt they would have gone too, but as it was I inherited them and sold them to pay for my passage here, and what is left will go towards buying the plantation.'

'And why is your heart so set on buying a plantation? Neither of us knows the first thing about growing sugar.'

'It just seems right, and besides, we can learn. Christopher will help us, and the Carstairses. They're the people we're staying with. They've been so good to us, Francis. You'll like them—I know you will. But besides that we must think of the future—not only for ourselves but for Elizabeth and Christopher too. There is nothing in England for us now—not until Charles regains his throne, and that may not be for a long time. Oh, Francis—say this is what you want too.'

Her face shone with enthusiasm and Francis smiled, a secretive, teasing smile. 'You really have been busy, but I don't think it will be necessary to borrow money from anyone.'

'Oh?'

'No. If buying a plantation is what you want then we will buy it together.'

She stared at him incredulously. 'But—but how?'

He laughed lightly at her confusion. 'How can I afford it? I had some money secreted away in Holland. Money which, if I had gone to France instead of coming here, I would no doubt have put into the King's coffers. But now,' he said, taking her face between his strong hands, his deep blue eyes looking down into hers, 'I can think of no better use for it than to build us a home. The first thing I must do is make you my wife. So come—if I am to be a planter then I have much to learn.'

Francis' arrival gave cause for much rejoicing at Carstairs Hall, and his reunion with Christopher brought a constriction to all their throats. He wept unashamedly when Francis clutched him fiercely in his arms. Although three years had not elapsed since their last meeting, Christopher had changed almost beyond recognition. He was no longer the gangling youth Francis had left in Ireland, when the house had rung with his careless laughter. When Robert Grey had gone to their home on that fateful day the well-ordered, secure world, the only world Christopher had ever known, had fallen apart and he had found himself thrust into hell itself. He was faced with all the cruel, naked realities that life had to offer. The harsh circumstances which had been forced on him had made him grow up quickly.

They spent many hours alone together, getting to know
one another again, and Francis became fiercely proud
of his young brother. Proud of the way he squared his
shoulders and set his sights on the future, setting himself
against the past which they must all learn to do now.

When Jake Fox came back to Carstairs Hall he was
alone, but he had found Elizabeth living in the caves up
in St Andrew with other runaways. She had refused to
come back with him. He had been unable to convince
her that he was not employed by Sam Coleridge to track
her down. Louise had to return with him.

The next morning he set off again with Louise,
Christopher, Philip and Francis, and an extra horse with
plenty of food and drink packed into baskets by Mrs
Carstairs.

By mid-morning they passed into St Joseph, the
smallest of the island's parishes, and rode north towards
St Andrew. Louise was almost spellbound, seeing some
of the most stunning scenery she had yet seen on
Barbados. The landscape was rugged, the rustic, rolling
hills in the distance still raw and uncultivated spreading
out in front of her, so different from anything she had
seen on the island, and both she and Francis commented
on how much it reminded them of Scotland. Only the
sweet scent of heather was missing. There were green
valleys and little streams that during the rainy season
turned into angry, swollen rivers. They were riding along
a high, steep ridge and to the east stretched the great
Atlantic, its huge waves, white with foam, exploding over
the reef far out to sea. Louise felt the soft, cooling trade
winds caress her face and she could smell the sea.

They stopped in a cool enclave, the shade full of delicately laced shadows of fern. The wild figs and hanging
creepers and thick foliage created a welcome relief from
the hot, noonday sun. The trees around them were fed

by a waterfall which, in the dim light, was the colour of emeralds, falling in a gentle cascade over the shining rocks.

When they had eaten they carried on, eager to reach the caves in St Andrew. They saw more spectacular scenery of deep, wooded ravines, gullies and hills before dropping down to lower ground, where they began to see several caves set into the hillside and people scurrying to hide in the darkness beyond.

Louise was quite unprepared for her meeting with Elizabeth. She had retained the image of a lovely young girl with deep blonde hair, her child's body beginning to blossom into womanhood. She had been so fun-loving and full of life, her brown eyes always full of love and mischief. The woman who crawled hesitantly from out of the mouth of a small cave was nothing like her sister. She stood there for a long time, looking down at the small group of people. She recognised the dirty one in front. He was the one who had come looking for her. Her eyes moved on and became riveted on the woman in the pink dress sitting gracefully on her horse, her sleek brown hair drawn from her face, her skin protected from the sun's powerful rays by her wide-brimmed pink hat.

The group watched her move warily down the hillside, clinging on to the hanging creepers to prevent her feet from slipping on the small loose stones. Louise stared at her. Surely this stranger could not be Elizabeth? This dirty, hollow-eyed creature who moved with the nervous caution of a trapped animal. She was tall and so thin, her dark eyes slanting upwards giving her the appearance of a bird. Her hair, bleached white by the hot tropical sun, lay in tangled disarray about her shoulders.

Halfway down the hill she stopped suddenly, her eyes still fixed on Louise, and then she recognised her. Her thin hand rose and clutched at her throat and her mouth formed a name and then, in an instant, she came flying down the hill, calling Louise's name as she skimmed over the rocks. Louise jumped from her horse, a cry of joy escaping from her lips, no doubt in her mind any longer that this was her sister. She ran to meet her, although she became just a blur as tears blinded her. Their arms were about each other, both laughing and crying at the same time, too full of emotion to speak for a long time, and when they did, after looking deep into each other's eyes, it was Elizabeth who was the first to speak, dashing away her tears with her dirty hands.

'I never thought I'd see you again, Louise. When that man came looking for me I wouldn't believe him, because I truly thought you were dead. When I saw you lying on the ground that night—after the soldier hit you—I—I thought he'd killed you. Oh, Louise,' she sobbed, clasping her tightly once more. 'How I grieved for you—so much I nearly went out of my mind. If—if it hadn't been for Christopher at the beginning, I believe I would have.' She gulped down her tears and stood back and looked at her sister. 'Do you know about Clara, that—that she died on the ship that brought us here?'

'Yes. Christopher told me.'

Elizabeth frowned curiously. 'Christopher? But—but how——?' and then her eyes travelled past Louise to the young man who had jumped from his horse and was moving towards them. He stopped and looked at her and then very slowly he smiled and held out his arms.

She stared at him incredulously, as if she were seeing a ghost, but then, her tears frozen in huge droplets on her cheeks, a fierce joy flooding her eyes, she spoke his name softly. 'Christopher—oh, Christopher,' and then she was flying over the ground that separated them, straight into his arms.

But when they rode away from the caves it was Philip whose hands clasped her waist and lifted her on to her horse. He stared at her, unable to take his eyes from her,

and there was a tender glow in their depths, darkening
them so that they were almost black. She was lovely,
utterly, bewitchingly lovely, and because of her wildness
it made her different from any other woman he had ever
known. Suddenly the pain he had suffered over the loss
of Louise did not hurt quite so much.

Since Francis' arrival everyone had been caught up in
the excitement of the wedding that was to take place just
as soon as possible between him and Louise. Servants
were intoxicated with enthusiasm as preparations were
put under way, and the day was declared a holiday for
all on the plantation. Several guests had been invited
from among the Carstairses many friends, most of whom
Louise had already met on several occasions since coming
to the island, and who were now eager and curious to
meet Lord Francis Slade, the close friend and confidant
of the King, and to see for themselves if he was as
handsome as rumour had it. They were not disappointed.

With Elizabeth and Christopher they all gathered
around to watch the simple wedding ceremony which
was to take place on the green lawns of Carstairs Hall,
beneath the magical, contrasting shades of the giant
tropical trees and ferns. The air was filled with the heady
scent of a multitude of flowers of every colour and
description. Even the birds were singing more loudly than
usual on this, the happiest of days.

At a distance from where the ceremony was to take
place, so as to keep the smoke away from the guests,
meats were being cooked on spits over fires and the succulent odours of roast pork floated by. Long tables and
benches stood in the shade covered with the finest linen
and lace tablecloths of a pristine whiteness. All Mrs
Carstairs' treasures had been brought out for this truly
grand occasion. The tables groaned with every kind of
food, covering a wide range of tastes. Meat, poultry and

fish dishes, exotic fruits and vegetables, followed by desserts, dish after dish of exquisite flavours, all deliciously mouth-watering and to be washed down by some of the finest European wines.

All eyes were on the bride and groom, black and white faces alike split with smiles. Louise was resplendent in creamy brocade, embroidered with tiny seed pearls which glinted as they caught the sun. Her hands clasped a spray of white, scented lilies and her face was full of radiance as she moved towards Francis, waiting for her, gazing at her wonderingly, even now scarcely able to believe she was to become his wife.

Elizabeth had romantically scattered a carpet of flower petals of all different colours for Louise to walk upon, and their velvety softness brought back a poignant memory of the rose arbour at Kilcrae Castle on a summer's day. A vision of Charles Stuart floated before her gaze, a vision of a handsome King—only she hadn't known it then—in a blue velvet suit, with a dark countenance and sombre black eyes. A sadness filled her and her eyes misted over at the distant memory, as if it belonged to another world, and she sent up a silent prayer, praying for God to keep him safe until his people called him to his throne. But then the mist cleared and Francis stepped forward and took her hand. She was filled with a quiet joy, knowing that when, at last, he placed the gold ring on her finger she would cease to belong to herself, that she would become his, body and soul. How happy she was and how she loved him. He had already taught her the joys of love and now she waited with sweet anticipation for the time to come when she would be his again—only this time as his wife.

Before the makeshift altar, they uttered the ritual responses in turn after the minister, with their eyes locked together, and Louise said softly, 'Until death us do part.'

The minister raised his hand in a blessing and Francis
at last lowered his head and softly brushed his wife's lips
with his own. She closed her eyes, savouring this moment
of complete happiness, afraid to open them in case she
broke its magic.

Louise and Francis bought the Coleridge plantation,
along with another hundred acres of unworked but fertile
land, some of it still thick with forest. They renamed it
Highfield.

Six months after their wedding, six months of blissful
happiness, they stood on the site where the new three-
storeyed house with gables both back and front had
already started being built beneath the quiet, gentle shade
of the towering old trees, and let their eyes travel down
the avenue of swaying palms, the drive having been
cleared of the thick tangle of weeds, past the neat rows
of new slave cabins and the compounds for cattle and
horses with the newly mended fences and on over the
acres of rich green cane fields that stretched almost as
far as the eye could see. Louise's heart swelled with joy
and for the first time since leaving Ireland she was at
peace. She felt as if she had come home, and with Francis
by her side her happiness was complete.

With Christopher they had been living on the plantation for several months in a small log cabin. Jake, for
some peculiar reason, had taken to hanging about
Highfield, often sleeping on the porch, and oddly his
presence about the place reassured Louise, although it
seemed to amuse others the way he always followed her
around. He was still a quiet man, speaking only when
spoken to, his unkempt appearance leaving much to be
desired. But secretly he felt a deep respect and admiration for Louise and what she had achieved in Barbados,
buying the plantation with her husband, determined to
make a success of it, doing most things her-

self—things no lady of gentle birth in England would
have dreamed of doing. No—for a woman, he reckoned
she was all right.

The house Sam Coleridge had lived in had been
demolished immediately, but however unsavoury he
might have been, caring little for the welfare of his servants and slaves, no one could deny that he had certainly known how to grow sugar. The Slades had
experienced many difficulties over the past months, but
at last they were satisfied that the hard work of learning
how to run a sugar plantation and earning the respect
of its labourers was beginning to pay off. At last they
were winning, but they could not have done it without
Christopher, who had astounded them with his
knowledge of and skill at growing the cane. He had
worked tirelessly, personally supervising all the work in
the fields and in the mill, all the while teaching them the
art of making sugar. All the doubts and misgivings he
had felt about coming back to the place where he had
been so ill-treated had gone, but with Elizabeth it had
been different and she had remained with the Carstairses. Nothing and no one could make her go back
to the Coleridge place.

It was only now, after being tormented by fear that
someone would come and forcibly take her away, that
she was beginning to settle down and not jump every
time someone came up quietly behind her. At first she
had been silent and withdrawn, her eyes sharp and
forever watchful, and Louise realised sadly how the
events of the last two years had changed her. She spent
many hours alone and on Sundays, the day of rest on
the plantation, with the air filled with the scent of fragrant blossoms, she could often be found in the slave
quarters sitting on the grass with her knees folded in
front of her, drawn by their tribal rituals, the powerful,
mystical beating of the drums and their singing, mes-

merised by their bodies shining and hips swaying and
their dancing to the magical rhythm of the music—
sometimes frenzied—as if they were trying to cast out
evil spirits. For a time she was in a trance, one of them,
her mind lost in a great void and filled with a strong
spiritual force. When the music ended and she emerged
from her trance-like state she would rise and leave them,
a feeling of calm having descended on her.

Slowly the ugly memories of all she had been through
began to sink into the depths of her consciousness, and
the smile returned to her lips and a light in her darkly
beautiful, slanting eyes—especially in the presence of
Philip, who adored her. His love and strength had given
her a wonderful sense of security she had thought was
to be denied her forever.

Over the years Francis learned how to be a planter, a
good planter, and Highfield became one of the grandest
houses in Barbados, but unlike Christopher his heart
wasn't in it. It was across the Atlantic Ocean with the
King in France, still trying to regain his throne.

Louise, now the mother of his two fine sons, always
knew that one day he would leave Barbados, and that
day eventually came. It was eleven years after the
execution of his father that King Charles II finally came
into his own and was restored to his throne. Oliver
Cromwell was dead and the people of England, tired of
the stifling oppression of the Puritans, called for the
happy days of the monarchy to be brought back.

On a day of national rejoicing, when bells were rung
and bonfires lit throughout the length and breadth of
the kingdom, the King rode into London. It was his
thirtieth birthday. On his restoration all those who had
assisted him in his escape after the Battle of Worcester
and those who had remained loyal he remembered with
deep gratitude, and he rewarded them well. Not least his

good friend Francis Slade, whose estates in Devon were restored to him.

It was with a mixture of sadness and happiness that Louise left Barbados. Sadness at leaving Elizabeth, who had married Philip and lived happily at Carstairs Hall with their children, and Christopher, who was to take over Highfield, but happiness at the King's restoration and their return to England. But as Louise, with Francis' arm about her waist, stood on the deck of the ship taking them home, the island receding into the white, tropical mist, Louise would remember her years in Barbados as being the happiest of her life.

DON'T MISS OUT ON HOLIDAY ROMANCE!

Four specially selected brand new novels from popular authors in an attractive easy-to-pack presentation case.

THE TIGER'S LAIR
Helen Bianchin
THE GIRL HE LEFT BEHIND
Emma Goldrick
SPELLBINDING
Charlotte Lamb
FORBIDDEN ATTRACTION
Lilian Peake

This year take your own holiday romance with you.

Look out for the special pack from 29th June, 1990 priced £5.40.

COMPELLING FINAL CHAPTER

EDEN – Penny Richards   £2.99

The final novel in this sensational quartet tracing the
lives of four very different sisters.
After helping her younger sisters to find love. Eden
felt she'd missed her own chance of happiness.
Then Nick Logan blew into her life like a breath of
fresh air! His young good-looks threatened her
respectable reputation – but if this was her one
chance at love, Eden was determined to take it.

July 1990

W●RLDWIDE

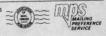